Charlie Williams was ~~~~~~~~~~~~~~~~~~~~
went to Swansea Univ ~~~~~~~~~~~~~~~~~~~~
for several years. He n ~~~~~~~~~~~~~~~~
his wife and children. ~~~~~~~~~~~~~~~~~

Charlie Williams was born in Worcester in 1971. He .... university, then worked in London .... now lives in Worcestershire with .... Deadfolk is his first novel.

deadfolk

charlie williams

Library of Congress Catalog Card Number: 2004100911

A complete catalogue record for this book can be
obtained from the British Library on request

First published in 2004
by Serpent's Tail,
4 Blackstock Mews, London N4 2BT

website: www.serpentstail.com

Typeset in 11/13.5pt Plantin by FiSH Books, London
Printed by Mackays of Chatham, plc

10 9 8 7 6 5 4 3 2 1

For Lisa

1

....

WOMAN DIES IN CLUB FIRE

Mangel Police have found the body of a woman inside Hoppers nightclub, which was gutted by fire in the early hours of yesterday morning. It is thought to be that of Mangel resident Elizabeth Dawn Blake, 25.

Lee Munton, joint owner of Hoppers, was taken in for questioning yesterday along with Royston Blake, 28, head doorman at the club and husband of the deceased. Munton was released without charge shortly thereafter. He was later unavailable for comment.

Blake remains in custody.

I were standing on the grass out by the East Bloater Road when the Meat Wagon came past. She slowed a bit then drove on up towards town. I were glad of that. Sight of the Meat Wagon never had been summat to warm a feller's cockles.

Standing on the grass out by the East Bloater Road didn't seem such a good idea now. A wind had started up from the North that went through your clothes like a gutting knife. But I couldn't go yet. Not unless I wanted to be passing the Meat Wagon on the way in.

So I paced around for a bit and smoked two fags, thinking how I really ought to stop coming out this way cos nothing were to be gained from it. Then I got back in me car and pointed her homeward.

She were a Ford Capri. I'd always driven a Ford Capri and always would do, long as I still had a choice in the matter. Despite the chill and the damp and the mood I were in she started first time, which cheered us up no end. As I slotted her into third she backfired like a bastard. Been doing a fair bit of backfiring of late she had. Hole in the exhaust like as not, and once you gets one of them they only gets bigger. Unless I got her down the garage for fixing she'd get louder and louder until the noise were hurting folks' ears. But that'd have to wait, being as I were skint. And besides, she started running smooth once I shifted her up to fifth.

Judging by the way the sun were slipping down beyond the Deblin Hills it were getting late. I put me foot down and swung her into the first long bend on the way back to Mangel. It were nice and straight for a mile or so now with woods either side and no other vehicle in sight. Rarely was folks out this way. Didn't lead you nowhere you might want to go, see. I opened her up and tipped her over the ton mark. Course, I were taking a risk shifting at that pace. But like I says, no one were about. And I were meeting Legs and Finney down the Paul Pry in a bit. If I missed the start I'd be on catch-up and I didn't like that. I liked to swill at the same rate as them I'm swilling with.

The trees was hanging over and it were right dark down that stretch, so by the time I saw the Meat Wagon parked longways across the road I were near enough atop it. I braked hard and thought about swinging her left or right around the big white van. But there were no room for that. It were the Meat Wagon or one of the big trees either side. And by the time I'd decided on which trunk looked softest it were too late for either of em. The Meat Wagon it were, with Lee Munton's eyes glaring out at us from the driver side and the shadow of Jess peering over his shoulder. I squeezed me eyes tight and pushed down on that middle pedal for all I were worth and a lot more besides. My head were filled with screeching rubber and a *thump thump thump* the like of what you'd never heard. When I felt the wheels flip out from under us I knew I were done for. Not from the car crash, like. But from what the Muntons'd do to us for fucking up the Meat Wagon.

The car stopped.

I kept me eyes shut, thinking how there hadn't been much of a bang on impact. Not even a little *pop* as bumper met panel. But I had an explanation for that one, see. I'd slammed into the van so hard that the noise had gone and bust me ear drums.

Then Lee started talking and I knew my ear drums was right as plumb wire. 'Alright, Blake,' he says.

'Alright, Lee. Alright, Jess.'

Jess moved his head a bit.

The Meat Wagon were but a few inches from where I were sat. Somehow the car had stopped with my window sideways-on to Lee's and back-to-front, like if we'd been passing each other in the street and stopped for a chat. 'Well,' says Lee, smiling like we was still mates. 'Reckon you needs yer tyres checkin'. Eh, Jess?'

'Aye.'

'Needs his tyres checkin' alright. See 'em slip out

from under him just now did you, when all he done were apply a bit o' brake pad?'

'Aye. Flipped out. Brake pads.'

'Know what my impartial advice to him would be?'

'Aye.'

'Go on then.'

'Dunno.'

'S'right, Jess. You dunno. And Blake here dunno neither. Thass why I gives impartial advice. Wouldn't bother if folks knew it already. Be no use to em, would it.'

'Reckon not.'

'S'right. Well, I'd say to him this: Bring yerself down Munton Motors and Baz'll sort you out.' Lee stared at us for a full half minute. When he piped up again he weren't smiling. 'For tyres, like.'

He knew I were skint. Every bastard in Mangel knew I were skint, I reckoned. But I put on a smile anyhow and says: 'Ta. I'll think about it.'

'You do that,' he says. 'Cos our Baz, he wants you to know that there's no hard feelin's. Sometimes he has a drink an' gets a bit lairy an' forgets hisself is all. But he didn't mean nuthin' by it. And he don't want you gettin' no wrong ideas about him by it. Juss get yerself down there and he'll sort you out for tyres. Alright?'

He stared at us until I says: 'Aye, alright.'

'Smart. Cos if there's one thing I don't like iss hard feelin's. And our Baz, well, he ain't got one of em in his whole body. Just a bit of a boy is our Baz. That right Jessie?'

Jess's lips didn't move at all. 'Bit of a boy.'

'Alright, Blakey. Alright. Long as everyone gets along, thass all I asks. Now Blakey, what was you doin' up yonder just now.'

'Yonder?'

'Aye. On the roadside up there. What was you up to?'

I looked past him at Jess. He hadn't moved once. Not even when he'd been talking. He were like a big statue carved out of sandstone. Only time he ever said summat were when Lee spoke to him. Even then it were only aye or summat. 'Well,' I says. 'Ain't much of a reason for it really.'

The Munton brothers stared.

'Just comes out here now and then to...' I tried to swallow but it weren't coming easy. So I coughed a bit instead. 'You know, look at the scenery an' that.'

There weren't much else I could say so I sat tight and waited, listening to Jess's breathing.

Lee stuck his big head out the window at us. When he spoke I could smell what he'd had for lunch. Mixed grill, I reckoned. 'Just so long as you ain't plannin' on leavin' town.'

'Leavin'? No one leaves Mangel, Lee.'

'S'right. Specially not you. Don't want our mates leavin', does we Jess? Wants em here where we can see em.' He fired up the engine, eyes still stuck on mine like a terrier's teeth on a robber's ankle. And suddenly he were smiling again, like he hadn't ever not been smiling. 'Workin' tonight?'

'Nah. Night off.'

'Just so long as you ain't got yerself sacked. Don't go gettin' yerself sacked, Blake. Not for a couple of weeks anyhow.'

'Ain't intendin' on it.'

'Smart. And remember – tyres waitin' for you at Munton Motors.'

The Meat Wagon lurched forward and headed townward. I pulled in on the verge and had a fag.

Then I looked at my watch and headed townward meself.

'So he says to us, he says: "Get off the fuckin' pitch or I'll have you banned from this fuckin' league." No, he did. That's what he bastard said. He fuckin' did you know.'

I were in the Paul Pry now, knocking em back with Legs and Finney like the sun had set for the last time. To be honest, the way I were feeling, I wouldn't have cared much if it had. I were in a hole, see, and no matter how hard I tried I couldn't climb out. Weren't just seeing the Munton boys just now. Seemed like I'd been feeling that way or thereabouts for a couple of years, and the old, easy-going Blake who everyone knew and loved were some other feller entirely and not me at all.

'I knows what I'd of done, mate.' Finney stood half a foot shorter than meself and about half as heavy, but you'd not have known it from the way he spoke sometimes. He never really knew it neither. 'I'd of smacked the fucker. Fuck the fuckin' league.'

Legs and Fin was doing all the chat, but I weren't paying 'em much heed. I knew they just wanted to take my mind off things. They meant well, bless em. They could see how I were, and they was helping us out the only way they knew how: lager and jokes. But it weren't working. How could I be interested, with all that worry rolling around up in me swede?

'What you reckon, eh Blake?' This were Legs again. Legs had a way with words. He were a milkman by trade, but from the way he spoke you'd have thought him town mayor. It weren't the words he said but the way he put em across. He had presence, you might say. Legs said summat, you listened. He were a big

enough feller by normal standards but not particu-
larly hard, far as I or anyone else knew. Except on the
footy pitch when the game got the better of him. To
be honest I hadn't hardly seen him in a proper fight,
so he were summat of an unknown quantity. But it
were his voice what done his talking, not his paws. No
matter what it were he said, you stopped drinking or
smoking or scratching yourself and you gave him your
full and undivided. If you didn't . . .

Well, there were no saying what if. You just did.

And so did I. 'Woss that, mate?'

'You'd of twatted him and all, would you?'

'Twatted him? Oh, aye.' I put pint to gob so I
wouldn't have to say more.

But it weren't fair on em, making all the effort that
they was and me stood there hanging my head like a
barren brood mare. No, they deserved a bit more
from us. So I licked the beer off me lips and got going
again. 'Twatted him and more besides. In fact I'll tell
you what I'd of done.' I pulled meself up nice and tall.
If you're planning on doing some talking you might as
well do it standing up straight. I faced Legs, acting
like he were the ref and I were him. 'I'd of stood in
front of him. Nice and tall, yet sorta loose an' all. Like
this, see. Look him in the eye a couple of seconds,
weighing him up like. Then this . . .'

Some fellers is good with their paws. Some knows
how to put the boot in just right. Then there's the
ones who always carries an item from the cutlery
drawer, or summat nice and solid from a toolbox. We
all needs a little bit extra at times. Specially in my line
of work. There's a time in every doorman's life when
he finds himself out of favour with one or two punters
and needs some support on his way home. And that's

why I had a monkey wrench stowed down the stitching of my leather. But such hardware is strictly for emergency use only and oughtn't to be required in most cases of argy-bargy.

Anyhow, my weapon of choice were none of them things. It were my head. I were skilled in every category of headbutt in the book. Straight, sidewinder, piledriver – you name it, I'd swung it. The secret, right, is to keep your neck relaxed and picture your swede like a demolition ball. Mark your target – nose or cheekbone is best – then swing that ball. I swung mine at Legs.

See, the other side of good headbutting is control. You've got to be able to divert your butt – or even stop it altogether – at the last moment. That's what I done. This were only a bit of a laugh after all. I called off the butt, forehead about an half inch from Legsy's cheekbone. All in the neck muscles, see. I did it all the time on the door. Swing it and stop it. Let em know how easy it is for you. And I hadn't ever nutted a feller I hadn't meant to. Until now.

Legs dropped his pint and went down like a sack of turnips. I swigged some lager and rubbed me forehead, wondering how that had happened and what best to do about it.

'You've gone and done it now,' says Fin after a bit, shaking his head.

'Didn't mean it did I.' I finished me pint and bent over Legs. His glass hadn't broke so I picked it up and put it on the bartop. There were a little nick below his left eye. It gave us a nasty feeling in me guts to look at it. 'Looks worse than it is.'

'Can't very well look much worser,' says Nathan the barman, who'd come over to give us a refill. 'I won't have that kind of nonsense in my bar, Royston

Blake. There's plenty of pubs in Mangel that'll turn a blind eye. But I'll not have my punters fightin' amongst emselves. Here.' He squeezed out a beer-sodden bar towel and chucked it down to us.

'Ta,' I says, and swabbed some of the blood off Legsy's face.

'Fer cryin' out . . . Thass fer the spilt beer there on the floor. Here's fer his face.'

This time he lobbed down a clean white flannel soaked in cold water. Legsy's face were alright now, barring the cut. So I used the flannel to clean the beer up off the floor.

'You've gone and done it now.'

'Shut it, Fin.'

'You can't leave him there,' says Nathan. 'Bad fer business.'

'Fuck sake, Nathan. What shall I do with him then?'

'Bad fer business. Try the hospital. They takes folks like him.'

'Folks like him?'

'Folks leakin' blood all over my floor.'

'Nathan, this is Legsy, one of yer top punters.'

'Not at this moment he ain't.'

'You've gone and done it now,' says Fin.

'Giz a glass of water, Nathan.'

'Water? Ain't usual fer you.'

'Juss giz it.'

'Still or sparklin'?'

'Fuck sake Nathan. Tap water.'

'Tap water's no good.'

'Why not?'

'I don't recommend Mangel tap water. Discoloured. Tastes of manure.'

'Fuckin' giz the water.'

'Alright. No call fer shoutin'. Pint or half?'

When Nathan came back I took the pint off the bartop and poured it over Legsy's face. It didn't have much effect, except washing some of the blood away.

'Woss that in aid of?' says Nathan. 'Good pint of lager that were. And don't think you ain't payin' fer that. Water's in this un here.'

'Thass why it never woke him up,' says Fin. 'Lager'll only make him feel more like he already is. Iss the water he needs.'

'Fuckin' shut it, Fin.' I opened Legsy's gob and poured the water in it. He went still for a bit, not breathing nor nothing. Finney looked down at us and I looked up at Nathan, who folded his arms and shook his head. Then Legs started coughing and spluttering and trying to sit up.

'Help him, then,' says Nathan. 'Least you could do, I reckons.'

I helped him onto his arse and wiped his face a bit more. Before long he stopped coughing and started breathing normal. Then he went to get up and landed on his arse again. I took hold his arm. 'Get off us,' he says. He tried again and got up this time, using the bar rail to steady himself.

'You alright?' says Fin.

'Aye, aye. Where's me pint?'

'Well . . .' Fin looked at us and shrugged.

Blood were starting to pour down Legsy's cheek again, but not half so much as before. It were a puckered little gob of a wound like they gets on footy pitches when two fellers jumps for a ball in the air. He brushed away the blood so quick you'd not have seen it if you wasn't looking for it. 'Well? Where's me fuckin' pint gone?'

Nathan looked at us and raised his eyebrows.

I started to say summat but my gob were dry and it came out silent. I coughed and started afresh: 'I spilt it, Legsy. Soz about that. Nathan, get Legsy another, will you? Don't hang about.'

Nathan stayed where he were for about ten seconds, staring back at us. Finney stared at us too. Legsy were busy sparking one up.

'Fact he ain't gat no beer ain't my doin',' says Nathan. 'I'm a barman. I'm the feller who gives beer. I ain't the one who taketh it away, now, am I?' Without taking his eyes off us he plonked a full pint of lager on the bartop.

Legsy took it and necked it in one. 'Where were I?' The blood started trickling down his cheek again. He didn't wipe it away this time. He didn't look at us neither. He hadn't looked at us since I dropped my head on him by accident. 'Oh aye. That were it. So, what you sayin', Blake? Sayin' I'm a cunt for not twattin' this ref, are you? That what you sayin'?'

I looked around. No one were looking at us. But I knew they was listening. 'No, I ain't—'

'Bottled it, did I? Let a ref make a cunt of us, eh, did I? Reckon thass what he's sayin', Fin? Cos for the life of me I can't think what else it might be.'

'Now hold up a minute,' I says before Finney could make up his mind which side of the fence he were sat. 'I didn't say twattin' him were the right thing to do, did I? All I said were that iss what I'd of done. And if my memory ain't lettin' us down, s'what Finney here said he'd of done an' all.'

'Don't fuckin' bring me int—'

'Hold up a min, Fin. Right? Now Legsy, just cos me and Fin here'd do it, don't mean you oughta of.

See, me and Fin here is peasants. We ain't got class and breedin' like what you has. I comes from a long line of sprout pickers, far as I knows. And Fin here...Well, I'd be shocked if his folks knew how to eat off a plate.'

Finney opened his mouth, but said nothing. He were spectating, see. He wanted to see us dig me way out of my hole.

'Violence ain't the answer to all life's ills,' I ploughs on. 'Them of us with a brain in our heads knows that. Even peasants like meself and Fin. But in the heat of the moment, when the ref is wavin' his red card and actin' like he's better'n you – thass when we forgets it. But you, Legs, you knows how to conduct yerself. You knows when to twat a mouthy cunt, and when to walk away from a decent feller who perhaps got up wrong side of his bed. S'all I'm sayin'.'

I took a huge swig from me pint and let my words sink in. I got a fag out and offered the pack round. Fin took one. I downed the rest of my lager, then called Nathan the barman over. It were my round.

'Well...' Legs were looking along the bar as he spoke. He had a little plaster on his face now which I hadn't seen him put there. Looked alright it did, like he'd no more than cut himself shaving. He still hadn't looked us in the eye, mind. 'Blakey's right, you know.'

I put on an earnest face. 'You know Legs, I reckon I am in this case.'

'Aye, you are. About you and Fin. Couple of fuckin' peasants.' He laughed.

Nathan came over and started laughing and all. Pretty soon a couple of birds up the bar was joining in. Then Finney cracked up, leaving me looking like the miserable cunt. Fuck it, I thought, and joined in.

'Eh, Legsy,' says Fin, holding his aching sides. 'So what did you do?'

'What did I do when?'

'The ref. Sent you off didn't he.'

'Oh, him.' Legs pulled on his fag and let it out through his nostrils. Nathan were watching him, putting my money in the till. The birds up the bar was watching him too, waiting. Finney had his eyes on him and all. I were watching the froth disappear on my new pint. 'Kicked him in the knackers, didn't I.'

But a moment later, when everyone had stopped rolling in the aisles and slapping Legsy on the back, I caught his eye. It were only a quick look, but it told us summat, loud as if he'd bellowed it. It said that things wasn't alright, that I ought not have butted him back there. It said I'd made a cunt of him, and he weren't too happy about that.

And I reckon that were about the moment when things started turning to shite.

2

....

You knows how sometimes you needs a kebab so bad
you're willing to walk thirty mile across rough
country, long as there's a large doner with chilli sauce
at the end? Well that's how I were feeling. And Fin
indicated he were getting that way and all. Luckily
enough, Alvin's Kebab Shop And Chippy were only
hundred-odd yard up the road from the Paul Pry.
Used to be called plain old Alvin's Chippy, course.
Ain't sure when the kebab bit got added on and I
don't reckon anyone is. Just happened some time a
few year back. Bit like the kebabs emselves. No one
knows for surely what the stuff they puts in em is.
Some says it's sheep, some says goat. There's them
who reckons doner ain't meat at all. But no one cares
much. If a thing tastes alright, folks'll eat it.

  We walked and ate for quite a while. Only sounds
was taxis, footsteps, and the chewing and swallowing
of scran. I had extra large doner with a bag of chips
bunged in, the lot swimming in enough of Alvin's
special chilli sauce to kill half a dozen younguns and
old folk. Fin had same, but with mint sauce atop his.
I'd long since given up trying to make him see that it

just ain't right for a feller to be selecting mint ahead of chilli. Some folks'll just never learn. Still, none of us is perfect. And I had my own fair share of imperfections. You'll be hearing about them soon enough.

Fin belched, farted, and chucked the empty kebab wrapper at a passing cab. The driver honked his horn. 'Know what, Blakey boy,' he says. 'You oughtn't to of done that.'

'Done what?' I says. A big slice of doner flapped onto my chin. I sucked it up, leaving a bit of chilli sauce that burned me lips even after I licked it off.

'Butted Legsy. Oughta of been more careful.'

I hadn't thought about that for a bit. It'd all been a long time ago far as I were concerned, water under the bridge and that. Plus I'd had ten or twelve pints since then and done me best to get on with it. Legs seemed like he'd forgot about it himself after a bit. And rightly so. An accident is an accident after all, and a grudge between pals is like drinking beer out of a teacup, as they says. It don't feel right and there's no point to it. Aye, he'd cleared off a bit early, before the night had got into the full swing of itself. But Legsy were a milkman, so you had to make concessions for him on that score. 'Legsy's alright,' I says. 'It were only a scratch anyhow.'

'Ain't the point, is it. Legsy don't like being made a cunt of he don't. You oughta know that.'

'Nah, he's alright.' I rammed the last handful of scran into me gob and started chewing. Like Finney, I screwed up the paper and went to lob it at a passing vehicle. Only it were the Meat Wagon, so I didn't.

'Fuck,' says Fin. 'You almost done it there.'

For a second the Meat Wagon looked like carrying on up the road. The Muntons had already bothered us that day and it weren't their practice to harass us more than the once the same day. But it slowed anyhow and pulled in a few yard up the way.

The two of us stopped, then started walking again, slowly. 'Woss up here then?' whispers Fin.

'Dunno.'

'You must know. Iss you they'm after.'

'Says who?'

'Never bothers with me, does they? Must be you. Always botherin' you they is.'

'Fuckin' shut up.'

We was getting closer and closer to the van. The back doors was filthy but no one had written in the dirt. No one ever wrote in the dirt of the Meat Wagon. The only words on the body was the MUNTON MOTORS painted black and red on the side. I were starting to get a bad feeling about it all. Fin were right – the Muntons was always bothering us. For the past two years anyhow. But all they was doing were keeping us in check. They never had cause to fuck with us and never would have. No, there were summat different about this, though I couldn't rightly say how so.

As we passed the front end I couldn't bring meself to look at the windows. They was blacked out anyhow so there were no point. But you could be sure Jess'd be on the roadside, Lee behind the wheel, and Baz like as not between the two of em if they could fit him in. And they'd all be looking for the whites of my eyes. I stopped.

Ain't sure why. I stopped right there next to the window. Fin stopped and all, though I could feel how hard it were for him. I turned and looked at the black window.

Aye, it were blacked out alright. But if that weren't

a face pressed up against it I don't know what it were.

I wanted to run. I wanted to peg it like Billy-o and not stop until the front door were bolted behind us.

And me a doorman.

Aye, I'll admit it. I were scared shiteless right then, hard as it might be for you to believe knowing my profession and reputation and all. But like all professionals I put on a straight face. Even managed a bit of a smile and nod. Then I set off again, nice and casual.

Finney bolted a few yards but slowed when he saw us still walking. 'S'alright,' I says. 'They'm shitin' us up is all.'

'Aye, they am that.'

'Ain't follerin' is they?'

Fin looked over his shoulder and shook his head. We walked for another two or three minutes before Fin spoke. 'What you gonna do?'

'About what?'

'About what? Fuckin' Muntons is what.'

I shrugged and flobbed into the gutter.

'Gotta do summat Blakey. Muntons is after you.'

'Muntons ain't after us.'

'Looks to me like they is. Looks that way to most folks.'

I stopped. 'Alright, woss folks sayin'?'

'Nut'n. What I just said, is all.'

'Woss you heared?'

'Nut'n, like I says.'

'Tell us.'

'Get off us Blake. You'll rip me shirt.'

I let go of him but kept my face up close.

'Alright alright,' he says. His breath smelt of spew. Finney weren't built like the rest of us. It were his habit to sly off to the bogs for a quiet chunder after eight pints or so. 'Folks is sayin' that...that the Muntons is after you.'

'Bollocks. Spit it out, you cunt.'

I watched him get up off the floor and brush the dust and dead leaves off his jeans. I reckon I must have pushed him a bit hard, him being steady on his feet even when pissed and never one to fall on his arse of his own accord. But I couldn't recall doing it. His elbow were bleeding a bit, and I'd feel a bit bad about that on a normal day, same as I'd felt bad about nutting Legs. But this weren't a normal day. This were the day when everything started turning to shite.

'They'm callin' you a...'

'Come on, fuck sake.'

'They'm callin' you a bottler. Blake. Blake, you alright?'

I got a fag out, lit it, and smoked it quarter way down in one pull.

'You alright mate?'

'Aye.'

'Looked fit to topple there a minute.'

'Well I'm alright.' I started walking up the hill. It weren't so easy now. The talk had sucked the sap out me legs.

'You knows what folks is like.'

'Aye.'

'Says things cos they don't understand. Summat about you and Baz Munton is all I knows. I mean, I weren't there so I dunno what happened. But I knows you ain't no bottler.'

I flinched. I wanted to change the subject but there weren't much else to talk about.

Fin licked his thin lips. 'So is you gonna tell us what

happened or what?' I'd known him since before either of us cared to recall. Went to school together, me and him and Legs. The three of us bunked off together, played in the road together, swiped our first handbag together, done our first house together. The first night I spent in the cells, Finney and Legs was right there beside us. Even bust our cherries together, we did. Not together, like. But with the same bird. One after the other. One feller climbs off, next climbs on. Debbie Shepherd her name were, from the flats behind the old Coopers Tannery. Cost us a tenner each and a bottle of voddy between us.

Aye, Finney were a mate.

But just being a mate don't mean you can trust a feller, do it? Telling a mate your innermost thoughts is like getting out your knackers and asking him not to kick em. Why put temptation under his nose? Ain't doing him no favours. And it weren't doing me none neither.

'Don't you go frettin' over me,' I says. 'I'm alright. Iss you I worries about, walkin' around with only half a brain in yer swede.'

He looked at us for a few seconds, walking along as we was. Perhaps he were trying to read me thoughts. Some folks can do that, they says. Stare hard enough and they can look right through your skull and into the bit of your swede what does your thinking for you. Dunno if it's true. Maybe it is. But if anyone can do it, that person ain't Finney. Finney couldn't find his own arse if you stuck a Christmas tree up it.

After a bit he shrugged and shook his head. He shook it for a few seconds, like as not trying to shake off all the thoughts that had taken root there but come to nothing. Then he started talking about footy, and

how he were secretly hoping to take Legsy's place on
the Paul Pry squad on a permanent basis. In truth, I
didn't think he could do it. Them two players was just
too different. Fin ran like a greyhound and dribbled
like a new-born baby. He were skill. But Legs were the
heart of the team. Passion, commitment, courage – he
had it all. He'd break your legs if it meant victory.
That's what'd got him in bother with the ref. Knacked
a feller's ankle under the whistle-blower's nose. And
shoeing him in the knackers couldn't have helped
neither. Looked like a season-long ban at the least.

Course, I used to play a bit and all. I were goalie,
and not a bad un if I says so meself. When I let one
past us it hurt. Hurt us more than any kick could. But
that were in the old days when Beth were still around.
Soon as she weren't there no more I stopped caring
about goals. They could fly past us like ping pong
balls in a gale for all I gave a toss.

This were what I were thinking while Fin carped on
about how this were his chance to make that number
nine shirt his own. I weren't listening to him. It's easy
to switch off to Fin's voice when he starts talking his
bollocks. Which is why I weren't exactly prepared for
what he said next.

'You what?' I says, thinking I'd heard wrong.

'Hoppers. How's it goin' down there?'

'What?'

'Hoppers. You know. Fuckin' place you works at.'

'I know what Hoppers is. Why you askin' about it?'

'Fuck sake, can't I ask about yer bastard job now?'

'Aye, well. Goin' alright, like.'

'Oh aye?'

'Aye.'

'Thass good.'

We walked on a bit. I were hungry again, despite the kebab. Either that or the odd feeling in my guts were summat else. A taxi rolled past. I looked at the couple on the back seat. The bird looked a bit like Sally. She'd said she weren't going out tonight. But she always had been a fucking liar. I ain't saying that in a bad way neither. Her lying were a part of her character, like. You took it or you fucked off.

I wished I were in the cab with her, mind. Even if she were with some pissed-up feller who had his paws on her tits and his tongue down her gullet. Suddenly I'd rather be in there than yomping up the hill with Finney. Why did me and him always end up walking home anyhow? Weren't like he couldn't afford the taxi fare. I turned to ask him just that question. But he got one in first.

'So what you gonna do about them Muntons, then?' he says. 'Hey, where you goin'? Blakey? Woss I said?'

A while later I were back in town, and Finney's whining were far behind us. To be fair it weren't just me wanting to get away from Finney. I knew he meant no harm by his verbal twattery. Truth were I weren't ready to go home. There were nothing for us there no more, since Beth had passed on. No one to give us a boot if I'd fell akip in front of the telly. No one to open the windows when the room got too full of fag smoke and farts. No one to pick up the empties and tip the ashtray. It were them things I were remembering these days. The good things. I knew there'd been bad stuff and all, shite that brung us down and made my head boil. But I didn't like thinking about that. And I couldn't go home.

I yomped up the one road and down the next. Getting away from Fin had done us no end of good. My feet was tingling, itching to keep going all night. The beer had mostly worn off, leaving my head nicely clear despite it being gone midnight. But I couldn't roam the streets forever. Folks'd see us and wonder what I were up to. Perhaps they'd start wondering if I were alright in the head all over again. No, I had to go somewhere. But nowhere were open this time of night, unless I wanted another kebab. And I didn't. So I carried on walking. Had some thinking to do anyhow.

Truth be told I'd been doing some thinking for a long while now without getting nowhere with it. The thoughts never went nowhere besides round in circles and up my own arse. But suddenly things was different. The goalposts had moved. And it were Finney who'd moved the bastards. It had been my problem alone before. A little arrangement between meself and the Muntons. They'd started it. I had to put up with it.

But now Finney and every fucker in town knew. And that meant it weren't a problem no more. It were a fucking crisis.

And it were for me to sort it out.

I walked down a few streets and scratched my head and thought hard. I tried to think crisis thoughts, not just problem ones. That seemed to do the trick. Soon they was in my head, big loud thoughts with flashing red lights around 'em. And then they got moving.

Round in circles and up my own arse.

I lit another smoke and turned into Cutler Road. My head weren't working. Must be somewhere I could go to get me mind off things and relax a bit. And then I thought of a place.

There were an offy halfway down Cutler Road. I went behind it and looked for lights on in the flat above. Kitchen window were glowing yellow so I climbed the fire escape and knocked. Grey and blue from the telly flickered through the knobbly glass of the front door. A familiar shape blocked it out and opened the door.

'Alright, Legsy.'

He looked at us funny for a bit, weighing us up no doubt. I wondered if it had been such a bright idea to come up here after all. Perhaps I oughta have left it a day or two, case he bore any quiet grudges regarding the headbutt. But I forgot all that when he said: 'Alright, Blake.'

He shambled back, leaving the door open. I followed him into the living room. It weren't a bad flat, and I'd always liked going up there ever since he'd moved in. It were a feller's flat, with no outside fiddling of the female variety. That's why I spent so much time up there after I got wedded, like as not. I'd go up there when Beth were getting on at us about summat, or just when I couldn't face going home and looking at her sour face. I've already told you about him being a good talker. But he could listen and all. We'd crack open a couple and I'd start joshing about this or that. And somewhere along the way I'd always get to Beth, and the way we didn't always get on so well. Course, they wasn't all bad times with Beth. There was good uns and all, else we'd never have got wedded in the first place. And I told Legs about them as well, sort of things Beth wouldn't have wanted airing outside of our bedroom like as not. But like I says, Legsy's flat were a place where you could talk man to man with a feller.

'Lager's in the fridge,' he says, collapsing length-ways onto the sofa and sending out a little cloud of bachelor's dust from the cushions.

I got meself one and sat down in the same armchair I always sat in. It were a recliner and kicked back just far enough. It were a big chair but fit us perfect, me being generously proportioned all over including my arse, and after a bit of creaking and buttock shifting I always found a nice position.

I chugged beer and watched the telly. A film were just finishing up. The feller stood there with blood on his beefy arms and what looked like old motor oil striped across his cheeks. He tossed down his carbine and took the belt of shells from around him. A bird with blonde hair and big tits threw herself at him and buried her face in his neck. I couldn't see how she could let herself do that, her being all nicely made-up and fragrant and him looking like he'd rival a pig farm for smelling bad. 'Is it all over?' she says breathlessly.

'It's over,' he says in a voice coming from some-where near his size thirteens. 'For now.'

And then the credits rolled past and the adverts came on. I drank some more beer and put my fag out in an ashtray on the little table next to us. It were one from Hoppers, from years back, well before Fenton had took it over.

'Legsy,' I says, looking over at him. You never could tell what state of mind Legsy were in just by looking at him. But I looked anyhow, out of habit. 'You alright, mate?'

He picked his nose, looked at it, then flicked it into the darkness. I heard it land somewhere behind the telly. The cut on his face looked nasty in the telly's flickering light. The plaster covered up the worst of it but the area all around were purple and swollen. 'Aye,' he says. 'You?'

'Aye. Soz about earlier.'

'About what earlier?' He lifted his arse up to get a pack of Regals out his pocket.

'You know. The, er...In the Paul Pry.' I looked at the screen. The adverts ended and the news came on. I didn't listen to what the feller in the tie were saying. No one ever did. And if they did they couldn't understand it anyhow. After a bit he shut up and they put on some pictures of the war. A line of tanks ploughing into a village, birds and nippers looking on. A missile tearing down a street in the middle of the night. 'I were just havin' a laugh, like. Never meant to—'

'I knows that.' There were a touch of the narky in his voice, which put us on edge a bit, us being mates and me trying to set things straight between us and all. But then he says, more friendly: 'I knows that. Take us for a fool, do you?'

'What, you? Heh, nah, I knew you knew it. Juss makin' sure like.'

We watched telly a bit more. Still pictures of the war. Bunch of soldiers taking aim out of a window. Shot of a bomb sitting in a silo, feller with a broom sweeping the floor around it like it weren't there, like it were a lamppost or summat.

Legs rubbed his nose and says: 'Gonna tell us woss really on yer mind?'

'Who says there's summat else on me mind?'

'Blake,' he smiled. He had a full set of teeth but one at the front was grey and dead. 'How long we knowed each other?'

'Long time. Years. Too fuckin' long.'

'Right. Too fuckin' long. And ain't we always been mates?'

'Aye.'

'Well don't you reckon a mate gets to the point where he spots things?' He hauled himself upright and sat elbows on knees, fists under chin, eyes on me. 'Like when there's summat on yer mind?'

Truth be told I were finding such talk a mite awkward. I mean, he were one of me best mates and all. And like I says, I'd told Legsy all kinds of things of a personal nature at one time or other. But you don't let on to anyone that you've got a bottle problem. Feller can't stick up for himself, feller don't get respect. 'Alright, there is summat on me mind. But it ain't a problem. I mean, iss summat I can deal with. Right?'

'Muntons on yer back? That it?'

'How'd . . . ?'

'Heared things ain't I.'

'Who off?'

'Don't rightly recall.'

I could feel my face turning a nice beetroot. It didn't do for such matters as these to be out in the open. 'Alright, I got a spot of bother with the Muntons. But I can handle it. Alright?'

'Right you are.'

Legs got up and went into the kitchen. He came back with two cans and two meat pies. He lobbed one of each at us. I tore the plastic wrapping off the pie and started munching on it. After the pie I chugged half the can and lit a fag, tossing one to Legs. I let out a smoky belch that lasted about five seconds.

'Right you are,' says Legs again, lighting up. 'But you need help with summat, you come to me. Right?'

I could feel me cheeks burning more than ever. I necked the rest of the can, hoping it'd cool my head down, and then rattled off another five second belch. 'Ta mate.'

Legsy winked at us. 'What mates is for, ennit.'

3
....

It were a bit like waking up next to a marquee the next morning. I ain't bragging nor nothing, but my tadger were good and tall and pushing up into the covers like a tent-pole. That's from sleeping on a full bladder that is. A bit odd when you thinks about it, seeing as when you finally wakes up and hobbles along to the bog you can't piss anyhow on account of your tent-pole.

Still, nothing's impossible. I kept trying, bending meself double so's to ease the pressure. That got some of it out, but not where I wanted it. Feeling that this were getting silly, and with piss all over the tiles and everywhere but down the pan, I stood up, closed me eyes, and thought about the Muntons. Sure enough the tent-pole packed itself away and left me hanging limpish. I pissed for a long time, sighing with the joy of it all. There ain't many feelings to rival that one. Two others that I can readily think of, in fact. And soon as I started thinking of one of em, up came the tent-pole again.

I went back to me bedroom, thinking that it'd been a couple of days since I'd last had my end away. If I didn't empty me sack soon my bollocks'd pack up on us. That's what happens with monks, I once heard. Their knackers ain't called upon, so eventually they stops producing the goods. Well, I hadn't fathered no nippers, far as I knew. And I had no plans of spawning none. But nor did I plan on becoming no monk neither. So I had a choice.

Pull meself off.

Or go round Sally's.

I climbed into the car and bombed across town. I loved that motor. Far back as I could recall, all I'd ever really wanted were a Ford Capri. There's summat about that long bonnet and low-slung chassis that makes angels sing in your ears. When I were a younguns I used to stop at every Capri I walked past and feel her all over, drawing grim looks off passing grannies and arsey shouts from Capri owners. I couldn't help it.

So as soon as I started earning – from robbing mostly – I started saving up. By the time I were eighteen or so I had enough to get meself one. Only problem were that the standard of Capris on the market had dropped a bit by then. And it'd been dropping ever since, same as the standard of everything else. You only gets what you're offered, and if shite is all they offers, shite is what you gets. Still, my Capri were a good un. Best one in Mangel I reckoned. And long as I could keep her going alright I were happy.

And happy I were, as I overtook a bus and stuck him two fingers in the mirror. All my worries seemed to have up and left us during the night. It were as if I'd worried meself round the clock and started at nought again. Or maybe I were just seeing things more clearer now. Things blow over. Folks move on and leave their shite behind. Just cos Finney and Legs and a few others knew about me and my problems with the Munton boys, don't mean everyone knew. Or maybe I'd got the Muntons all wrong. Maybe they was just pissing us about, and not intent on harming us at all. Aye, that were it, like as not.

And besides, I didn't fancy worrying no more. Life were for living, not fretting. Right?

No one were answering when I buzzed. But that didn't mean much. She liked her sack, did Sal. I reckon she liked it best when she had a feller in it, but she were partial to a bit of kip and all. Specially after a night on the pop. I buzzed again, holding me thumb on the button for half a minute.

Still no answer.

Then I remembered walking home with Finney last night and thinking I'd seen Sal with a feller in the back of a cab. I looked at me watch. Half-three. If she had someone in there he'd have pissed off by now. Sal weren't the sort to let fellers hang around after she'd had her fun. Only I were allowed that privilege. And that's cos I weren't just a feller. We had a special arrangement, see. When she needed a bit of protection, she came to me. And I went to her when I wanted . . . well, a shag.

I heard a motor starting up round the corner. Noises like that don't as a rule catch my attention, but this were a deep rumble – summat powerful, like what you don't often hear round these parts. I leant back to take a gander. But that were when Sally's voice piped up on the intercom.

'Who the fuck is that?' she says in her best telephone voice.

'Alright, sweetheart.'

'Oh, hiya.'

The door clicked. I pushed it open.

I walked up the stair feeling nice and easy. Halfway up I stopped and lit a fag. Alright, she'd had a feller last night. So what? Weren't the first time. And I were no monk meself. Weren't like we was married neither. Not even close, mate. She liked a slap and I liked a tickle, and between us we had an alright time when it suited us. Healthy feller and a fit bird – nothing wrong with that. But it didn't mean nothing else, right?

She were still in her dressing gown. But it weren't that what set us on edge when I walked in the flat. It were the smell. You know the smell you gets in your living room when your pissed-up mate kips on the sofa? A manly smell, mixture of beer, sweat, stale aftershave and farts. Your typical feller don't notice it much round his own house, it being the normal way of things for him. But in a bird's place he will notice. 'Who were he?' I says, all cool and can't give a toss, like.

Sally had flopped onto the couch and lit a fag. She took a long pull on it and says: 'Don't you go gettin' jealous on me, you daft bastard. You knows you ain't meant to mention things of that sort.'

'Things,' I says, looking at the floor. 'Things of what sort?'

'You know. Things . . . Oh Blake. I turns a blind eye to what you gets up to and you does same for me. Iss the way we is, Blake. I don't tell you what to do an' you—'

'Who were he is all I asked,' I says. I shoved my hands in me pockets, where they clenched into fists. 'Go on, who?'

'You never asked before,' she says, snatching up her dressing gown around her chest. Bird can't show her wares when she's got a mood on. 'You never asked before because that's the way it suits you. Gets to shag yer way through every little slapper in town, you does.'

'I never asked before cos I never had to sniff the fucker's farts before. Now answer us. Who were he?'

'Leave us alone. I hates you sometimes.' She picked up her fags and lighter and cleared off into the bedroom, leaving us standing there like a twat.

Just because it were the way it were, don't mean I liked it. I did know about Sally's dalliances. And so did half the town. Sally'd always been that way. Specially when she had a few Pernod and blacks inside of her. Scrumpy did the trick and all, but it took longer and gave her wind. She'd been that way at school, popular with the fellers and vicey-versa. She'd carried on that way when she left and got a job cutting hair. You couldn't blame her for craving a bit of male company after crimping all them old ladies' barnets all week and listening to their gossip. It's a fair bet she got even more that way after taking up stripping, what with all them fellers seeing what she had on offer. And she were still that way when I bumped into her in the job shop a couple year back. Sal were Sal. And like I says, I didn't always like it too much.

But it weren't my place to complain, were it.

So there I were sniffing some feller's farts. And suddenly it weren't right. It just fucking weren't. And don't go pestering us about the why neither. Some things just is what they is or ain't. There's right and there's ain't right. And this weren't right. Alright?

I opened a window and wafted the curtains around a bit. Then I went and knocked on the bedroom door and gave it some more of the cool and can't give a toss. 'You tell us who this bastard is, right? You tell us now. And why's he still here at half-three in the afty?'

'Ain't still here.'

'Ah, so he were here. Come on, woss his name?'

'Ain't tellin'. You don't know him.'

'Come on. Tell us, you dirty little slapper.'

'Stop shoutin' at us. And don't call us slapper.'

'Why? What you is ennit, a slapper?'

'Least I ain't no bottler.'

My heart stopped beating. I thought, that's it. That's me finished. Thirty year old, keels over of heart attack in his bird's flat in the middle of a row.

But then he came back, beating like a bad un and making up for all the beats he'd missed. And I were alive and breathing and standing at Sal's bedroom door with her on the other side screaming at us. And she'd just called us a...

'What'd you call us?'

'Bottler.'

'Now Sally, you just can't go—'

'Ah, ain't so tough now is you. Ain't so big now I've found out yer little secret.'

'Come on, tell us what—'

'Bottler bottler bottler.'

Sal had jammed a chair up against the handle. But it weren't a problem. I just kicked the door a couple of times and the chair fell away. Meanwhile Sal were still shouting. She weren't calling us bottler no more. I were a bastard now, in her book. Bastard were alright. But I couldn't have the other. No fucker had ever called us bottler face-to-face and got away with it.

She threw herself onto the bed when I came in. That were summat of a trademark for her, throwing herself at things. Any other time I would have thrown myself on there with her, seeing her dressing gown come away like that and flashing her arse cheeks and a bit of hair. But this weren't no normal occasion. I had other priorities.

I stood over her. 'Who's callin' us bottler?' I says. I were calm. Aye, I were calm. I fucking were, alright?

'Call yerself a doorman? What doorman gets slapped in the face and does nuthin' about it? What doorman lets a feller in after pushin' him round an'... an'... callin' him names?'

My poor heart couldn't take much more of this. I had to do summat, say summat. But no words came. I grabbed her ankle.

'Get off me, bastard.' She flipped herself over and swung a foot at me knackers. I fell to me knees. She sat up, panting. 'Oh, I gets it,' she says. 'Thump a woman would you? Can't stand up to a man, but a woman? Well...'

I stayed where I were. Not cos she'd landed one in me spuds. They hurt a bit but I could handle that. It were because she were right. You shouldn't touch a bird in anger. Even if it's just grabbing her ankle. Even if she's hoofing at your bollocks and doubting your manhood. I fell forward onto the bed and buried my head in me hands. That were all I could think of to do. And as it stood it were the right thing to do.

I felt her arm creep around us. That's the other thing about our Sal. That little heart of hers were made of gold. 'Oh Blake, I... You...' She massaged my shoulders a bit and pressed her tits against my back, filling up the silence with her body. 'It'll be alright.'

But I'd spotted summat on the floor next to her bed. And I knew it wouldn't be alright. I had a feeling that it wouldn't ever be alright again. I reached down and picked it up. 'Woss this?' I says. But I could see what it were. I just wanted to hear her say it.

'Dunno. Lob it in the bin.'

'How'd it get here?'

'I says I dunno, didn't I? Room's a tip ennit. Might of been hangin' round for months—'

'Room ain't a tip. Carpet's tidy except for knickers and this little card. Now you tell us what it is.'

'I...I dunno. Looks like a tradesman's card or summat.'

'What do this say?'

'Ain't got me glasses on.'

'Wossit fuckin' say?'

'Alright. It says Munton Motors.' I knew all Sal's ways. There were nothing she could hide from us. When she got nervous she got lairy. When she got scared she went all sweet, like she were trying to flirt her way out of her troubles. Right now she were being a bit of both, massaging me shoulders with her fingernails. 'So fuckin' what?'

'So fuckin' what,' I says and all, grabbing her gently by one wrist and pulling her round to where I could see her. 'So fuckin' not much, I reckon. Just you has a feller up here not ten minute ago, you calls us bottler, then I finds a Munton callin' card next to your trolleys. How long has it been goin' on?'

'I fuckin' hates you,' she yells, spit flying all over my face. 'Let go me arm.'

'Come on. How long you been seein' Baz again? Couldn't stay away from him could you. Or perhaps it weren't Baz. Perhaps you're tryin' out Lee and Jess now. Eh?'

'Piss off.'

'Which one were it, you dirty slapper?'

'Fuck off. It were Baz. Baz were here with us. An' I'll tell you what ... I'll tell ... I ...'

'Aye? What? What you gonna tell us about Baz Munton?'

She touched my arm and moved her hand up to me face. I let her do it. She'd shagged one of the Muntons. Baz Munton, for fuck sake. But I still loved it when she put her fingers on us. I could feel my anger draining away. Weren't much I could do about that. She had us by the knackers, in a way of speaking.

She put her other hand on my trouser front, just to drive the point home. 'Come on, Blake,' she says all soft. 'It were just a shag. Nuthin' else. A shag for old times. Didn't mean nuthin'.'

'So why'd he leave his card?' I says, suddenly feeling sulky like a youngun who knows what's what but don't like it.

She shrugged. 'Must of dropped it.'

'And what'd he say about me?'

Her hand left me. The look on her face changed. It were hard to describe how. I hadn't seen her like this before. She'd always treated us like I were lord of the fucking manor. Even when she were calling us a cunt. 'Don't matter, Blake.'

It don't matter. 'It don't fuckin' matter? Tell us.'

'Oh Blake ...'

'Tell us.'

'Alright alright. Get off me arm. Alright. He says you're a bottler cos he went down Hoppers and everyone knows the Muntons ain't welcome in Hoppers and he slaps you round the chops and calls you a cunt and pushes you out the way an'... an' you stands there like a lemon and lets him get in. And that ain't no way for a proper bouncer to be behavin', he says an' all.'

I stood up and walked over to the window. Outside two younguns was poking and prodding my Ford Capri. I opened the window and shouts: 'Hoy. Get off me Ford Capri you fuckin' little bastards.'

They was about ten year old I reckon, and they started off pretty swift when they heard us bellowing out of Sal's window. Then one of em stops and looks up at us. He says summat to the other, who stops and all. Then the two walks up to my motor – my Ford fucking Capri, for fuck sake – and sits on the bonnet. 'Piss off, old bottler,' shouts the one of em.

Well, I reckon I turned about hundred different shades of white and red for the next few seconds. No youngun had addressed us like that since I were one meself. And even then it had been a case of me smacking the cunt in the teeth before he could do it again. But now... Well, they was just younguns. It'd be wrong to smack a youngun in the teeth. I shut the window and went back to the bed.

'Oh Blake.'

'Don't worry, Sal.'

'About what?'

'What they'm sayin'. Fuckin' liars.'

'Don't matter, Blake.'

'Liars. I ain't no bottler.'

'I know.'

'Ain't no fuckin' bottler.'

'I know.'

'Ain't no bastard fuckin' bottler.'

'Blake...'

'Ain't—' Sal led my hand under her gown and pressed it into her tit. That always had the effect of calming us down, then geeing us up again in a different way. But it weren't working this time. I didn't fancy her. I couldn't. How could I feel her up when she were still warm and wet from Baz Munton? 'Don't matter, Sal,' I says, getting up again.

'Come on, Blake. I'll just pop in the shower.'

'Ain't in the mood. And besides, I gotta be at work soon.'

4

Reckon there ain't much you needs telling about the Munton clan. Unless you growed up in the woods you'll have heard all about em. Mangel ain't ever seen such a family as them besides emselves. There were talk once of erecting a statue of the three boys and their late pa right in the middle of town. I hope they does and all. Give folks summat to lob things at. Cos sure as bollocks there ain't no one round here touched a real Munton and lived to brag about it down his local. Except meself, course. But that were Mandy Munton, who were a bird. And I don't brag about that.

Anyhow, I were thinking such thoughts and smoking a fag as I drove townward. Your Capri 2.8i is worth a ton-thirty on a long straight and seven and half seconds up to sixty. On top of that it has power steering and manages twenty-eight mile to the gallon. That's what your manual says anyhow. Mine weren't quite like that. Power steering were fucked, fuel injection were shot and, like I says just now, the exhaust were starting to blow. But I still loved her.

I parked her behind the Paul Pry and strolled on in.

Half-five it were. Nathan were reading a paper, propping himself up by the elbows on the bartop. He stood up when he seen us. 'Alright, Blakey,' he says.

'Alright, Nathan the barman. What you doin' readin' that for?'

'What? The paper? Most folks reads it so's they can stay in touch with local events, Blake. And thass why I reads it an' all.'

'Aye, but difference between you an' most folks is you knows it all already. Feller can't fart in this town without you gettin' wind of it, so to speak.'

'I wouldn't say that, Blake.'

'I would. You might as well write the bastard paper.'

He made a sort of growling sound. Not that he were comparing himself to a wild animal. Nathan weren't by any stretch a physical man. He were simply making it be known that he felt uncomfortable talking openly on such matters.

'Usual, is it?' he says.

'Aye,' I says, though he'd already half-pulled the pint. You had to feel sorry for him in a way. Things must get boring when there's nothing you don't know. 'Woss on special today?' I says.

'Pie.'

'Again?'

'Aye.'

'Alright, do us pie and chips then.'

'Be ten minutes.'

I gave him a note and he handed back some coins. It were just enough for some fags and a bottle of milk later on. I pocketed it, wondering why I were always skint even though I spent most of me time working in a bar and not drinking in it. Then I remembered that it were pay day and cheered up a bit. I turned the paper round and tried to read it. It were the *Mangel Informer*. I didn't get very far with it. Every page were filled with what passed for news in Mangel them days. If they only knew, I thought, shaking my head. If they only knew what real news were. How could I give a badger's arse about someone landing a twenty-pound barbel in the River Clunge when the Muntons was doing their best to ruin us?

Your feller off the street might be able to take in his stride accusations such as I had suffered. Being called a bottler weren't the worst thing that could happen, they might say. Better than having your bollocks lopped off with a rusty pair of shears anyhow. That's what your average feller'd say. But he ain't a doorman, is he? He's a bricky or a milkman or . . . works down the slaughtering yard – summat that don't demand the total respect of his public. For me – Head Doorman of Hoppers Wine Bar & Bistro – losing your knackers is the easy bit. Least no one can see you ain't got no knackers.

'Eh, Nathan.'

'Aye Blake?' he says, shoving a plate in the microwave.

'You heared things about us?'

'Well, I reckon not,' he says, walking up to the bar and smoothing down his tash. As tashes go there weren't much to smooth down. It were not unlike a centipede taking a nap on his upper lip. A far cry from my own effort, which were wide and thick and filled the gap between nose and lip quite amply. In my opinion if a man can't grow a proper tash he's better off shaving. But nobody's opinion counted for shite with Nathan except his own. 'No, I reckon not. Only that thing with the Muntons. Baz Munton in particlier.'

Like I says – no one can see you ain't got no knackers. But every bastard with two ears knows if a doorman's courage is called into question.

Asking Nathan didn't prove nothing, mind. Just cos he knew, don't mean everyone knew.

'Alright, Nathan. Ta.'

I got started on me pie. It were alright. About as alright as you got at the Paul Pry anyhow. But I couldn't enjoy it. I couldn't enjoy nothing while that big yellow question mark were hanging over my head. Even the lager tasted flat. Life had lost its flavour. And far as I could see there were only one way to get it back. Show folks that my bottle were intact. Show em that no bastard – not even a fucking Munton – could keep us down.

I polished off the scran and sank another pint. Some of the taste were coming back now. That's what happens when you makes a decision. Life's flavour comes back. Only some of it, mind. You don't get the whole lot until you've done what you decided on doing. But that wouldn't be long in coming. I looked at me watch.

Time for work.

That's the good thing about decisions. Soon as you makes one you feels better. Never occurs that doing what you've decided is another matter entirely, and liable to have you feeling bad all over again when you fucks it up.

'Alright, lads,' I says, in my fatherly way. It gives em a nice feeling as they goes in, gets em in a good mood so they don't mind splashing out a bit at the bar. This were just one of the little touches that had made me Head Doorman of Hoppers Wine Bar & Bistro.

Only it didn't seem to be working on this occasion. There was five of em, all underage. By rights they ought to have been kissing my boots for letting em in. But no. All I got were sniggers and smirks.

But I couldn't let it get to us. There was other punters to think about.

'Lookin' lovely tonight, ladies,' I says not five seconds later. And I'll tell you what – they was lovely. This were one of the things I loved about my job. You got to act like the host at a posh party, winking at all the birds and patting em on the arse as they frolics past. And they loved it.

Usually.

'Get yer filthy hands off us,' the one says. I'd seen her around ever since she'd sprouted tits and were thus old enough to get into pubs. She were normally the friendly sort, full of winks and licking lips and rubbing herself up against us when the crush were on.

'Alright, doll,' I says, taking it in my stride, me being a doorman and all. 'No harm done, eh.'

'I seen what you done, dirty old bastard.' This were a different one now. All three of em was facing us, pointing at us with their pushed-up bosoms. 'You molested her.'

'Hey,' I says, still smiley of face and sing-song of voice. 'Calm down, right? Juss me bein' friendly ennit.'

'Friendly? Blinkin' over-friendly if you asks me.' This were the first one again – the one whose arse I'd molested. 'I've a good mind to...'

I stopped. A crowd of punters had formed behind em, laughing and rubbing hands together like it were bonfire night and I were Guy Fawkes. I thought I spotted Legs amongst em, but it were hard to tell. No, couldn't have been him. Legs would have backed me up. I were starting to feel a mite dizzy, truth be told. All I wanted were for them birds to shut it and move on. Then the crowd would piss off and things'd get back to normal. I were only doing me job after all. I were only meeting and greeting and making punters happy.

'Call the pigs, Kel. Folks like him needs puttin' away and castratin'. If we don't do summat about it he'll go off and molest someone else.'

'Reckon he's one o' them pervies, Kim?' she says, looking at us and squeezing her lower lip between finger and thumb. 'Here, go inside an' call the coppers for us will you.'

'Call em yerself. You he raped ennit.'

The crowd were still growing. It weren't a crowd no more, it were a mob. Seemed half the town were coming down to see old Blakey in his darkest hour. Meanwhile I'm stood there, hands behind back. What else could I do? I were a doorman. My job were to welcome them what's welcome and send the others on their way. Only no one were interested in coming in. They was all coming out onto the street. They all wanted to watch me and Kel and Kim and the other lass.

'Go on Kim. I ain't feelin' alright an' I don't reckon I'd make it to the phone.'

'Fuck off. Standin' up ain't you?'

'*Please* Kim. Go on.'

'Woss goin' on here then?' It were hard to tell whose voice this were. It came out of the crowd, from amongst the laughs and hoots and cat-calls. But in my heart I knew straight off who it were. It were one of them voices that'd been fucking with my head every night of late – winding us up and calling us names and telling us things I'd rather not have heard.

It were Baz Munton.

And suddenly he weren't in the crowd no more. Suddenly his fat face were looming up behind Kel. Or Kim. I forgets the which. 'This cunt botherin' you, ladies?'

'Hiya Baz.'

'Hiya Baz.'

'Oh, hiya Baz.'

'He molested her,' says Kim. 'Gettin' the pigs onto him, ain't us.'

'Oh aye? Touched her up, did he?'

'Aye, grabbed her arse. Tits an' all.'

'Deary me. You ain't joshin' us?'

'I ain't. Gospel truth it is.'

Baz shook his head slowly, eyes on mine. 'So he touched up an innocent child?' he says. 'That what you're sayin', Kel? Grasped her pure white flesh and turned it to his own mucky ends?'

Kim looked at Kel.

'Aye,' says Kel, her face screwed up with the pain of it all. When the tears started rolling they took half her slap with em, leaving dirty great stripes down her face. 'He used me.'

You might be thinking I were just standing there like a cunt, taking it all. Well, that'd be about right. But you tell us what were I supposed to do? I searched the crowd for Legs, but I couldn't see him no more. Maybe I hadn't seen him the first time. All them faces looked the same to me. Eyes dark and burning, lips hanging open, gagging for my blood.

But I had to say summat. I were a doorman. 'Come on ladies and gents. Show's over, ennit. Move along now. Come on—'

'Are you tellin' us to fuck off?'

'Hey now, Baz. There's no need for—'

'Is you? You is, ain't you. You molest these innocent birds here, an' then you tells us to fuck off. Well make us. Make us fuck off, Blakey boy. Come on.'

He pushed me hard, slamming us into the brick wall. I were still standing, but he'd knocked the wind clean out of us and I tasted blood in my mouth. 'Leave it Baz,' I says, searching inside for the old Blake who used to take shite off no one. I ran the tip of my tongue against me lower lip, feeling where I'd bit it.

He went to take a swing at us, stopping his fist a few inches from my eye. But it were too late. I'd flinched. I'd flinched fairly out me skin. And I knew how that looked to the onlooking horde. He came up close and spoke low, so as only I could hear. 'I heared things about you. Things you wouldn't want these good folks to hear. Things you wouldn't want coppers to hear neither, seein' as these things I heared makes you a killer. Wife killer an' all. Reckon to that, eh? Eh?'

His breath smelt of fag butts and old sewerage pipes. But I'd rather smell that than hear what he were saying. I kept quiet and looked sideways.

'I'm the last cunt you wants on yer back. Know why, Blakey boy? I'll tell you why. Because I hates you. I hates you and I'll see to it that you goes down. An' go down you will. Maybe tomorrer. Maybe in a few year. We'll see.'

He patted us on the cheek and moved off. I dunno if he went inside or not. I didn't notice anyone go in or out after that. I couldn't look at their eyes. I knew that they'd be looking back at us, see. And I knew what they'd be thinking. After a while I fucked off for a bit. If I can't see who's going in and out what's the good in standing there? I walked round the back, smoking and kicking pebbles about. I knew I were out of order. I were a doorman. What kind of a doorman abandons his door? It weren't right, but I couldn't hack it back there. Maybe that were it.

Maybe I weren't up to being a doorman no more.

When I went back inside I had no fags left and Rachel were just calling time. I stood by the door, watching em all pile out slowly and nodding only to them what nodded at us, which weren't many. Rache had sent the other bar folk off early, so by midnight the place were empty save her and meself.

I got meself a pint of lager and sat at the end of the bar, watching Rachel go about her business. I weren't really watching her. Eyes was just riding on her well stacked frame while my brain got on with other matters. She weren't paying me much heed neither, getting her chores done quick so she could piss off home. Her eyes was avoiding mine for once. I might have found that odd on any normal night, sociable as she were by character. But I thought nothing of it at the time.

Like I says, my brain were tied up elsewhere.

'Ta-ra Blake,' she says at last.

'Alright, Rache. Er, Rache?'

'What love?'

My gob were hanging open but nothing were coming out. I ought to have known better. You can't go to birds with your problems. Never works it don't. You can't put em across right to a bird, and even if you does they don't hear em right. Nah, there's only one kind of folk who can help out with shite of that sort. And them's your mates.

'What is it Blake?'

'Ah, never mind.'

'You alright love?'

'Aye.'

'Here,' she says, handing us an envelope. 'That'll cheer you up.'

I opened it up and counted the five brownies. I'd been so up me own arse over the Muntons I'd forgot about it being wages day, which made us feel even more shite. Specially with all me subs took off it.

'Ta-ra Blakey.'

'Aye, see you Rache.'

I pulled meself another pint.

Took us half a minute to notice she weren't starting. Wheezed and choked she did, but stayed put. Some nights your Ford Capri can be like that. Temperamental. And there's no point in getting all het up over it neither. A Capri is like a beautiful woman, and ought to be treated like one and all. If she don't wanna play... Well, that's up to her ennit.

So I walked. I yomped the half mile or so to Cutler Road, keeping my eyes a yard or two ahead of me boots. 'Cunts,' I says every time my foot fell. 'Cunts. Cunts. Cunts.' When I started climbing the stair to Legsy's flat I tried to get out of that mood. I always wiped me boots on entering a feller's house and the same stood for the shite in my head. I rang the bell.

I stood on the doorstep scratching me bollocks and thinking how thirsty I were. Kitchen light were on again, along with the telly, flickering shades of green into the hall. He shambled up to the door again, same as he always done.

'Alright, Blake.'

'Alright, Legs.'

I got meself a cold un and plonked my arse down in the usual spot. I looked over at Legs, who were crashed out on his beloved sofa, punching buttons on the remote like I weren't there. It were always the same with him. I reckoned if I just sat there and kept mum he'd happily watch telly in silence, then get up and head for his pit, turning all the lights off on his way. He kept flicking to and fro between channels, which were getting irritating being as he gave us just enough time to get interested in each one before switching to another. One were showing nothing but adverts for things I couldn't afford and they didn't sell in Mangel anyhow. One were showing a bird dancing and swinging her tits on a misty stage. The other one had news on, and that's what he plumped for.

The war were on as usual. Some talk were going on in the background but I couldn't hear it proper. Forty or so deadfolk was lined up on the floor on their backs, most of em covered up with sheets, leaving a foot or hand sticking out here and there. Soldiers was standing all around, guns at the ready. But there were nothing to shoot at. They was looking at the cameraman and down at the deadfolk and then up at the cameraman again. I wondered if they was weighing him up for a dead man himself. They could take his gear and flog it for a few quid, like as not. But I knew it weren't likely. If they shot the cameraman they wouldn't get on telly.

'Much else on?' I says.

Legs flicked again and found a film. It were on a street corner at night. A feller were waiting in the shadows on the one side, flick knife out and glinting. Up the other way were coming a bird with big tits and blonde hair, swinging her handbag and singing to herself. It were the same bird who'd been stripping just now.

I didn't want to interrupt him. Looked like he were having a good time watching his telly, though he were pale and frowning. But if I kept quiet it made no sense me being there. 'Legs,' I says. 'We was talkin' just last night on a certain matter.' I lit one up and took three or four deep pulls on it. 'I'm on about the Muntons, the problem I got with em.'

'Oh aye,' says Legs, tearing his eyes away from the bird on the screen who were just now getting raped. 'What of it?'

'Moved on a bit, you might say.'

'Better or worser?' He got a fag out and lit it, which were a good sign. Legsy always sparked up when he were concentrating.

'Worser.' The bird were trying to scream but the feller had his hand across her mouth while he pumped into her. I were seeing all this but not really paying no mind. 'Gettin' so I can't do me job. Know what happened just now?'

'Oh aye? What?'

I thought about it for a bit, then says: 'Ah, more of the same really. Nuthin' new.'

'No.'

The next scene were in a police station. Legs flicked over and found a western. I watched it for a bit to see if Clint Eastwood were in it. Legsy must have been doing same, being as he flicked back to the news when it became clear there were no Clint.

He seemed happy just to let our conversation hang in the air, so I pressed on. 'I were thinkin' on what you said last night.'

'Aye?'

'About the Muntons.'

'Aye.'

'Said you'd help us out, right?'

Legs flicked the telly off, stubbed his fag, then sat upright and rubbed his hands together. 'Now then. I'm glad you came to us with this. Done a bit of thinkin' on it meself, I has.'

'Oh aye? Nice one Legsy. I knowed I could rely on you.'

He sparked another one up. 'I reckons you oughta stand up to the fuckers.'

I played it over in my head a couple of times before replying, just to be sure he'd said what I thought he'd said. 'You what?'

'Face up to em. Only thing a bully understands that is. Soon as they sees you ain't a soft touch they'll leave you alone. Ain't worth their bother doin' nuthin' else.'

I scratched the back of my neck and took a long swig. 'Well, ta Legs.'

'S'alright.' His hand were already reaching for the remote. 'Any time. Can't help out a mate, who can you help? S'what I says.'

We watched summat for a bit, then I says, 'Only I reckons it ain't as simple as all that.'

'What ain't?'

'Me standing up to the Muntons.'

'Why ain't it? Worst you can get is a beatin'. Had one o' them before ain't you?'

'Like I says, ain't that simple.'

'Why the fuck not?'

'Cos I...' I swirled the beer around in the can, searching for the right words. But I knew in my heart there were only one way of putting it. 'Cos I lost me bottle. Thass why.'

Legs looked at us. I couldn't meet his eye. I were ashamed to, and were glad the light were low and he couldn't see us turning beetroot. But all the same I had a feeling a little smirk were hovering round his lips. 'You?' he says. 'Royston Blake, Head Doorman of Hoppers? Lost yer fuckin' bottle?' He made a farting noise as if to rubbish such a barmy idea. But then the smell reached us and I realised it were a real one.

'Fuckin' hell Legs,' I says, wafting it away.

'Aye, soz. Pies ennit.'

'I ain't joshin' around here. I lost me bottle. Simple as that.'

There were a bit of silence. Weren't the silence that a couple of mates can sit in and not worry about talking. More a silence filled with turmoil and fart gas. Then Legs stood up. He walked over to the window and looked out of it. There weren't much to see out that window during daylight. Couple of brick walls and a few chimneys, some pigeons if you was lucky. And at night there were even less of a view. But he looked out anyhow. 'You ain't lost yer bottle,' he says. 'You just been lettin' it all get to you.'

I thought about that. I knew it were wrong. I'd lost me bottle, plain and simple. But I thought about his words anyhow. Letting it all get to us he'd said. Maybe that were part of it.

He stepped back away from the window and started walking the room, hands behind back, fag in gob. When he spoke again it were in that voice of his that you had no choice but to listen to. 'You know, with some men, their reputations is all they's got. Proud men. Men of honour. Them's the sort always been bred in Mangel. In the old days, leastways. And when someone takes that reputation away from em . . . Well, like takin' their life away ennit.'

He passed the fag from one hand to the other to drive his point home. Then he walked around a bit more, thinking out his next bit.

'Now you can set us straight if I'm wrong on this, but I reckons you're a man o' that sort, Blake. Man o' reputation.'

I stared into space for a moment. Man of reputation. I hadn't thought of meself in such terms for a long while. Sounded about right, mind.

'And now you're hurtin', cos that reputation o' yours has taken a few knocks. When it goes down, you goes down. And them Muntons goes up. That the way iss gonna be, Blake? Happy about you goin' down and them up, is you?'

It took us a while before I noticed I were shaking my head. And then I shook it harder. 'No it fuckin' ain't.'

'What you gonna do about it then?'

'Dunno.' I put tin to teeth and chugged. It were empty. I lit a fag instead. But no matter how hard I puffed, it just didn't do the same job as lager. 'Bit of a mess ennit.'

'Not such a mess as you can't fix it. Don't require no deep thinkin', Blake. Just a bit o' courage. Woss the first thing a man like you does when someone gives him grief?'

I wanted to be as honest as I could, so I thought about it for about twenty seconds before answering. 'Nut him.'

'Right you are.'

'But I can't nut the Muntons. There's three of em and they'm the hardest f—'

'You can if you gets one of em alone.'

'I . . . But . . .' The lit end of my fag were about an inch long, and glowed brighter when I pulled on it. It were like a beacon, pointing through the dark to where Legs were stood. Listen to him, it said. Legsy knows what's what.

'Trust us, Blake. Get one of em alone. Trust us. Trust yerself.'

That were that, far as that conversation went. Some of his words echoed in my head for a while. Specially the ones about trusting meself and him. I dunno if I dropped off or not, but summat happened. The darkness got darker. It got so dark that most things disappeared. Legs weren't over there on his couch no more. I weren't even sure the couch itself were there. And I dunno what happened to me fag. Then I spotted one or two things in the blackness, things what wasn't there before. Seemed like faces.

But I couldn't be sure. More of em was popping up all around the room, though it weren't really a room no more. I could see they surely was faces now. Fellers and birds – cheeks white, eyes wide, mouths hanging open like they was watching summat on telly that they didn't like the look of but couldn't turn away from. It were me they was watching, course. And they was the crowd outside Hoppers.

I were curled up in a ball, cowering. I knew it weren't no Munton that were getting to us. It were the crowd. They was hissing at us, jeering, spitting. I had to do summat. I had to turn em around.

And then it were morning.

Neck were stiff and gob felt like it'd seen use as a pickling jar overnight. I sat up and stretched a bit. Legs weren't on the couch no more. I could hear snoring somewhere not far off so I reckoned he'd crashed out in his pit. I went to the kitchen and swigged two pints of water, then lit a fag and looked in the fridge. It were full of beer and pies. I weighed it all up for a while, then shut the fridge and went out the door, closing it quietly behind us. Watch said half-five. It were early for us, and I thought about turning back for a kip on the recliner. But then I looked around us.

Sun were out already. It had rained overnight. The slate on the rooftops glistened like the calm surface of a river. Everything smelled fresh and earthy, though there were nothing but concrete and stone outside Legsy's flat. I walked down the stair and off down the Hoppers to pick up my vehicle.

I had things needed doing.

5

. . . .

She started first time. That were always her way. Blowing hot and cold. But when she blew hot she didn't half. I pulled her out of the Hoppers car park, thinking how it were only natural that she'd be right as rain and ready to go this morning. I were feeling that way meself. And last night, when she'd played up on us, I'd been feeling like shite.

We went home. After a wash and change of clobber I went down the stair and set about getting some scran together. There weren't much in the cupboard so I made do with half a dozen eggs, eight sausages, a few fried slices and a cup of tea. Then I sat down in front of the telly and watched this and that for a while. I didn't have a remote control so my habit were to stick with whatever I found. A weather report said the sun were due to shine all day, which were alright by me. Then the war came on and I drifted out for a couple of hours.

A bit later I got back in my car and drove her back into town, me touching her the way she liked and her taking us the places I wanted to go.

Namely the Paul Pry.

I don't reckon I'd ever been down the Paul Pry at opening time before. Never had much call for pop at eleven in the morning, even if I were awake at such an hour. And that were the way with most folks, it turned out. The place were empty besides Nathan.

'Alright, Blake,' he says.

'Alright, Nathan.'

'Early fer you.'

'Aye.'

'Usual, is it?'

'Aye.'

It were when I'd touched bottom of me second pint that he says: 'Business?'

'You what?'

'You up and about at this hour. Business, is it?'

'Oh, right. Well, matter of fact I does have a bit of business to sort out. Aye.'

'This wouldn't be to do with what we was talkin' about, would it?' He refilled my glass and plonked it back in front of us.

I picked it up and necked half of it straight off. 'And what might that be?'

'Well... Muntons.' He folded his hairy arms and squinted at us. 'Baz in particlier.'

'Don't be barmy.' I laughed and shook my head and swilled the rest of the lager down. While it were settling in me gut I thought about what he'd asked and how I'd answered it. It were one thing keeping your designs to yourself. Specially if they involves violence. But what were the point of doing what I had planned unless folks knew about it? How would I get my reputation back if folks didn't know I'd done what I were about to do?

They wouldn't, is how.

Not unless someone told em. And I couldn't hardly go round town bragging about it meself. That'd be asking for it. No, it had to start as a rumour, just like the rumours that had been besmirching my name of late. And who better to start a rumour than Nathan himself?

'Matter of fact, Nathan, you ain't too far from the truth there.' I winked and raised my empty vessel.

'Oh aye?' He put his polishing rag down and looked us in the eye. 'Well you just be careful. Times is hard and I can't afford to lose custom. And thass why I'll not be puttin' another fill in here.' He picked up my glass and put it behind him, next to the till. 'Not until you comes back afterwards anyhow. Alright?'

It weren't alright. I were thirsty and I needed to get me strength up. But I saw his point and liked the idea of it, saving my thirst for the victory toast and that.

I got up. 'Ta Nathan.'

'Bye Blakey. He'll be turnin' up at the Bee Hive shortly, by the way. Thereafter at Munton Motors. On yer guard, eh?'

'Oh aye. Ta.'

Norbert Green, as well you knows, were and is the hairiest bit of Mangel. Some might say Muckfield has its moments and all. It had to be said – some hard fellers had come from out Muckfield way. But it were still safe to walk there for most folks, long as your face weren't wrong.

Norbert Green, on the other hand, were a different proposition. Folks went missing out that way all the time. Folks who weren't from Norbert Green that is. Even the coppers wouldn't get involved if they could avoid it. Not that they had much call to stick their snouts in. Far as they was concerned, them what ventured there did so at them's own risk. Norbert Green mostly policed herself. And if on occasion she didn't, there was always the Muntons to step in and sort matters out.

If Norbert Green were a boil on the devil's back, right in the middle of it were a big yellow bag o' pus known as the Bee Hive. I pulled in about thirty yard up the road from it. My watch said five past one. Either he were already in there or he'd be along any second. I had to think quick. I had to decide on where best to do it. I could go straight to Munton Motors and have it out with him on his home turf. Or I could surprise him on his way back from the pub, long as he weren't driving.

Get one of em alone, Legs had said. That's all I had to do.

Alright, I thought. Alright alright alright. So I'm here in Norbert fucking Green, waiting outside the fucking Bee Hive in me fucking back-firing Ford fucking Capri in broad bastard daylight. But it were alright.

Get one of em alone.

Never mind that any cunt walking past on his way to the pub might clock us and walk inside and spill the beans. Never mind that Baz Munton would get on the blower to Lee and Jess.

'Alright,' I says aloud, holding open hands up in front of us and nodding slowly. 'Calm down.' I took a deep breath, closed me lids, and listened to Legsy's words in my head.

Trust me.

Trust yerself.

When I opened em again me eyes latched onto a fat

arse wrapped in grimy denim shambling down the road fifty yard up yonder, away from the pub. It were the arse of Baz Munton, and it were swaying left to right across the pavement as the beer in his large belly sloshed hither and thither. I waited till he were out of sight. Then I turned the key.

Only she weren't starting, were she. I tried her again a few times, but no. I opened my gob to call her summat rude but held me tongue. And thank fuck I did. A man who abuses his car – even verbally – is a man who don't respect himself. I stroked the dashboard and said a few calming words. Then I had a think.

The idea came at us like a mugger out of a dark doorway. Well, it weren't much of an idea, such as it were. More like the boost I needed to go through with the only thing I could do. I got out of the car and hared off down an alley.

Fuck knew how many pairs of Norbert Green eyes clocked us as I zigzagged through side-street and short-cut, hopped over fence and darted across lawn. But stealth weren't of the essence. Long as it ended in a face-to-face with Baz it didn't matter who seen us. The more the better, long as none of em was members of the Munton clan. No point in me blacking his eye or breaking his nose unless the whole of Mangel knew that old Blakey were behind it.

I got there in about five minutes. Or maybe it were one. Time didn't matter. I were there, lurking behind the big oak tree in the graveyard halfway between the Bee Hive and Munton Motors. I could hear Baz's boots crunching gravel further up the path, getting closer. It were too easy in a way. Too easy to do what I went and done.

That were my last moment, I reckon. Leaning there

up against the bark, entertaining barely a flicker of a doubt that what I were up to were for the best. That were the last time I still had a choice. I didn't have to go through with it. I could skulk away quietly, like an old tomcat who knows his prime's behind him and henceforth he'll take more hidings than he can give. And maybe I would have done that, if I'd looked into the future and seen the shite that'd kick off shortly thereafter. But I weren't no old tomcat and I couldn't see into no future.

And Baz Munton were pulling level right about then.

'Alright, Baz.'

'Alright, Bla—' He stopped, wobbled a bit, and gave us one of the dirty looks for which his family were famed. But there were summat else there and all. I wondered if he weren't cacking his pants just a mite. Summat along those lines were going on anyhow, and that were enough for me. You latch onto these things when you finds em.

'Woss matter, Bazzy boy?' I says, laying it on thick like. 'Lost yer voice or summat?'

He licked his lips. 'What the fuck you doin' here?'

'Well, mate, I'm here so's I can lean against this here tree, see? I mean, if I weren't here in this graveyard I'd have to lean against some other tree. An' I don't want that. I want this un.'

He were becoming more himself as the seconds ticked by. 'Best clear off before I gives you a smack.'

'A smack, eh? Would that be a smack on the arse? I bet you'd like that, wouldn't you. Smackin' a feller's arse.'

He shot us another of them nasty glares. This time it were a good un, marred by none of the fear that he were surely feeling inside. It didn't work on us though. We was all alone. Far as I were concerned he were just a fat chicken who hid behind his brothers. They all was, when you thought about it.

'Didn't you hear us last night?' he says. 'I got some shite on you, Royston Blake. Bad, bad things is what I been hearin'. Shite that'll put you away for a long un. Been a naughty boy ain't you. Murder's a very naughty thing to get up to I reckons. Speshly when iss yer own dear wedded wife on receivin' end.'

I'd been expecting summat along them lines, and I weren't planning on letting it get to us. I didn't even blink. 'No one can touch us on that one. Not even the coppers. Tried to make a charge stick on us already, didn't they. But it wouldn't.'

'And why were that?'

'Dunno why you're askin' us. Whole town knows about it and I don't mind if they does, bein' as I got fuck all to hide. No evidence, Baz. Nuthin' sticks cos there's nut'n to stick.'

'Ah, but that ain't true. There is summat. Summat that'll stick to you like a burr on a mongrel's arse.'

I'd been keeping a cocky grin up alright until then but suddenly it shrivelled up and dropped down me throat.

'Woss matter, Blakey boy?' he says. 'Lost yer voice?'

'Alright, you reckons you knows summat. Tell us then.'

'Never mind that. We knows what we knows, see? And thass a lot more than you wants us to know, I can tell you. So you best clear off, and hope that I don't spill the beans too soon. Know what I means? If I were you I'd shift arse out of Mangel. Pack up and move somewhere else, far away. And never come back. Hearin' us alright?'

I opened and closed my gob a couple of times. Then I licked me dry lips and says: 'Leave? No one leaves Mangel.'

'Ain't my problem is it. Oh, and you can take yer tart with you if you likes. You could say I've had her every way a man can, an' I'm pretty sure there's nuthin' special to her. Course, I tried her out the other night one more time, just to be sure. But a tart's a tart, ennit. Keep her.'

I stared at him.

He stared back. His eyes was crystal blue against the pink of his fat cheeks. We was stood a few feet apart but I could smell the beer on him. He'd looked half-cut coming out the Bee Hive. But he didn't now. It were me who were half-cut.

He stared at us.

I stared back. His fists was clenching slowly, like a gunfighter inching hand to holster. I wanted to look down but I couldn't. All I could do were stare back and bide me time. I were Clint Eastwood and he were Lee van Cleef. A fat Lee van Cleef. And a heavily built Clint Eastwood if I'm honest. I stared, and I knew me eyes looked just like Clint's. My leather jacket were a poncho and, though my scalp were sporting nothing but a quarter inch of hair, I truly believed I had a cowboy hat perched up there.

My eyes started watering. Clint's eyes never started watering. Not that you saw anyhow. I thought about it for a second and decided his eyes must water sometimes, all that staring and squinting and sand blowing about in the dry air. And if Clint's eyes watered then he'd have to blink. He were only human after all, weren't he? Aye, course he fucking were. And if he blinked, it were alright for us to blink. I just about had too, tears welling up in my eyes and getting ready to spill down me cheeks as they was. Wouldn't want Baz to reckon I were crying, would I.

So I closed my eyes.

It were only a scrag end of a second later when I opened em again. But already it were too late. His right fist pinged off my head around the left eyebrow. I closed me eyes again, thinking how that were the fist he wore his sovereign on. I opened em to find same fist closing in on me right kidney. I crunched that side up without thinking about it, like you'll always do if you've grown up scrapping. It stopped the worst of it but he still knocked half the wind out of us. I stepped back to give meself a chance, but the oak tree were there and I lost me footing and went down. Baz put the boot in straight away.

I curled up in a ball and tried to guess what Clint might've done if he were us. It were a fair bet that he'd never have found himself on the deck getting a shoeing in the ribs in the first place. But if he ever did you could be sure he'd get out of it somehow. And he'd not waste all that sweat and blood fighting back neither. He'd do it clever. He'd have lost his gun by now, else he wouldn't be getting a kicking. But he'd have summat else hid away. Summat like a knife.

Well, I didn't have no knife down me trouser leg. But I did have the old monkey wrench tucked away in the lining of me jacket. As I slipped my arm in to get at it Baz left off the ribs and started on the back of my head, which made it hard to think but easier to ferret around in me leather. I don't know how long it took cos it were hard to keep track with Baz shoeing my head, but after a bit my fingers curled round cold hard metal.

I rolled over and took one in the face. He tried to pull the leg back but I grabbed it and twisted, wanting him to go down. That didn't work. He stopped the kicking and hopped around a bit, but stayed up. While he were busy doing that I pulled meself up using his leg for support. Soon as I were level with him I swung the wrench. And swung it again.

And again.

And . . .

A noise.

I looked up, feeling summat hot and black and solid drain out of us. A mongrel were sniffing around a headstone not ten foot away. He were a tatty old cur, with not too much hair and only one ear. That didn't seem to bother him, mind, wagging his tail as he were. He cocked his leg and started pissing. I watched the steaming flow darkening the old grey stone, and a little knot of worry took hold in my belly. I looked down at Baz, and felt me breakfast clamouring for daylight.

I turned about and chucked me guts on the path. As the chunder spewed forth I shook my head. It'd never been like this in the old days. Spilt blood were summat to be proud of back then. A mashed face were the mark of a job well done, not summat to make you sick. I stood up and tried to calm meself. Couple of deep breaths ought to do it. Stretch the back and loosen up them neck muscles.

Baz were lying still where I'd left him. Didn't look much like Baz now, mind. More like one of Alvin's kebabs with extra chilli sauce. I laughed. In a good-natured way, mind. We was all mates underneath. Even if we was acting like enemies. One day we'd all be codgers sitting in the pub blabbing on about the good old days when we used to thump each other ragged. But I stopped laughing when I noticed that Baz weren't moving.

Right on cue his head shifted a bit, like he were trying out his neck. His mouth opened and closed. Didn't sound too good. Sounded like he'd need a bit of wiring there. Plus all the stitches. Maybe I'd gone a bit overboard. I had to admit, I hadn't left no one with a face like that before. But I couldn't blame meself. It'd been a long time since I'd had a scrap, so I'd had a lot of steam to let off. Baz knew that and shouldn't have pushed us. I felt more chunder stirring in me guts. But I couldn't hang around for none of that. Nobody were about, apart from the mongrel. And now he'd pissed off somewhere looking for a fight or a bone or a shag. But you never knew who'd be along next. I took off.

Summat made us stop after three or four strides. I dunno what it were. Might have been the Good Samaritan in us, taking pity on the poor battered Munton lying roadside. Whatever it were, I found I couldn't walk no further. Not without going back for another gander at him. Just to be sure he were alright and that.

Course, it were only when I found him eyes open and not breathing that I knew he weren't alright.

He were dead, weren't he.

I scratched my ear, wondering how that had happened. I got the monkey wrench out and looked at it, shaking my head. But them who talks of workmen and their tools is right, you know. I had to shoulder some of the blame. Specially after all I'd been saying about monkey wrenches and being careful with em and that.

I knelt down beside Baz. 'Soz about that, mate,' I says. 'I er... I reckon I dunno what came over us like. You'll understand, won't you? Aye, course you will. Well, er... I'll be off then. Bye.' I pushed his eyelids down, but they crept up again. I tried again a couple of times, then gave up. He'd always been an awkward cunt and he were no different dead.

I stood up. A bus chuntered past alongside the graveyard. A dog barked. A plane flew overhead, likely heading somewhere better than Mangel. I had to do summat, I supposed.

I hauled the carcass behind some nearby bushes. There were a big pile of dug earth amongst em which didn't seem to be doing much in particular. So I dumped Baz next to it and kicked some soil over him. Not much, mind. I had to be able to find him again. When his face and hands was covered, and he looked like a few old rags in the dirt when you stood a few yard back and squinted, I legged it.

I headed back same way I'd come, seeing even less of it this time. All I could think of were Legs, raising his fatherly eyebrow in that way of his and telling us I'd done alright. It were barmy to ponder along such lines, I know. But it were better than the other – to think about how I'd just killed a Munton.

When I got back to the Capri the engine started first time. If I were a man who lived by omens I'd take that as a good un. I crossed me fingers and let the clutch off. If there were one time I needed her to purr nice and quiet like a good pussy, it were now.

And she did.

I nigh on floated through the streets, heading back to the graveyard. I didn't dare think about what the hell I were to do once I got there. It were broad bastard daylight, fuck sake. And driving your motor across a graveyard ain't exactly the most discreetest of things a feller can do. How were I planning on getting Baz inside the car? I weren't even sure he'd fit, your Ford Capri being a bachelor's coupé and not well suited to what I had in mind for it. I pulled up a block away from the graveyard and gave the situation my full and undivided.

If I left it until dark some bastard might find him. Or some dog more like. No, I had to get him out fast. At least if I took Baz that'd be the evidence hid. And it were better to be seen hauling summat into a car now than to have folks find a dead feller later on. Wouldn't take many brains to link the corpse to meself. Not even Mangel brains.

From my vantage point at Capri-level I could see a fair bit of the graveyard a block down the road, including the foot of the old oak tree, which is where Baz and I had come to blows. My eyes stayed on that spot as I sat behind the wheel and tried to think. But a sudden movement set my heart thrashing like a landed trout. Someone were coming up the path towards the bushes and the dirt heap.

Some bastard with a shovel and barrow.

I gunned the engine and charged into the car park. I weren't sure what I were up to. All I knew is what I had to do – stop the gravedigger finding Baz. The car crunched to a halt. I got out. The digger were still where I'd first spotted him. But now he were staring at us, gob agape. I reckoned the dodgy exhaust had finally earned its keep. I ran up to him, wondering what the flaming Betty I were meant to say. But then, like it always do if you leaves yourself open to it, providence steamed in clutching a little plan in his sweaty paw.

'Hoy, mate,' I hollers, all urgent and scaredy-eyed, which were how I were feeling anyhow so I didn't need to put it on. 'Yer, uh . . . Yer bird's had accident, like.'

'Me burd? Who?'

'Aye. You know. She's . . .'

'Me gurlfriend?'

'Aye. Thass her.'

He were a young feller, as gravediggers went. But bald as a duck egg. 'But I ain't got no gurlfriend.'

'No?'

'No.'

'Oh.'

'Me woife, you means?'

'Oh aye. She's had accident.'

'Ain't got a woife neither.'

I scratched my head, which I sometimes found to work at times like this un.

'Could be . . .' says he, rubbing muddy paws together.

I were looking at the heap of soil across the way, not ten yards from where we was stood. One of Baz Munton's clumping boots were sticking up clean out of the earth, announcing quite clear to the world that he were lying there, dead. 'Oh aye?'

'Aye. It could be that you means me muther.'

I slapped meself hard across the cheek and says: 'Thass for me bein' so blinkin' thick. Course I means yer mother.'

'So woss happened to her?' he says. I were starting to think it were normal for his gob to be hanging open like that.

'Run over. She got run over. You gotta go to her.'

'Who let her out?'

'Eh?'

'Ain't got legs, has she. Who had her out in the road?'

'Well, she were in a wheelchair, weren't she. Out in the street.'

'Lord almighty,' he says, rubbing his pate. 'Who done it? Who gone an' ran over me muther?'

'It were . . . Well, iss a bit hard to talk about. I were a passer-by, like, just by-passin' and mindin' me own an' that. I . . . Oh hell . . .' I says, all quivery and rubbing me eyes.

'You're alright, mate. Go on an' tell us.'

'Well, there was so many coppers and ambulances, you see. You ain't seen the like of it before. I ain't anyhow. Thass why I comes to tell you ennit. All the coppers and that was all busy sweepin' up the road and lookin' after hurt folks.'

'Who were it? Who ran her over?'

'Sure you wants to know?'

'Aye.'

'Alright. Well it were a bus, big red double-decker. Just ran out, didn't she. In her chair, like. Driver had no chance. Passed away instantly, she did, by all accounts.'

'A buzz?'

'Aye. A bus.'

'Flamin' heck.' He dropped the barrow and hared off homeward.

Alone as I now were, I got to work. I hauled Baz up into the barrow along with plenty of loose grave dirt. Then I wheeled him over to the Capri and lugged him, after much grunting and sweating on my part, into the boot. I put everything back as it had been, checking that no item had fallen from Baz as I'd tossed and lugged him about. I even had presence of mind to turn over the bits of blood-stained gravel with me boot, where I'd given Baz his final hiding.

I drove out of Norbert Green, thinking how I might just be alright if I hit the right buttons and scored a few nudges. Aye, long as I took care of Baz's body alright. And long as no bastard knew I'd gone after him.

I slammed on me brakes.

The heavy object in the boot near came through onto the back seat. What were I thinking of?

I set off again, heading for the Paul Pry.

A few cars was parked out back when I pulled up. It sank my heart to see em, but nothing were to be done about that. I got out.

I called in at the bog first. I looked in the mirror and didn't recognise the feller in it. My hands, face, and hair was covered in dirt and blood. But after the shock wore off I reckoned it weren't so bad after all. Clothes was mostly alright, which were the main thing. It took us fairly five minutes to get all the shite off my hands and clean up me head, but needs must. When the dirt were off me face the cut above my eyebrow from Baz's sovereign didn't look so bad. I felt the back of my head. It were starting to ache like shite, but I couldn't find no major bumps nor cuts, which were a bonus. A couple of fellers came in for a piss during that time. 'Alright, Blake,' they each says on seeing us.

'Alright, mate,' I says back, not even looking.

When I got to the bar I called Nathan the barman aside.

'Alright, Blake,' he says.

'Alright, Nathan.'

'You'll be wantin' this now, I reckon,' he says, getting the glass he'd put by earlier.

'Oh . . . aye.'

He were looking at my head as he filled her. 'I hopes he came off worser'n you, mind.'

'Aye, well. You know what I were sayin' before?' I says, low of voice and shifty of eye. No one else were near, but too careful is summat you can never be.

'Aye. Find Baz alright?'

'Shhh. Do us a favour, will you? I never told you about Baz. Alright?'

His eyes narrowed. 'Funny, I reckons you did.'

'I knows I did, but I wants you to reckon I didn't. Gettin' us?'

His eyes narrowed until they was more or less shut. 'Why would I reckon summat like that?'

I knew what he were getting at. I pulled out my wallet, hoping to fuck that he'd be happy with what were in it. I had a last loving feel of the five sheets lying therein, then palmed em and put my hand on the bartop. 'Cos you're a businessman,' I says.

He licked his lips, greyish tongue brushing the lower reaches of his tash, then turned about and served another punter. I were sweating. I could feel the notes getting damp under my hand. I wondered how long they could stay there without turning to mush. But Nathan came back and nodded at my untouched pint. 'Payin' fer that, are you?' he says, and winked at us.

I handed him the notes.

He walked to the till, counting em, then stuck em in his back pocket when he saw the other punters was busy drinking and not paying him no mind.

I drank the lager, hoping that that were that, far as that went.

I were fair worn out when I got home. Swede were anyhow. It were plain to us that deciding on a final resting place for Baz at this stage might well be a mistake. I didn't want to dump him somewhere and then go back a couple of days later, when I could see straight, to shift him somewhere else. And besides, there were no hurry.

I had a cellar, see. A big bastard of a cellar that went down two levels, getting cooler with each one. In fact the cellar were as big as the upstairs, and I'd often thought about putting a little gym or a pool table down there. But I never ended up doing that. Never had the money, and couldn't be arsed even if I had. Weren't really my house. It were me old man's, though he were long dead. I only dossed there.

But Baz'd be alright down there, for now.

I hauled him out of the boot by the armpits and lugged him down the stair. His mashed face were all dry and caked and puckered round the edges, like raw meat left outside on a hot day. He were getting heavier and all. I promised meself, as I sat him up in a corner of the bottom cellar, that when I brung him back up again it'd be in at least ten bin liners.

I didn't hang about at home. There were still a fair bit of afternoon left before I were due at Hoppers. Be a pity to waste it. I ain't the sort to be holed up all hours like a hermit. I likes to get out there amongst em. And besides, I didn't fancy spending much time under the same roof as Baz. He smelled manky at the best of times, and being dead weren't liable to change that.

On the way out I noticed my shaking hands. I went to the kitchen and took a big swig out of the whisky bottle I'd lifted out of Hoppers a couple of weeks back. It went down my neck like molten lava and settled in a warm pool somewhere in me guts.

When I opened me eyes again my hands was steady. I wiped my eyes and took another swig, just to be on the safe side.

I got back in me car and took the usual route across town. I were starting to feel alright.

'What?' she says after I'd rung the bell.

'S'me ennit. Let us up.'

'Who's you?'

'Me, you dozy cow. Let us up.'

'Fuck off,' she says. But that were just her way. The door clicked.

I pushed it open with my boot and went up the stair.

'What the fuck happened to you?' she says. 'White as a glass o' milk, you is. Sick or summat?'

She were sitting on the bed in her black undies. Maybe she'd been waiting for us. Maybe she'd just been getting dressed. It mattered not a jot to me. She were there, is all. And there were a bed. She saw the look in my eyes, and showed us the one in hers. I pushed her back on the bed. She bounced back up, giggling, and started pulling at my belt. I pushed her back hard this time. And she knew.

She knew alright.

It were all over my face, whatever it were. She couldn't take her eyes off it. Not even when I were pressing it on her flesh and pumping it inside her. She had to have it.

I gave it to her.

6

....

I fell fast akip straight after, as were my habit, and started dreaming, which were not my habit. I gets em all the time now, but dreams never used to come easy to me. These days I can't rest my eyelids for a couple of seconds without dreams popping up out of the darkness. Sometimes seems I'm spending more of me life dreaming than waking. But that's now, and I ain't here to talk about the now. I were talking about back then, after I'd topped Baz Munton, stashed his body, tried me best to take my mind off it all by rogering Sally, then nodded off.

Well, as I says, I had a dream. A nasty one, although you wouldn't reckon so if you had one such yourself like as not. I were in a dark room. It were the kitchen in my house, curtains drawn and no light on. No light were on cos there were no bulb in the socket, and that's what Beth were berating us over. Despite fact I hadn't seen her since the day she died, it were no surprise to see her. It were no shock to hear her sharp tongue neither. She were at my right ear giving us all kinds of verbal hell. And I were sat at the table, taking it in one ear and doing me best to flush it out the other, as were my habit back when Beth were about. But there were some sort of block in the U-bend and the shite weren't flushing out proper. And slowly my head were filling up with it. All in all, things was just as they had been leading up to her demise.

It were because my brain weren't flushing it away that I had to give up finally and listen to her. She weren't moaning about the light-bulb as it turned out. Not no more anyhow. Now it were summat else, summat that she had no business carping on about, being as she were dead and all.

'I made a pie for you, Royston. I made a nice big pie with meat and taters and onions in and a nice brown puff pastry just the way you likes it. But you left it, Royston. You didn't eat yer pie. You left it on the table until it got cold and the pastry went hard. Wasn't hungry, you says. But I knowed you was hungry cos you went out and ate a bag o' chips. And while you was gone, Royston, while you was gone someone came along and ate the pie.'

'No.'

'Come on Blake, I'm starvin'. An' don't shout like that.'

'Leave us alone. Get away.'

'Blake. Wake up you dozy wazzock.'

'The pie . . . Wha . . . ?'

'You're dreamin', sweetheart,' says Sal. And, if you can believe it, her voice were tender as the first warm breeze of spring.

I opened my eyes and squinted at her, trying to convince meself that she were real and Beth were a dream. But that weren't easy. Sal looked and sounded like a dream herself, all dewy eyes and soft caresses. I were afraid to trust her, as if she'd be snatched away from us and replaced with Beth, face all screwed up with spite and nastiness.

'Hey,' she says. 'S'matter? Gawpin' at us like that, eyes fit to pop out.'

'You called us sweetheart, right?'

'I did.' Her voice were soft and gentle like someone else's. Anyone's but Sal's. 'So?'

'Well . . . Summat of a shock, ennit.'

'But sweetheart,' she says again, even going so far as to stroke my face. 'Sweetheart, you knows I loves you.'

I didn't know it, as it happened. And on any other occasion I'd not have welcomed hearing it. But it seemed alright just then. So I put my arm around her and pulled her close. I were still jumpy from the dream, and the closer I pulled her the better I felt. 'Aye,' I says. 'I reckon I do know that.'

She looked up at us, big blue eyes containing none of their habitual hardness. 'Do you love me, Blake? Do you? Answer us honestly.'

Beth had asked me this once, as it happened. I hadn't known quite what to say to it then, so I'd guessed the answer. And guessed it wrong. But you learns from your mistakes, and I weren't about to walk into that trap again. There's only one answer when a bird asks you that question. And let me tell you now – if you don't get it right, you're in for trouble. I opened my eyes and winked at her. 'Aye. Course I do.'

We snogged for a bit. Just as I were getting going again Sal got up and walked across the room. I watched her arse cheeks go up and down and out the door. When she came back soft music were floating through from the living room. It were 'Endless Love' by Lionel Richie and some bird. I watched her tits bounce back to the bed. Instead of getting back under the sheets she climbed atop us and sat looking down. It weren't a bad view from my angle, and I started moving under her. But she wanted to talk.

And when Sal wanted to talk she talked. 'Then why don't we move away?'

I gave her a good look in the eyes, probing for signs that she were joshing. Or maybe I'd banged her so long and hard that I'd knocked her brain askew. Why'd she come up with such barmy ideas? That's what I wanted to know. But I couldn't ask it. Hurt her feelings it would. 'Woss matter with you?' I says instead. 'We can't move away.'

'Why not?'

'Lives here, don't us. Always has done always will do.'

'But—'

'No one leaves Mangel, Sal. It ain't an option for folks like us. There's things standin' in our way, keepin' us in.' She knew what things I meant. Everyone did. But I didn't like to say em out loud. No one did.

'Oh Blake,' she yells, eyes blazing, tits wobbling, Lionel warbling on in the background about not being able to resist some bird's charms. 'Why don't you see? What kind of a life does we live here, eh? Same thing day in, day out. Ain't no hidin' here. Every bastard knows every other bastard. Everyone calls me slapper. And now they've all taken to callin' you bottler.'

'That won't be happenin' no more,' I says, all deep and flat. Bit like Clint Eastwood actually.

'How come?' she says, crossing her arms across her chest and looking at us funny.

But I knew it would be happening. They'd go on

calling us names unless I let on to folks about what I'd done to Baz. And I weren't likely to do that. 'It won't be happenin' because...I'll show em that it just ain't true.'

'Oh aye, what you gonna do? Top one of the Muntons or summat?'

After a pause I says: 'That'd be goin' too far I reckons. But don't you worry about it. Opportunity'll arise soon enough.'

She stretched out beside us. We stayed like that for a while. My eyes went to the net curtains, which was rippling gently in the warm breeze. Outside the sun were packing up and hauling tent for some other part of the world, making way for an evening that'd all but moved in already. I wanted to stay just where I were, leaving all them out there to fight and name-call amongst emselves. But it never worked out like that. Sooner or later someone comes along and knocks on your door. And if you don't answer they lobs a brick through the window.

That's what I were thinking. And maybe Sally were thinking it and all. Either way, we gave each other a squeeze.

'I oughta shift,' I says. 'Work tonight.'

'Blakey...'

'Aye.'

'I ain't no slapper.'

'I knows that, love,' says I, pulling up me trolleys.

'An' I won't give no one cause to say I am. Not ever again. Them days is gone.'

I gave her a kiss. A nice long one. And I had a feeling she meant it. 'Sal,' I says, pausing in the doorway. 'Lend us a tenner?'

'Fuck off. Ain't got a tenner have I.'

'Go on Sal.'

A few seconds later she got out of bed and went to her handbag on the dresser. 'Here. Fiver's all I got.' She held it over her shoulder, keeping her back to us to make a point.

I put my arms around her and kissed her neck. Then I took the bluey and pissed off.

I drove home, feeling better all round. Soon as I got in I took my gear off and put it in bin liners. I weren't expecting trouble from coppers, but sticking to the safe side never did no one no harm. I smelt Sal all over my body as I stepped into the shower, which got us excited all over again. Then I saw the grave dirt under me fingernails and went limp. I started singing to take my mind off it. I sang 'Always on My Mind' for about twenty minutes, then got out of the shower.

Afterwards I splashed me neck with aftershave and pulled on some clean trolleys. I were thinking about Sal again as I opened the wardrobe. Not in any sentimental way, mind. I went over what we'd done back there at her flat, before I'd fallen akip. It had never been like that before. Some bits I couldn't recall, like they was a dream. But I knew they wasn't.

I thought about the real dream that had followed, and straight away looked at my bed, the one that I'd shared with Beth. I dunno what I were looking for. Maybe I were expecting Beth to be lying there, long blonde hair spread out across the pillow like straw, snoring like a trooper with sinus trouble. But she weren't there. And she never would be again.

'Calm yerself,' I whispers, catching my eye in the mirror. 'You don't act calm, folks'll wonder woss wrong, ennit.'

I buttoned up a white shirt and made sure the dicky bow were a mite askew, the way dickies is meant to be worn.

I wondered if Sal had meant it, about leaving Mangel. She were full of it, that girl. She knew as well as anyone how leaving town weren't what Mangel folk did. Truth were, I couldn't see meself living nowhere else, nor her neither, even if it were possible. Products of our environment, that's what we was. Used to learn us at school that we was all leaves on the same tree, and when a leaf drops off it withers and dies. We can't live without the tree, and it can't get by without us. That sounded about right when we was younguns. And most folks accepted it as gospel. And if I drove out to the East Bloater Road now and then and looked on the fields lying yonder, what of it? I were just looking, weren't I?

I donned black trousers, black jacket, and black boots. I were primed and ready. But I didn't go. Not right away. I looked at meself in the mirror a while longer, turning and posing like you do. I were looking alright, I reckoned. Bit puffier these days than when I were younger and done more training, but you has to set that off against other things. Like my features maturing with age, coming into their own like. Beth used to say I looked a bit like Clint Eastwood, as it happens.

'Beth,' I'd say to her. 'Who do you reckon I looks like?'

She shrugged and didn't look up. 'Dunno. No one really.'

'What about Clint?'

'Clint who?' She was lying on her bed in knickers and bra, painting her toe nails.

'Eastwood. You knows him.'

'Oh him. Aye.'

'Woss that? Aye, you knows Clint Eastwood? Or aye, you reckons I looks like him?'

'Aye.'

'Thought so. Ta.'

'What you grinnin' at?' she says, finishing one foot and moving on to the other.

'Clint Eastwood ennit. I looks like him.'

'But Blakey, it ain't about looks, is it. It's about the things you does. Actions. Thass what counts.' And that were the end of that conversation.

I trotted downstairs, looking at my watch. I were late. I went out the front door and fired up two point eight fuel-injected litres.

Beth had a point you know. About putting yourself across. It don't matter how much of a hardman you looks. It don't matter how wide your shoulders is or how short your hair's cropped. Looking hard amounts to jack shite. You want folks' respect, you got to show em what you can do. Remind em what'll happen should they choose to meddle.

These was the issues I were tossing around inside me swede as I touched sixty up the Wall Road. Things seemed clearer now. Maybe it were the wind whistling through the window. Maybe it were the fag I were smoking. Maybe it were the pleasant feeling in me loins that dogging Sal all afternoon had left us with. But I didn't reckon so.

Not really.

It were because I'd killed Baz Munton.

Hoppers weren't far short of dead when I stepped in. It were early, mind. Normally I'd have a pint or two near the door until the pace picked up, maybe share a joke with Rachel. I were planning on doing just that when Fenton comes out his office holding a cigar.

'Alright, Mr Fenton.'

'Blake, can I have a word, mate?'

Fenton had bought Hoppers a few month back, when it were still a burnt-out shell of a place. It were a classic case of an outsider sailing into town in a big car scouting for prime land to stick his flagpole in. No one knew shite about him, besides him being a poncey cunt from the big city with a flash motor and a posh voice. But folks didn't need to know much. It were enough to know he weren't local. If you ain't from Mangel, folks round here tends to wonder why. Why ain't he from Mangel when every other fucker is? And if he ain't from Mangel, how'd he come to be here? They wondered, but no one ever had the bollocks to ask him. See, your outsider in Mangel commands a certain grudging respect. He's been out there, ain't he, seen places that Mangel folk ain't seen nor never will see. Folks might not like him but they won't touch him neither, just gawp at him like he's got two heads and three arse cheeks.

I'd never seen him that way meself. For starters he had floppy hair past his collar, which made him bent in my book. Feller's hair ought to be short, unless he's a tramp. Then there was other things about him I didn't take to.

He didn't understand what made Mangel folk tick, for one. That don't add up to much of a problem in a street sweeper or a warehouseman, but when you runs one of Mangel's premier drinking holes it does. Right from the off he were spouting newfangled ideas about running Hoppers. I reckoned em just talk at first. But then I seen the way the new Hoppers were taking shape. It weren't right. He'd turned a perfectly good piss house into a fucking tart's parlour. Take the name for starters. Plain old Hoppers it'd been up to then. Nothing wrong with that and no need to change it. But Fenton had to go and tack on 'Wine Bar & Bistro', didn't he. I'd never seen no one drink wine in there and fuck knows what a bistro is.

Course, when the punters saw his changes they gave it the arse and stayed away in droves. And to his credit Fenton recognised where he'd gone wrong and changed most of it back again, except the new name. Still weren't right in my book, but it were an improvement. And folks seemed to agree. Hoppers weren't the place it once had been but it were a place to get pissed. Punters came back. And after a while you got used to the name. It were classy, when you came to look at it. Classy in a way only a feller from the outside could pull off.

'Aye,' I says to his question about him having a word. 'Why not.'

'What happened last night, Blake?'

'Last night? What of it?'

'You disappeared.' He were wearing a dark grey suit with a green tie. Fucking twat, wearing a suit when he didn't have to. No need for it. But suits and ties is what he always wore. 'There was some kind of scene out front and you disappeared. I need to know why.'

He were right, you know. After the thing with Baz last night I weren't feeling much like being a doorman. So I popped round back for a bit of air. Fair enough, you might reckon. But I hadn't ever done it before. And Fenton had a point: a doorman oughtn't to desert his door. I'd forgot about it since, what with everything. Not even walking into Hoppers had jogged my memory. But it weren't a problem no more. I'd sorted it.

'Look,' I says. I were feeling better now I had everything straight in me head. You couldn't blame Fenton for being a wanker. Like I says, he weren't from round here. He didn't know what's what more than a cat knows how to make gravy. 'Look, it ain't a problem,' I says. 'Won't happen again.'

'What won't happen again? Tell me what happened.'

'Some shite, thass all. Nut'n to—'

'Blake.'

'Eh eh eh,' I says, nice and calm. I noticed I were stood square to him now, arm aloft in a placatory gesture. It were only when he looked at it that I noticed there were a fist on the end. It shut him up mind, which is what placatory gestures is meant to do in my book. 'Cool it, right? As I were sayin', some shite came to pass and it ain't worth frettin' over the entrails. Alright, I shouldn't of deserted me post an' that. But I had a little problem an' now iss sorted, see? Nuthin' like that'll ever happen henceforth. You mark my words it won't.'

He said nothing. You could almost hear his brain whirring away beneath them floppy locks.

'Tell you what,' I says, smirking a bit. 'It happens again, I'll hand in me dicky bow. Feller can't play fairer.'

'Blake... Look, I really don't want to fight about this, but I need you to understand something. When I took you on there were certain conditions attached. Remember? Do you remember them?'

I did. And I thought em a bit strange if I'm honest.

But it were a doorman job and it were Hoppers, so I'd shrugged and said I'd do it. 'Aye.'

'And do you remember what they were.'

This were a bit harder, being as it'd been a while back and I don't like to think about the past too much. But I had a quick think and came up with summat. 'Aye,' I says. 'Work five nights a week and don't have holidays unless you has em same time.'

'That's right. And watch out for anyone strange coming in. That was your special job, Blake. That's why I needed a good doorman.'

'And you fuckin' got one.'

'I know I did. But I need to trust you.' He sucked on his cigar. It'd gone out. 'Can I, Blake? Can I trust you?'

I tutted and looked up the bar. Punters was coming in. 'Fuck sake. I'm the best fuckin' doorman—'

'—in Mangel. I know, Blake. Look, let's forget about this, OK? No hard feelings. But just please be vigilant on that door. It means a lot to me. If you have to slip away for any reason, tell me. And watch out for those—'

'Odd folks.'

'Yes. Strangers. One other thing, Blake.'

'What?'

He relit his cigar and brightened up a bit. 'I've been thinking about Hoppers. I've got plans. Big plans. Plans that'll turn this place into something the people of Mangel have never seen.'

Oh, for fuck sake. Couldn't leave it alone could he.

'First off,' he says, 'the name Hoppers has got to go. Even with the Wine Bar & Bistro suffix. I know we've tried this before and it failed, but I think the timing was wrong. It'll work this time. It's been called

Hoppers for too long and people have made up their minds about the place years ago. No, we need something new. Something that people will find irresistibly glamorous and exotic. I'm thinking Café Americano. What do you think about that, Blake?'

I rubbed me chin. 'Ain't a caff though, is it. Only scran a feller can get here is a bag o' nuts. And there's Burt's Caff twenty yard up the road for a fry-up.'

Fenton burst out laughing like I'd tickled his armpits. Then he stopped so suddenly you'd never have known he'd been laughing just now. 'Blake, the word "café" has connotations beyond the greasy spoon. I aim to bring in some catering anyway. That's part of my plans. Just a selection of light bites.'

'Americano. Woss that mean? American? Hoppers ain't American though is it? It's in Mangel.'

'That's the whole point, Blake. I want to bring a slice of otherness to this town. I want to give people the excitement of foreign culture without them having to leave town.'

'And you ain't American neither. How can you call Hoppers American?'

'Ah, don't worry about it,' he says, turning. 'Just wanted your opinion.'

'Aye, and I gave it you.'

'Right.'

I got the impression folks saw us a bit different that night. There were none of the last night's sneering and jeering. There were no trouble, which makes for a good night when you're employed as a doorman. And there were no talk of bottling.

But there weren't much else neither. No joking from them who was in the habit of being funny. No asking after my wellbeing from them who was often as not solicitous after it. A lot of looks, mind. A lot of long stares and sly glances from them what ought to know better, eye contact being the main root of aggro round these parts. Plenty of looks from the birds and all. And when I gets that kind of attention I reciprocates in kind. You shouldn't look a gift horse in the muzzle, says I. Not even when she's got fat legs, cross-eyes, and a hair lip. You never know when your luck'll change and someone like that might be all you can snag.

Course, I knew these folks couldn't be acting on knowledge of what I'd done. They couldn't know. If they knew then the Munton boys knew as well. Them what was remaining of that clan anyhow. And chances were the coppers'd know by now and all.

But I couldn't help thinking that somehow folks did know, without knowing it, like. I knows I ain't making much sense here, but if you just bears with us I'll do me best to spit it out in such a way as you'll understand. Some things folks knows without realising it. Sometimes you can tell what kind of a thing a feller has done simply by looking at him. And it's not in your swede where you feels it. It's in your heart. So they knew, I reckoned, without really knowing what they knew, why they knew it, or whether they knew anything at all. Alright?

And whatever they felt about us, I felt it and all. I felt like I could have kept a randy bull out that night, no matter how many pissed-up cows was inside.

Didn't last long, mind. About halfway into the evening them other thoughts started creeping in, ones about the Muntons. Who the fuck were I joshing, reckoning I could top Baz and dump him in me cellar and go to work and hey-ho, here we go? I were joshing no one, is who.

Least of all the Muntons.

They'd know it were me alright. It were plain as the hairs on my arse. They'd know. Them and every other bastard in Mangel. It were all clear now. The way folks had been looking at us – fellers backing off, birds licking their lips. They knew what I'd done, who I'd done it to, and how I'd done it.

I passed the rest of the evening turning these things over in my head, looking for any sign of light up the end of the dark tunnel that had opened up before us. I didn't even notice the folks going in and out of Hoppers after a bit, other than that none of em was Munton nor copper. There were no light to be found in my tunnel. And no matter which way I turned I knew it only came out one place: the back of the Meat Wagon, me tied up and gagged and heading for a carve-up in Hurk Wood.

I finished up for the night at midnight or so, and pulled meself one before pissing off. I reckoned I'd go and see Legsy again. I wouldn't let him know what had happened to Baz, less he'd already guessed it. But I could tell him what else were happening on the Munton front. He'd tell us what to do. And maybe it'd be best to spill the full tin of beans after all. Legs were a mate and I could trust him. He'd not be able to help us unless I told him about Baz.

Aye, that's what I'd do.

But somehow that didn't make us feel a lot better. It were with a leaden heart that I downed the whisky and traipsed out back. Each footstep were a step further into the dark tunnel what only had one end.

Even if I stopped and turned arse the other way, it were still a step further. There were no way out. Legs couldn't help us out of this one.

No one could.

I opened the door and climbed into my car, thinking how going to the coppers might not be such a bad idea. I'd go down for years. But at least I wouldn't find meself dressed in concrete at the bottom of the river, arms and legs lopped of and head shoved up arse. And it were because I were preoccupied with such thoughts that I didn't notice the feller on the back seat.

'Alright, Jess,' says I as he pulled himself upright.

7

....

Right here seems a good place to say a few more words about the Muntons, reduced in number as that clan now were. You've heard the stories. Can't very well hear about Mangel without hearing a thing or two relating to the Muntons. And you've heard what I've already told you, so I'll do my bastardest not to retread old ground, so to speak.

But there's one thing about them that you won't have heard. It's a secret alright, sure as shite is brown. And if it ain't a secret and you has heard it before . . . Well, I don't rightly know what. Who told you?

Happened two summers before the time I'm telling you about. I were working for the Muntons back then, as I had done for the few years previous, and intended on doing for as long as they'd have me. It were good work, see. I were doorman at Hoppers. Head doorman.

Heard it before, eh?

Well, Hoppers were a different kettle of kippers back then. These days it were a Wine Bar & Bistro, as you've come to hear. But in them days it were something of a local entertainment venue, as well as being a place to get right pissed. Every night there were summat on. Funny man Tuesdays, topless mud wrestling Monday and Wednesday, karaoke Saturday, strippers other nights. And happy hour every night between five and seven. It were popular and all. Not just amongst town folk. They came from miles around, from Barkettle in the north to Tuber in the south. Once I even welcomed a coach party from East Bloater, believe it or not.

Hoppers were the Mangel Mecca in all but name. And presiding over it were the Munton brothers. Course, it were their old man who made it what it were. Tommy Munton.

Aye.

Tommy Munton.

Let me tell you summat. Everything you've heard about Tommy Munton is true. True as grass is green, trees reaches upward and turnips grows in the ground. Even the one about him ripping off the post office in Lower Flapp dressed as a nun. And the shoot-out in Felcham where he shot their heads off and walked away with nary a pellet up his arse. Course, that's how Hoppers got started, with all the money he'd robbed. How else do a man borned in a skip and growed up in the gutter get his paws on that kind of coinage?

But none of his misdeeds mattered if you looks at em as a means to an end. That's the way most folks reckoned it anyhow. Hoppers were the smartest premises in Mangel. And when Tommy died of old shrapnel he passed it on to his younguns.

Which were his first and last mistake.

Now, you can say what you likes about schools and books, but far as I'm concerned teachers and writing can't give a feller a business brain. He's either born with one or he's picking sprouts with the rest of us. And Tommy Munton were born with one. That's how he'd made Hoppers the success it were. Helped him with the bank jobs and all, like as not. You'd need to know where they keeps the safe in a bank, for example. But whatever business brains he had, he'd held em back when fathering his boys.

You'd never have known it to look at the surface appearance of things. To the untrained eye Hoppers looked healthy as ever under the Muntons junior. Folks was drinking, which were all that counted to my thinking. And that's why it were summat of a shock when Lee took us aside one night after lock-up and told us what he had in mind.

'Burn the place down?' says I.

'Aye. And you're the torch.'

'Hang on, hang on—'

'Can't hang on too long. You're doin' it, Blakey.'

'But . . . Lee, this is Hoppers. You can't very well burn down Hoppers. Iss . . .'

'I'll tell you what it is. Worth more to us burnt down than stood up is what it is.'

'But Lee, you can't.'

'Right. I can't. So you do it.'

And so it were to be.

The date were planned for the Thursday night a week hence, which were a stripping night. Lee's thinking were that coppers and insurance folk would point the finger at local opposition, there being a backward element in Mangel what reckoned a bird oughtn't to be exploited in such a way as they was at Hoppers. That's how his thinking went anyhow. Can't say I'd ever met any such folk meself.

Well, the night came. I started it as I always done, standing by the door. I weren't being as friendly with folks as were my custom. It weren't only impending commitments playing on my nerves. There was other matters getting us down and all. One of em – the main one, perhaps – were that I'd not been getting on too brightly with Beth of late. Like any happily married couple, we'd had our ups and downs. But you know how it goes. It gets to the point where the downs just keeps on going down, making up for all the ups you had at the start.

Anyhow, them was the sorts of worries that nagged at us as I stood there at the door of Hoppers that night. To cut a long un short, I weren't feeling up to the task in hand. Torching Hoppers were a big job, and one which demanded the kind of juice that frankly weren't in us. So I took a young feller aside, showed him a few twenties, and asked him to get it done for us.

Finney being Finney, he accepted the task with nary a moment's reflection. Said he'd do it for nothing, twat that he were. But seeing as I had the money out ready and all, he took it. Come back a couple hours after closing, I says to him.

Getting that sorted had no end of a soothing effect on me nerves. I were able to spend the rest of the night being my usual self – cheerful and up for a laugh but any trouble and I'll have you, mate. Even had a couple of pints and caught some of the show. Sally were up there that night, skin all oiled-up and glistening under the spotlights. She'd only been working there a few weeks. Course, she were Baz Munton's bird then. But when a feller lets his bird go up on stage like that and show off her wares he's asking for trouble. I dunno how long I watched her for. Got to feeling like no one else were there, it did. Just me with me lager, and her up there dancing for us. Things'd be alright soon, I recall thinking.

After lock-up I went out to the car park, trying not to think about the future too much. Just get this out the way first. Burn Hoppers down, collect me torch fee from Lee, and see what happens. Only problem were that the Capri wouldn't start.

I had me swede under that bonnet for half an hour. Can't recall what the trouble were. You knows what Capris is like. I went back inside and rang Beth. Get some kit on, I says, it being late and her in bed and all. If I were still stuck in fifteen minutes, I told her, she'd be hearing another ring from us. Else she could go back to her kip. True to form, she hurled thirty seconds of complaint down the line, studded with words choice enough to have a bull terrier blushing purple. I shrugged and hung up. I knew she'd come if I asked her, just so she'd have a reason to get at us for the next few days. She'd fucking better. Finney'd soon be here with a tank of paraffin and a lighter.

But then the car started, so I never called her back.

I took one last look around the place, made sure the door were unlocked for Finney, then hared off home.

When I got there I cracked open a can and sat down a while, thinking how lucky I were that Beth were sound akip. I turned on the telly and watched the news for a bit. They was talking about the war, as always. That were about the time they first started showing that big bomb sitting there in the silo. I had a flick and found my way to a film that looked like it had potential. Sure enough, within a minute or two a feller were taking the bird's bra off and feeling her up all over. It were smart, like the stuff you ain't meant to get on telly. Before I knew it I had meself out and ready. It didn't take long. I didn't really need the telly neither. All I had to do were close my eyes and think of Sal, up there on stage, half a can of motor oil rubbed into her tits and arse. I imagined it were me who oiled her up before her turn. And I had a feeling it soon would be, though the stage'd be charcoal by then.

After I'd had a bit of a doze I pulled me kecks up and went to the front window. You couldn't see Hoppers from where I were standing, but there were a dull glow in the sky above a certain spot in town. I had a funny feeling at that moment, like a frozen clot of blood passing through my heart. But it passed. It were no real shock to see that Hoppers were blazing. Finney might have shite for brains, but if he says he'll do summat he'll do it. He were still standing there now, like as not, warming his hands and laughing. Fucking twat.

It were with a heavy sigh that I switched off the telly and went up the stair. I opened the bedroom door as quietly as born clumsiness allows. I weren't planning on kipping in there, mind. That'd be breaking the habit of twelve months. I just wanted to... Dunno, really. See that Beth were akip, I reckon. But she weren't. She weren't in bed at all.

She weren't anywhere in the room.

Hang on, I thought, scratching my head. I know what she went and done. She went to pick us up anyhow, even though I hadn't called her back. She went to get us so she can lay into us, bitter and enraged as she were.

'Ah, fuck...' I says, downstairs again now, glancing outside at the warm glow over Hoppers. It were a clear night. Stars in the sky, full moon. Smoke billowed up like a grey genie out of a dirty old beer bottle.

My throat already knew the feel of cold steel. My old man used to threaten to slit it on a regular basis. Just verbal threats at first, little reminders that one day he'd cut me neck open and hang us up over a tin bucket. After a while I noticed a pattern – the threats'd come when I looked happy, when I walked around the house whistling or bouncing on my heels. Then I started coming home with birds. Hiding em from dad, course. But he always knew. He'd get the family silver out soon as she were out the door. 'Thinks your life'll turn out just how you wants it, don't you,' he'd say, throat rattling with all the fags and whisky. 'Reckon it'll be nice and happy, eh? Well forget it. Didn't turn out that way for me did it. And I'll make sure it don't for you neither, you little bastard.'

'Shift,' says Jess, nodding at the controls and sliding the blade off my skin.

I knew he'd nicked us. I could feel the drop of blood reaching into my chest hairs and tickling us. But I didn't wipe it away. I got the motor started and put her in gear. 'Where to?' I says as we joined an empty Friar Street.

'Strake Hill.'

'Car park?' I looked in the mirror and saw his nod. Weren't much else about him I could see besides his big silhouette. Reminded us of Baz. I'd never thought em alike before. 'Been puttin' on weight there Jess?' I says.

He didn't move. Or his silhouette didn't. He just sat tight, filling my mirror. A car turned up ahead and flashed headlights in his face. I looked away. I liked the silhouette better.

'Whereabouts, Jess?' I slowed down, seeing the turn-off up yonder. 'What we goin' there for?'

He leaned forward and rested his knife hand by me right shoulder.

I pulled into the car park and straight away spotted the Meat Wagon parked in the far corner. Everyone in Mangel knew the Meat Wagon. No one seemed to know for surely why it were so called. Not even meself, and I'd been quite close to the Munton boys in the past. From the moment Lee were big enough to drive one they'd driven around in a white van known as the Meat Wagon. And before that Tommy Munton used to drive one, also known as the Meat Wagon. But I hadn't ever met a soul who could tell us for surely why. Weren't like they was butchers nor nothing. Most folks wasn't interested in the why anyhow, long as they never ended up riding in the back of it.

Jess pointed a finger at the van.

'Look, Jess . . .'

With his other hand he twocked the back of the blade across my head, which weren't nice.

I rolled up to the Meat Wagon nice and slow, trying not to wake it up. It were solid as a Sherman tank and had no windows besides them up front, which was blacked out anyhow. I says it were white, but it weren't white right then. It were plastered in shite and crap and couldn't have been cleaned in a year. I pulled up next to it.

What if I makes a break for it here? I suddenly thinks to meself. What are the chances of them having guns? I ought to outrun Jess, big feller as he were. And Lee never ran. Lee never done any kind of legwork. Aye, it were a good plan. Open the door and peg it like Billy-o . . .

I felt Jess's hot breath on the back of my neck. 'Try it,' he says, in a voice coming from somewhere between Norbert Green and the bowels of hell itself, which ain't too far separated I shouldn't think.

The passenger door opened.

Lee got in.

He were dressed same as he always were: black leather coat, black boots, blue jeans. There were no hairs on his head besides a neat beard that covered up some of the scars he'd earned as a youngun. Other facial scars was visible and all. There were no hiding the deep groove that started on his right cheekbone and went through his nose like a mountain pass. But some scars you don't want to hide. Some scars is a part of your character, and say more about you than any pissed-up pub tales.

'Alright, Blake,' he says.

'Alright, Lee.'

One thing were in my favour: they couldn't do it here. Not in this car park in the middle of town. Their style were more out in the sticks, Hurk Wood in particular if rumour had it right. They was always careful in their enforcing, even if they didn't know shite about running a business. That's why they was so legendary. All them stories about em, no convictions.

No, if they was planning on doing us in they'd take us outside of Mangel town. And that meant more opportunities to escape. That's what I kept telling meself anyhow.

Lee wiped his mouth with the back of his hand and coughed up some phlegm, then swallowed it loudly. 'Got some things to discuss ain't us, Blake.'

I couldn't help but feel like a farmer who'd fell in

his own slurry pit. 'Aye,' I says, letting the slurry swallow us up. There comes a point where all you can see is brown and all you can smell is shite. And when you reaches that point... Well, there ain't no more struggling. 'I reckons we has.'

Lee gave us a funny look. One of them looks that you feels rather than sees. 'You does, does you? Well, alright.' He shifted in his seat to facing us. I didn't move. I'd rather be hit on the ear than the face. 'So what d'yer think? Reckon it's a goer, or what?'

'Eh?' I says.

'How much homework you done?'

'What?'

He laughed. 'Hear that, Jess? Some things never changes, does they. Moon keeps comin' up, river keeps on flowin', an' Blake keeps on playin' the twat.'

I looked in the mirror. Jess weren't moving.

Lee went on: 'Alright, Blake. I'll play. I can see yer angle. You works there, so you gotta play thick, right? Just in case. Well let me get things started so's you don' have to. Your boss. Fenton. Poncey little arse bandit. How much you know about him?'

Well that's interesting, I were thinking. I reckon I'll go along with this. Long as we're singing this song we ain't singing no other one. And there was a nasty little song we could have been singing, if only Lee and Jess knew the tune. 'Fenton? Well, like you says, he's me boss. Poncey, aye. Arse bandit? Quite possibly. That hair of his...'

'Tellin' us nuthin' new there Blake.'

'Alright. So, er... What is it you wanna know? Can't say as I've peered too closely at his affairs like.'

Lee shifted in his seat. His leather jacket creaked like an old barn door on a quiet night. 'I'm talkin' business. You knows what I'm after. When do he bank his cash? Where's his safe? Any peculiar security arrangements an' that? Woss his weak spot? Shite like that. Come on. Spill.'

I looked at him. 'You wanna do the place over?'

'Eh,' says Lee, turning to Jess and creaking some more. 'Did I say this feller were a twat? Do us a favour, Jess. Slap me wrist. Go on, slap the fucker. Slap it hard.'

I could feel my shoulders loosening up. I could almost remember times when I'd had a laugh with these two cunts. 'Alright lads,' I says, laughing a bit meself. 'Knock it off.'

'Aye, we wanna do the place. And when I says "we", I means us and you.'

'Me? Fuck off, mate. Ain't doing it.'

'Why.'

'Why should I? Me fuckin' job ennit. I likes me job.'

'We'll give you a job,' he says. 'Proper job. Legal an' that.'

'You? Doin' what?'

'Can't say yet. Secret.'

'Ain't interested. Ain't interested in doin' over Hoppers neither.'

Lee looked at Jess and shook his head. Then he says: 'By the way, Blake, seen Baz?'

My shoulders froze up again. 'Baz?' I made a clueless face and started shaking my head. Then I remembered what the whole town knew: Baz had given us a hard time only the night before. They'd know about that for surely. 'Oh, aye, he were round Hoppers last night. Last time I seen him, that were.'

'Aye, we heared about that one. You'll have to excuse our young brother. Blows a bit hot and cold like. Once he gets idea into his head he ain't liable to shake it. But we admires that trait, don't us, eh Jess?'

'Bit hot and cold like,' says Jess.

'But not in this case.' Lee lit a fag without taking his eyes off us. 'This time he came close to lettin' the cat out the fuckin' bag, I hears. But he didn't, did he. He just about kept the bastard in there.'

As it happened a dirty old tomcat were mooching around just then in the one corner of the car park where my eyes was focused. Dirt had spilled over from surrounding borders, which was filled with more pop cans, fag packets, and used johnnies than flowers and shrubs and what have you. The cat circled four times, then arched up and laid a big one. 'What bastard?' I says, wishing I were a cat.

'The bastard about you toppin' yer wife.'

I looked at Lee. Then Jess. Then Lee again. 'What?'

'Bastards,' says Lee. 'We'll talk about bastards a bit more, shall us? See, this is your bastard, Blakey. You fathered it when you sent Beth down Hoppers that night to burn. And now the bastard's comin' home to claim kin. Now's time to face up to yer fatherly responsibilities an' that. What you reckon, Jess? Blake oughta do the right thing by his bastard or what?'

'Aye. Fuckin' bastard.'

'What about you, Blake? Gonna be a good father?'

The cat strolled off up the car park. He didn't even kick any dirt over his business. There's summat wrong with cats these days. None of em bothers to cover up their muck. 'Who told you all this?' I says.

'So you admits it?'

'No. Just wanna know who's been spreadin' muck.'

'Don't matter who spreads it. Muck's there. Stinks.'

'Ain't true.'

'Stinks though.'

I stared Lee right in the eye. 'It fuckin' ain't true.'

'So you'd be happy if I pops in to the copper shop to spread it a bit further? Tell em what I heared, like? Won't mind if they hauls you in and takes a close look at you? Sure you didn't send Beth to her death, Blakey boy?'

The cat stopped when it got to my Capri. It nosed the air a bit and had a good gander through the windows. Then it made up its mind about us and hared off. I closed my eyes and saw Baz's dead body propped up in the corner of my cellar. 'Woss yer problem, Lee?' I says as calmly as I could. 'Why give us this shite?'

Lee gave us the eye for a few seconds. 'Less juss say this: You're in a position to repay your debt to us.'

'What fuckin' debt?'

'The one you rung up when you turned a little accidental fire into a murder inquiry, which had the coppers snoopin' a bit closer than normal and callin' it arson. The debt you got into when the insurance cunts refused to pay out.' He grabbed me collar and twisted, putting his screwed-up face up against mine. 'You fucked us, you fuckin' bastard.'

'Shall I kill him, Lee?'

'Leave it Jess. We does it my way.'

'I'll kill him.'

'You fuckin' will not,' he barked at the back seat. It were nice to have his face out of mine. 'Every man deserves a chance to repay his debts. Even cunts like him.'

'But it weren't me,' I says. 'I didn't kill her. I dunno what she were doin' in there an' it weren't . . .'

'Weren't what?'

'You know. She were inside and . . . I were . . .'

'Ah, save it. You're gonna help us out and you knows it. Come on Jess.'

They got out and stomped over to the Meat Wagon, Jess walking to the right of and a bit behind Lee. When all three brothers was together Baz'd be on the other side, slightly lagging. They wouldn't be doing that no more, and I felt quietly proud to see their little V-shape spoilt so. Before he reached the van Lee turned and shouted: 'That exhaust of yours needs fixin' by the sounds of her. Get down the Munton Motors why don't you. Baz'll get it done while he's doin' yer tyres. He'll be back on the morrer, like as not.'

They got in and slammed the doors. Lee swung the van out with the recklessness of one who wants every fucker in town to know how good at reversing he is. Then they bombed into the road.

I sat where I were for a while, tapping me fingers on the wheel. I lit two fags, one after the other, and smoked em. When I were nearing the end of the second one the cat jumped on the bonnet and glared at us. It settled down, legs tucked under, never losing eye contact. I turned the key and gave the throttle a good dose. The cat jumped in the air, did a bit of a somersault, then pegged it back into the bushes. I went home.

When I got there I went to bed.

8

Phone woke us next morning about ten. I picked it up and says: 'What time of the bastard night does you call this?'

'Ain't night. Mornin' ennit.'

'Alright, Finney.'

'Alright, Blake. Out for a drink the night?'

'Nah.'

'Come on, feller's gotta keep his strength up.'

'Nah, mate. Workin' ain't I.'

'Ah, right. The morrer, then?'

'Er . . . Dunno about that.'

'Woss matter? You always comes out drinkin'.'

'Workin' ain't I.'

'No you ain't. Never works on that day.'

'Oh, I dunno. Don't reckon I'll fancy it.'

'Fuck off, Blake. You always comes out drinkin' with me an' Legs an' thass what you're doin' the morrer.'

It were too much effort to argue. Specially with sleep still dragging us down and umpteen different worries lurking behind it. 'Ah, alright you cunt. I'll be there.'

'Thass the spirit, Blakey.'

'Bye.'

'Hang about.'

'What, for fuck?'

'I ain't said where yet.'

'But we always drinks in the Paul Pry.'

'Thass right, Blake. We always drinks in the Paul Pry.'

I laid back on the pillow. But I knew sleep were beyond us now. Finney were a cunt. I knew he meant no harm, but he were always doing just the thing you didn't want him to. It'd taken us all night to get to sleep. I'd finally dropped off at eight near as not. And sleep hadn't gave us what I'd wanted of it. I wanted some time away from me woes. I got another bastard dream instead. Same shite as last time – me at the kitchen table with Beth slagging us off nearby. Only the row had moved on a mite. 'How could you do it, Royston?' she were yelling. 'How could you do such a thing to yer own wife? Not that you ever treated us like a proper wife. All I ever done were try an' make you happy. And this is what I gets. Tell you what, Royston, I deserves better'n the likes of you. I married the wrong feller, is what I gone and done.' And it went on like that.

So all in all I were knackered.

I got up, had a shower, shaved, and trimmed me tash. A tash does no good when it hangs too low. All it'll do for you is tickle your top lip and soak up beer. But a well-kept one is the mark of a proud man, a man who knows what he is and why he's it. Then I put on me track suit and went down the stair.

I took a long time over breakfast, even though I were only having a few bits of toast and some bangers. I were planning on going training see, and there's nothing worse than exercise on a full belly. I rounded it off with a few cups of tea and three raw eggs. Then I went to the cellar door.

I were doing me best, see. I were trying to sort everything out and keep atop the steaming dung heap that my life were getting to be. A man who were liable to pull wool over his eyes wouldn't have even got as far as the cellar door. He'd have made himself forget all about the corpse in the cellar and josh himself that life were alright and no one had carked it. I'd seen it before. We'd done a house over up in Muckfield when we was younguns. Finney, Legs, and meself. A spot of opportunism you might say. Legs spotted an old bird locking up and staggering off down the shops with her walking stick. So we went in for a gander. Looked same as any other codger's house on the surface. Shite old furniture in every room and nothing worth robbing. Then we opened a door upstairs.

The stink fair bowled us over. Once our eyes stopped watering we saw where it were coming from. The old feller were lying there on the bed, all mouldy and blackened. Flesh looked like it were melting off him, like he'd been left in front of the fire too long. And the bed were all dark and wet beneath him where his fluids had leaked out. It weren't quite what we was after, all in all. But it learned us summat.

Folks don't want to face up to facts.

Anyhow, that were then and this were now. I opened the cellar door and looked into darkness. Then I shut it again. I weren't ready.

I weren't avoiding nothing. Honest I weren't. I just couldn't face it yet. I'd be alright soon. I just had to... I got in me car and went down the gym.

I hadn't been training in weeks. Months, come to

think on it. There'd been a time, when I were doorman at Hoppers first time round, when I were the biggest feller in Mangel near as not. And that's saying summat, bearing in mind folks round here is bred for the fields. Ah, them was the days. Eighteen stone and half of pure beef I were back then. Barely a bird could walk past us without squeezing a bicep and giving us that special look.

But then Hoppers burned and Beth died.

I were seventeen stone now. And most of that were maintained by eating and drinking alone. Besides a spot of bouncing I barely used me muscles at all. Couldn't see the point in training no more, since Beth. Lifting's about building yourself up to whatever you reckon you ought to be. You reckons you're a mountain, that's what you'll build towards. Truth were, since Beth died I didn't reckon I amounted to much. Seventeen stone of dormant muscle had seemed about right for us. But now I were starting to think again about that.

I were thinking eighteen and half stone again.

My back were still tender from the shoeing Baz had gave us, so I got to work on the bench press. I slapped on the sort of load I used to start with in me big days. Alright alright, don't get at us about it. A feller who's out of condition ought to start light and build his way back up. I knew that, alright? But I wanted to see if I still had it in us. It ain't about physical strength, see. It's about what you're prepared to do. It's about how far you can push yourself. I wanted to see if I could be a mountain again.

'Gonna lift that, mate?' some bastard says behind us, ruining my concentration. 'Only you've been lyin' on the bench like that for five minutes. Other fellers wants a pop an' all.'

I sat up. It's hard to get yourself from under a bar when your fists is all bunched up tight and ready for aggro. But my hands relaxed when I saw who it were. 'Oh, alright, Legs.'

'Alright, Blake. Uh, soz about that mate. Didn't... er... Didn't reck'nise you like.'

I looked at him, wondering if I ought to say summat about... About lots of things really.

'You alright there mate?' he says, noting the look on my face.

Whether I ought to or not, here in the gym weren't the place to tell him about Baz. I'd go and see him later, perhaps.

'Aye I'm alright. Didn't expect to see you down here is all.'

'Oh aye, trains a lot these days I does. Can't you tell?' He flexed a bicep that were a lot more ripped than mine but weren't that much bigger. 'You ain't seen us cos you ain't been comin' yerself. Gettin soft mate.' He patted my shoulder.

I went back under the bar and tried to lift it. Too heavy. 'Bollocks.'

'Take a bit off shall I?' he says.

It gave us just the spur I needed. I closed me eyes and pictured his face smirking at us, suggesting that I were an arse bandit. Soon I were seeing nothing but red. Then I pushed the bar. It went up this time. Only five reps, mind. I used to open up with eight. 'Woss you been up to then, eh?' I says when I'd done em.

'Me?' He got under the bar himself without changing the load, and did ten reps straight off. 'Oh, this an' that. You knows how it is.'

'Heared about Finney?' I says, swinging back my arms to loosen the pecs.

'What?'

It were my turn again. I added another couple of plates and got under. 'Gettin' yer number nine shirt an' that.' Soon as I were under the bar I knew I couldn't do it. I needed summat to fire us up and I couldn't use Legs again. Weren't fair on him, even if he were getting on me tits a bit just now.

'Got summat to say, have you?' he says. And there were an edge to his voice that I didn't much care for.

I pictured him and me having a fight. It were in the street outside Hoppers, half of Mangel standing around watching us. Legs had tried to get through the door but I'd handed him off and told him to leave it cos he were banned. That were what the fight were about. I had my arm round his neck, fist pumping again and again into his face.

Nine reps.

'No offence, mate,' I says.

'Oh, don't pay us no mind,' he says, getting on the bench. He did ten reps, then says: 'Some bastard has to wear number nine. Least while I'm banned.' Then he did another five.

I put on some more plates and went down. I closed my eyes. It were clear now how to fire meself up. And Legs wouldn't mind long as he didn't know. We was outside Hoppers again. He'd got out of my arm-lock and had us on the deck, knees pinning my arms down, slapping my face like a bitch. 'Blake ain't got no bottle. Blake ain't got no . . .' he were singing over and over. The crowd was singing and all. It were up to me. I could lie there and take it. Or I could do these six reps and . . .

'How's it going with them Muntons?' he says.

What strength I had suddenly drained away. My

arms felt like a pair of bamboo sticks holding up a steam roller. I huffed and puffed for a bit, then got off the bench. 'What about em?'

'Do what I said, did you?' He crouched down to pull another couple of plates off the rack.

'Nah.'

He slid em on the bar and sat down. 'Why not?'

'Ain't seen him.'

'Ain't seen him? You don't wanna wait for him to come to you. Go out and find the fucker. Go to him. Corner him when you wants him and then do him.'

Well, as a matter of fact Legsy, that's what I did do. I cornered the fucker on his home turf and done him good. Only it weren't the way you planned it, you mouthy cunt. I done it my way didn't I. I fucking topped him.

But them was just thoughts. What I says were: 'Well, we'll see eh?' Then I turned my back and did some stretching. My pecs was burning. Felt like a couple of hot irons strapped to me chest. Maybe I'd just sit on an exercise bike for half an hour.

'I heared Baz went missin',' he says, barely puffing after his ten reps.

I wanted to get to the bike and pretend I'd not heard him. But that wouldn't be right. 'Oh aye?'

'Aye. Know what folks is sayin', do you?'

I shrugged and closed my eyes. But it weren't darkness I found under the lids. It were my cellar at home, Baz propped up there in the corner with his face done in.

'Folks is sayin' – heh heh heh, pardon us for takin' it lightly – but folks is sayin' you knocked him off.'

'You what? Who?' I scanned the gym for snoopers. Most was grunting and lifting. Others was jabbering or wearing headphones. I turned back to Legs, wondering where my answer were. But he were giving it another ten reps. When he'd done em I whispers: 'Who the fuck is sayin' that?'

'Ah, fuckin' joke ennit. Don't get yer knackers in a twangle over it.'

'Woss funny about it?'

'Come on Blake. You and him outside Hoppers the other night. Everyone seen it.'

I wanted to kill him. I know it weren't his fault, but I didn't like what he were telling us. Plus he were the one got us into all this. So aye, I wouldn't have minded killing him right then.

'Look, don't get us wrong, Blake. I'm yer mate, ain't I? Only passin' on what I've heared. Thought you'd best know. And like I says, iss a fuckin' joke. Folks knows you wouldn't really knock him off.'

That were alright then. Until you thought about it. 'Who says I wouldn't?'

'Come on. You says it yerself t'other night, about losin' yer bottle. Well, I didn't wanna rub it in at the time, but it ain't zackly a secret is it. Ever since that trouble with Beth you ain't been same. I'm sorry an' that, but thass what they says. I ain't sayin' it, mind. They is. You knows I know you ain't lost yer bottle.'

'Wankers,' I says, kicking a pile of plates. The pain shot through my toes and up me leg. But I held it in.

'Fuck em,' says Legs, curling his fingers around the bar. 'Least it ain't true. You'd be under Hurk Wood if you had of killed Baz. Right?'

I reckon I'd pulled a muscle or summat in me shoulder. All the way home I kept getting shooting pains across me chest and down my arm. And that as well as the bruising all over me back. Course, didn't help that your Ford Capri is an awkward animal to steer, more so when the power steering is knacked. But that were your Capri for you. She had her ways and you put up with em. I told you that earlier. Ain't you listening?

Soon as I got home I went to the bathroom and applied some muscle rub to the afflicted area. Then I applied it to the area all around the afflicted one, just to be sure. By the time I were through everything between chin and belt were covered. I lay down on my bed for a bit, waiting for it to set in. A bit later I went down the stair, poured some whisky, and walked around chugging it for a while. I poured some more and went into the living room. Nothing much on telly that time of day besides news, and after a bit you gets tired of watching folks you don't know blow emselves up in some place you ain't never heard of. I got *The Good, the Bad and the Ugly* off the vid shelf and went to slot it in. But then an old tape caught my eye and I picked that up and all. *ROCKY 3* it said on the front in my best handwriting. I slapped it in the player and slumped on the sofa.

I dunno if you've seen this film. Most folks has, I reckon. Most folks rates it as the greatest film ever made. But to me it were more than that. And I'd never really known why. Not until now, as the opening credits rolled.

The story starts with Rocky as World Champion. He's rich as a plum pudding and only fights chumps. Reckoning it best to go out on top, he announces his retirement. But along comes a new feller called Clubber Lang, mouthing off that Rocky's a fairy and offering to give his bird a seeing to. Well, the natural happens and they ends up in the ring. But Clubber's harder than Rocky reckoned. And Rocky himself is softer than what he thought. Clubber wins, and Rocky's washed up. A former champ.

And that were where I were coming in. I'd been watching this film again and again and not knowing why. But now I knew. I were like Rocky, see. I'd known glory in the past. Ever since nipperdom I'd walked the streets of Mangel like a lion prowls the jungle. Folks was afraid of us. And rightly so. But it weren't like that now. Not since Beth. Now folks laughed at us and called us bottler. I'd killed a Munton and what did folks do? Made a fucking joke out of it and laughed a bit more.

But, right, Rocky weren't happy about being a former champ. And nor were I. He had a mountain to climb if he wanted his glory back. It were steep and hairy in places and it didn't look like he were up to it. But he started climbing anyhow.

I watched the film all the way through. Rocky won. He stood atop his mountain and held his fists high. I cried a bit, then dried my eyes and turned the telly off.

As well as me finally seeing that Rocky's situation and my own was the same, like, there were summat else in the film that made us think. Rocky won, but he'd done it with the help of Apollo Creed, former enemy and now bestest mate. It were Apollo who trained him up to take on Clubber again. And it were Rocky's wife who talked him out of the dumps he'd fallen into. He'd got help from them what was close to him, in short. And it got us to thinking.

Who could I call upon for help?

There was Legs, course. I'd already turned to him,

and his advice had led us to more shite. Weren't his fault, mind. He hadn't said go and kill the fucker. Only twat him he'd said. But he'd been a bit off in the gym and I didn't fancy calling on him again just now.

Who else were there besides Legs?

Finney, course. But he weren't the sort you'd want help from. Bit of a twat, like.

Sal. Well, what about Sal? I know we was only seeing each other casual like, for shagging and that, but hadn't she said she loved us? And I reckoned she meant it and all. I could tell by the way she always had a nice welcome for us. Couldn't help with my problems, mind. She were only a bird after all. But maybe I ought to give her my ear a bit more, like Rocky done with his bird. Wouldn't do no harm and there might be a shag in it for us.

That were all by the by anyhow. Mates and birds can only go so far. When Rocky got in the ring, he did it alone. No one can do his training for him and no one can throw his punches. I were dancing around the room as I were thinking this, doing a bit of shadow boxing. I were feeling alright. The muscle rub had sorted out my aches and pains. Or perhaps they was still hurting but I didn't care.

Didn't matter. Things was looking up. I were a fighter and I could feel a fight coming on.

A big one.

I danced around the house, punching the air and thinking about what I had to do to get my glory back. Well, folks was going round calling us a bottler. And I couldn't come out and tell em all what I'd done to Baz. So I reckon I had to show em a bit more of the same. In the name of my job, course. A doorman is always within his rights to break noses and loosen teeth. That ought to get em all talking about us the right way.

Going to the gym had shown us how out of shape I'd let meself get. Compared to Rocky anyhow. 'Let's get back to where we started,' says Apollo at one point, talking about training. Well, I'd been eighteen and half stone when I started out as a doorman. So eighteen and half stone were what I had to be again. There were summat else to do and all, and I'd put it off long enough. 'Alright,' I says, standing in the hall. I were sweating all over now and breathing hard. Sooner I got meself into shape again the better. But I were alright, far as lugging dead bodies were concerned. 'Alright then Blakey boy. Less do it.' I pushed the cellar door open.

Apollo Creed were holding my hand as I stepped down them steps. He were pointing the way with his red gloved fist. But when I hit the bottom of the first flight he were gone. I were on me tod. And I knew that were the way it had to be. 'You made a mess, Blake,' I says. 'Now clear the fucker up.'

The lower cellar had no light. I felt around on the shelf where I kept a torch, but it weren't there. That didn't surprise us. Last time I'd been down there I were hauling a tonne of dead fat and not thinking straight. I might have left the torch any place.

I sparked me lighter and ventured downward.

I'd never liked that bottom cellar. There were nothing down there besides a couple of bags of cement, an old bike frame, and Baz. It were a place I never went. That were why I'd stowed Baz there, see. If I never went there, nor did anyone else neither. That were my thinking anyhow, such as it were.

The flame flickered up against the bare brick walls.

There were a problem with damp down here and every surface were slimy and greenish. I took each stair nice and steady, making sure I wouldn't fall arse over. I got to the bottom step without so much as a spider landing on my head. 'I ain't afraid of no bastard,' I says. And my voice echoed back at us all mangled and creepy and sending a shiver up and down me spine. I went over to where I'd dumped Baz on the far side.

But the cunt weren't there, were he.

9

....

I searched that cellar high and low. But to be honest there weren't much searching to be done. Baz were gone, no matter how much light I shone on the matter. I ran up the stair, tripping on the steps and hitting me chin. I searched every room of the house – under beds, in wardrobes, behind curtains.

Nothing.

I were barely aware of the little whooping noises coming out of my gob and the sweat pouring into me eyes. I went back down to the cellar and searched it again, both floors. Nothing. No sign of him at all. Not even a shoe or a pack of fags or a hanky.

I slumped down on the kitchen floor with the whisky bottle. There was two things might have happened here. First were that some cunt had broke in and had off with Baz. I didn't want to think about that one. Who'd have done such a thing? Muntons? If it were them I'd have been strung up and bled by now. But if it weren't them, who?

The other thought were a bit more worrying. What if Baz had got up and walked? I hadn't doubted that he were dead when I put him there. But what if I'd only knocked him out or summat, and he'd woke up and fucked off? Then I had another thought.

What if I'm barmy?

But I never thought about that one for long. I'd thought about it enough in the past and found my way to a conclusion I were happy with: If I'm barmy, so's every other bastard, so it don't really matter if I is or ain't.

I thought about this and that for a while, sucking at the bottle until there weren't much left of it. Then I decided there just weren't no answers to be found in this life, and I might as well get on with things.

'What's this?'

'Dunno. Looks like a bit o' cable.'

'What's it doing behind the bar?'

'Dunno,' says Rachel. 'A sparky left it or summat.'

'Come on, people. I want things organised around here. If you're not organised you're not in control.' Fenton shook his head. 'Blake.'

'Alright, Mr Fenton.'

'Can you take that rubbish out back please? This place stinks.'

I looked at my beer and frowned.

'And do it soon, will you?'

Fenton went into his office. I sat where I were for a while, drinking and smoking.

'He's got a head on him today, ain't he?' says Rachel. Unlike most folks in town she were treating us with a bit more respect now. No doubt she'd heard the rumours about Baz and come to the right conclusion. I wondered how she felt about that.

'Aye,' I says. 'Time o' the month, perhaps.'

She giggled a bit, eyes sparkling. Then she went up

the bar and did something with some empties, glancing sideways at us now and then, a smile trying to break out all over her face. I winked at her. When she came back over we chatted for a bit. Not about anything in particular. Just this and that and the other. Soon she were sitting in front of us across the bar, leaning on her elbows and offering us an eyeful, which I gratefully took. I were wondering how far I could go with her if I played my hand the right way, when Fenton comes back.

'Hey,' he says, mincing over in his suit and red tie. 'Hey. What do I pay you for? Come on. Tell me.'

Rachel's eyes went from his to mine to her finger-nails.

'Come on. What do I pay you for?'

'Well, Rache here keeps bar, and I mans the door.'

'Is that so?'

'Aye.'

'How about you, Rachel? You agree with that?'

'Yes Mr Fenton.'

'Right. I guess I should be grateful that you're both aware of half your duties. I'll tell you the other half, shall I? Rachel, your contract says tend the bar and keep it stocked and maintained at all times. Look at those glasses there. You're going to leave them there are you? And Blake, are you not aware of the miscellaneous other duties listed on your contract?'

I shrugged. 'Dunno about no contracts, me.'

Rachel giggled.

'No, I guess you don't at that. Well let me enlighten you. Miscellaneous other duties means taking out the fucking rubbish.'

'Mr Fenton,' I says. 'There's a lady present, and no call for language like that.'

'Don't tell me what there's a call for in my own bar. I'll tell you what there's a call for. There's a call for people to get their arses into gear around here.' He stomped off out back again, shoes clickety-clacking on the wooden floor.

'Bastard,' she says after he'd slammed his door behind him. 'I always gets my work done. He ain't had no complaints about me. Fuckin' old tosspot.'

'Wild un, ain't you.' I winked at her again.

'Cheeky sod.' She turned her back on us, giving us a prime view of her well rounded arse cheeks. 'Go on. Take out yer rubbish before old tosspot comes back.'

'Rightio.' I hauled the bags out back, whistling 'My Old Man's a Dustman'. When I got back I sat down again and set about chatting up Rachel. It were plain as day she were loving it. Specially when I stroked her arm and she squirmed against my hand, brushing her tits on it. I were loving it and all. In fact I were fancying Rachel more and more each time I seen her these days. It were one of them things where you knows summat'll happen sooner or later, so there ain't no sense rushing it. Neither of us was going no place. And the longer we held it off, the better it'd be when we finally—

'Alright darlin',' says a voice behind us in a funny accent.

'Oh, hiya.' She stepped away to serve the punter. I didn't like that. If we was canoodling, we was canoodling. Nothing to be ashamed of. Just cos a punter walks up don't mean she has to jump to attention. I swigged on me pint and lit a fag, ignoring the two of em.

'Smart boozer this,' he says, picking up his pint. 'Who runs it?'

He sounded like he were from the big city. I slied a gander at him in the mirror behind the bar. Big cunt he were. Pilot jacket and jeans, cropped head, no facial hair, about my age. Mind you, not as big as meself at my biggest.

'Who runs it?' says Rache, sounding a bit thick. Put her on the spot he had. Ain't the sort of question you hears in Mangel. 'Well . . .' She looked at me.

'Don't matter, don't matter,' he says, looking around. 'Just interested in bars. In the trade, you know. Hear you gets a bit of trouble of an evenin', mind. Ropey door staff, is it?'

'Ropey?' I says, turning at last but not getting off my stool. Why should I get off me bastard stool? He might be big but he were an outsider. I were Royston Fucking Blake and I were on home turf. 'Who the fuck is you callin' ropey?'

He shrunk to about half his size for a moment. Then he pulled himself up and says: 'Look, I dunno who you—'

'What does I look like, eh? Eh? Woss this round me fuckin' neck? Reckon I put on a dicky bow for a laugh?'

'Calm down Blake,' says Rache, touching my arm. 'He's only askin'.'

I pulled away. 'Askin'? Stickin' his fuckin' snout in more like.' I turned away from him and got a fag out, then put it back when I saw I already had one lit. I were boiling inside and gagging to knock him so hard his hair'd grow out a couple inches. But I smoked my fag and drank me beer. I weren't rising to it. Not in front of Rachel.

'Now hang on a minute,' he says. I had me eye in the mirror. He put his weight on one foot and leaned against the bar. He opened his gob to say summat, then shut it, turning to Rache instead. 'Well, ta anyway love.'

She shrugged and made some noises. I knew she were trying to apologise without me hearing.

'Never mind,' he says, moving off. 'Maybe I'll see you again.' He went out the door, leaving a full pint behind him on the bartop.

Rachel left us alone for a bit. At least I reckon she did. If she spoke to us during that time I didn't notice. I were busy drinking and smoking, see. After a bit I noticed I were hungry so I asked her for a bag of nuts.

'You alright now, Blake?' she says, dumping em in front of us.

'These is dry roast. I don't like dry roast. Giz some salted uns.'

She gave us em and says: 'Don't let that feller get to you, eh? He were only chattin'.'

I put a handful of nuts in my mouth and started chewing. They cheered us up straight off. I likes me peanuts but I can't stand dry roasted. 'Don't like outsiders,' I says. 'Outsider, weren't he.'

'Aye.' She smiled. But her eyes was off somewhere else. 'Reckon he were from the big city, do you?'

By half-eleven the punters had all pissed off and the place were quiet. Rachel and the other bar folk were busy clearing up glasses and bottles. There were nothing left for us to do. And I were dog-arse knackered after everything I'd been up to of late. So I said me byes and fucked off.

'Fenton wants a word,' says Rache as I reached the door.

'You what?' I says. 'Fuck him.'

Back at home I changed into me favourite track suit and crashed out in front of the telly. A film about a feller going round killing lasses were on, so I cracked open a tin and sat down. I thought about going down the cellar again and checking for Baz. But that wouldn't do no good. He were either there or he weren't there. I'd checked earlier and he weren't, so that were that. The film were a bit boring. Every time he pulled his blade and went to cut her the scene changed to summat else. I had a flick and found a channel where two birds was tonguing each other and feeling their tits. It were alright. I got meself out and let the story take us.

Afterwards I felt more relaxed than I'd felt in a while. Like as not cos I were knackered.

I closed my eyes. Just resting the lids for a second, mind. I weren't kipping nor nothing.

It were the phone what woke us. Or the banging on the front door. Ain't sure. Whatever it were it weren't a nice thing to wake to, I can tell you. I zipped meself up and got on my feet, wondering what the hell were going on. I opened the front door.

'Alright, Blake,' says Lee.

10

Lee wanted us all to go downtown in the Capri, but remembered the fucked exhaust and changed his mind. We went over to the Meat Wagon. For a moment I thought they was gonna open the back up for us, and I froze. I'd rather be knifed in the guts than put in there. But I were fretting over nothing on this occasion. Lee opened the front passenger door and waved us in.

When we was all sitting pretty he fired up the engine. It were a fair bit quieter than my Capri, diesel-powered though it were. I sat in the middle. Jess were on the left cleaning his nails with a Stanley knife. All the way into town Lee kept his eyes on the road and asked us questions about Fenton. I answered em best I could, but to be honest I weren't paying em much heed. I were planning ahead, thinking where might be best to slip away. But I'd come up with nothing by the time the van stopped. Slipping away weren't summat you could do for long in Mangel.

We parked in Felcham Lane and yomped the quiet way across town. No one else were about. We came at Hoppers from round the back, walking a bit down the

Wall Road and then scrambling up through the scrub between it and the back wall of Hoppers. Lee clambered over the wall first. Then me. Then Jess. Lee grabbed my face and reminded us of what would happen in the event of a bottle-out, then we went up front and I let us all in, locking up again behind us..

Lee walked a few paces, breathing deep, eyes smiling and set on summat. He were looking at where the stage used to be, which were now just a raised boozing area. 'Ah, them was the days,' he says. 'We had em all ere. Berty Fontana. Tina Topless. Jungle Jane vs. Cowgirl Cath. We had em all, Blake. An' we'll have em all again soon. You'll see.'

'How's that, Lee?' I says.

But he were already off out back, rubbing his hands together.

I followed em. 'Stock room,' I says, coming up behind Lee, Jess behind us. 'Up there on the left. Safe's in there.'

'Oh, right,' says Lee, giving us a bored look.

Jess had the safe open in two minutes. It were a skill his old man had passed on to him, and other than cracking heads it were his only skill.

'Not bad. Come on,' says Lee, counting the wads. He were off out the door.

I followed him, scratching me head and wondering what else were worth pilfering. But Lee had his own plans. He were standing outside Fenton's door, pointing to the lock and calling Jess over. I went and stood by em, watching Jess at work. For a big feller he had dainty hands, which helped with the business of lock-picking. And if that failed he could always flatten the door with his massive shoulder. Or his head. Lee were watching him and all, smoking a fag. He didn't offer us one but I weren't too put out by it. I hadn't been to blame for him losing out on the insurance two year back – honest I hadn't – but I had topped his brother, so fair's fair ennit. I got one of me own out and lit that.

After a bit Jess got the lock done and pushed the door open. Lee stopped with his foot half in, then stepped back and shut the door quietly. 'What the fuck is this,' he whispers to us.

'Eh?'

'You. What the bastard fuck is you tryin' to pull?'

'Nuthin'. What?'

'Go on then.' He shoved us at the door.

I turned the handle and opened. I weren't feeling so relaxed now. My back were squirming. Having Muntons behind us right then didn't seem clever of a sudden. But I didn't have much of a choice. When the door were open enough I looked into the room. The desk lamp were on, facing downward. A ways away from it were a rum bottle, empty. Fenton's leather swivel chair were facing the window. Some of his floppy locks hung over the back of it. I reckoned he were fast akip, being as he were snoring like a tractor starting up on a cold morning.

I wanted to back out and piss off before he woke up, but Lee were right behind us, shoving us on. I walked quiet as I could across the floor. Someone's boots was creaking like rusty door hinges, but I couldn't worry about other folks' boots. I walked on, getting closer to Fenton, praying he wouldn't wake up and spin about in his chair.

Weren't so much that I wouldn't know what to say to him. I'd say nothing like as not, there being nothing to say besides the truth. It were the thought of what Lee or Jess'd do if he woke.

But he never.

I pulled up alongside the chair and peered down at him. He were fast akip alright. No man can make them sorts of noises while he's awake. He were in dark trousers, white shirt unbuttoned at the top, and a loosened orange tie. Across his chest, hands resting atop it, were a twelve-bore shotgun. My heart started hammering nigh on loud enough to wake him. I turned and started back, shaking my head at Lee. He had a black balaclava on now. He opened his coat and pulled out a sawn-off, pointing her at us. 'Open it, Jessie,' he says.

I put finger on lips. 'Fuckin' calm down,' I whispers. 'You'll wake the bastard up. And woss the—'

'Tell him,' says Jess, also now wearing a bally.

Fenton's snoring were turning into grunting and throat-clearing. He'd be awake in a moment for surely. 'Ain't there a bally for me?' I says.

Lee shook his head. 'Wanna see the look on his face when he sees who's robbin' him, don't us.'

'Aw, come on, I'll get locked up for it. Can't we blindfold him?'

'Scared or summat?'

'Aye.'

Lee laughed. Jess joined in. I didn't, hilarious though it all were. Fenton's head were moving side to side. If he didn't wake with all that noise there were summat wrong with his ears. On cue he made a noise – a bit like 'fnlagh'. Lee lamped him on side of the head, knocking him plum off his chair.

Jess were kneeling down in a corner now, moving a filing cabinet aside. His sleeve had slipped up his arm, showing a tattoo I'd seen once or twice and wondered about. SUSAN it said, in what were like as not Lee's handwriting, being as Jess couldn't even sign a cross

for his signature. Behind the cabinet were a hole in
the wall with a little safe in it. Jess sighed and shook
his head like a builder doing an estimate. 'Foreign, is
it?' he says.

'Hoy, talkin' to you he is,' says Lee.

'Dunno does I,' I says. Cos I didn't. Only safe I
knew were in the stockroom.

He looked out the window, shotgun dangling by his
side. Neither of em seemed interested in pointing
guns at us no more. I thought about pegging it out the
front door. Now we was here, the whole thing seemed
about as bad an idea as a feller ever had. Any moment
now Fenton were due to wake up and clock us. And
no one'd said nothing about firearms. And what the
fuck were I thinking, trusting Lee to split the proceeds
three ways? But running away weren't no better of an
idea neither. You can't hide in Mangel, least of all
from the Munton boys. Then I glanced at Jess's sawn-
off lying on the floor behind him and started having
other ideas. Better ideas. That's how they seemed at
the time anyhow.

'Can't open it,' says Jess. He got up and kicked
Fenton's foot. 'Wake up you cunt.'

Lee sat on the desk and folded his arms. 'Just open
the fucker.'

'Says I can't didn't I?' Jess grabbed his gun and
clutched it to his huge chest like a teddy bear. 'An'
don't fuckin' shout at us.'

'I never shouted. I just says open the fucker.'

'You fuckin' shouted.'

'I never.'

Fenton coughed and says: 'Fnlagh . . .'

'Bastard's wakin' up now,' says Lee. 'Blake, tie him
down or summat.'

'What with?'

'Dunno do I. Find summat.'

I had a quick ferret around the office but came up with nothing. I weren't really concentrating, being as I had these other thoughts, sort of thoughts you can't shake once they takes hold.

'He's wakin', Blake.'

I ran out front. Fenton had been whinging earlier about some cable, so I rummaged around behind the peanuts and found it in a bin liner. While I were there I picked up an optic and squirted some drink into the back of me throat. I didn't know what it were. Didn't matter. What mattered were that it made me throat burn and eyes water.

I had another quick think about what I had planned. It were one of the shitest ideas a feller ever came up with, but I reckoned it'd work if I held me nerve. The key to it were Fenton's shotgun. I had to get my hands on it. If I could do that I could make it look like Fenton had finished off two burglars – known crooks – who hadn't banked on him being present and armed. Like I says, as ideas went it were barmy. But sometimes it's the barmy ones that pulls you through.

Lee were kneeling on Fenton, who sounded like he were cursing, although you couldn't hear what he were saying on account of Lee's knee being in his face. I couldn't see where the shotgun were so I had to go along with things for the time being. I bound Fenton's arms behind his back with the cable, pulled the bin liner over his head, and made a little hole so he could breathe. He kept on yelling and screaming at first, but the bag were suffocating him so he had to calm down. He were quiet for a while after that, catching his breath. Then he says: 'Who's here? What do you want?'

Lee got off and pulled him up. 'Woss the combination?' he says in a deep voice, gruffer than what came natural to him.

Fenton breathed in and out. 'Who are you? How'd you get in?'

'Come on. Woss the number for this here safe?' He picked up the shotgun and crouched down next to Fenton's legs. Fenton breathed a bit harder. 'Come on, cunt. Get us into the safe or I'll hurt you.'

'I don't know the combination.'

Lee slapped him across the face. 'I'll tell you what – whatever's in there ain't yours no more. Iss mine. So get over it and tell us the number.' He moved up and down Fenton's leg with the gun, prodding it here and there. His finger were on the trigger. 'Know much about shotgun safety? Oughta be aware of shotgun safety, you ownin' a shotgun and all.'

'It doesn't matter what you do to me.' Fenton were sounding a bit calmer now, like he'd been expecting this all along and were alright about it. 'I don't know the combination, and that's a fact.'

'Always keep yer muzzle pointed in a safe direction. Never point her at person, animal, nor object what you doesn't intend on shootin'.'

'What do you want me to say? Look, there's another safe . . .'

'Keep her unloaded. Make habit of openin' and checkin' yer chamber whenever you picks her up. And keep the bastard empty and open til you're ready to use her.'

'There's two days' takings in the stock room safe.' Fenton weren't so calm now. His voice were getting louder and the bin liner were going in and out his mouth again. 'Take it. Please don't—'

'Keep yer finger off the trigger,' says Lee, holding up the gun and keeping his finger off the trigger. 'Fight the natural urge to put yer finger on the trigger when you holds the gun. If you must curl it round summat, use the trigger guard. The only time yer finger oughta touch the trigger is when you're ready to shoot.'

'Please. I'll give you anything else. Oh god. Just—'

'Stop,' I says.

The Munton brothers looked at us. Fenton's bin liner went still.

I know I said it, but it didn't seem like I had done. It were like the word had come out of my mouth of its own accord, like. Didn't sound like me neither, which I were glad of. I waved Lee over to us.

He spat on Fenton and came over. 'I oughta shoot the both of you,' he says. The barrel were pointing at my guts, but I reckon that were just the way he were holding it. 'Woss you playin' at?'

I whispers: 'You can't—'

'You what?'

I looked at Fenton, then whispers a bit louder: 'You can't fire that thing in here.'

'Why not?'

'Folks'll hear.'

'So? Let em. Part o' the fun ennit?'

'They'll call the coppers.'

'Coppers is slow round here.'

'They might be passin'.'

He thought for a short while, chewing his lip. 'Alright. You wins. Hold onto this.' He passed us the gun, then picked up a marble ashtray off the desk and crouched next to Fenton. 'Giz yer hand,' he says. Then: 'Giz yer hand, less you wants to lose it.'

Fenton reached out a shaking right hand. Then he pulled it back and held out his left instead.

Lee stretched it out flat on the carpet, fingers nice and spread out. He brung the ashtray down on em. Hard.

While Fenton were screaming I moved round the other side of him and curled me finger round the trigger. The bin liner were going in and out his gob, and soon he stopped screaming and started breathing funny, too fast like. Lee pulled it away from his face a bit to give him some air. 'Alright mate? Don't worry, I'll have these fingers loosened up no time. You juss sit back an' relax.'

More screaming.

I lifted the gun.

Lee looked up at us. 'Oi. Didn't you hear what I says just now? Never point yer weapon at folks, beasts, nor objects you ain't wantin' to shoot. Basic shotgun safety ennit. An' watch yer finger there—'

I pulled the trigger.

11

....

I were about fifteen when I killed my old man. Weren't much of a killing, mind. No knifes, clubs, nor shotguns was present that time. Didn't need em, see. When your enemy spends half his life drunker than a tadpole in a cider vat he's easy pickings.

I were upstairs in my room, flicking through a wank mag. I were swilling out of a big placcy bottle of lager and all and like as not half-cut, but you couldn't blame us for that. It don't matter how much shite you sees when you're a youngun. Don't matter how many times the old man comes home and knocks you about. Don't matter how often you goes hungry cos he's pissed his dole up the fucking wall. None of that amounts to shite. You're still gonna end up thirsting for the warmth and numbness that comes from necking sauce. If you're bred for it, you can't escape it.

Front door slammed.

I closed the mag and slipped it back under the mattress without thinking about it. My ears filtered everything else out and listened for my old man. You learns to concentrate like that when you shares a roof with someone like him. He were messing around in the hall, getting his coat off and muttering to himself. I went to my door. It were open a crack. I tried to hear what he were grumbling about. Any information helps when you'd rather avoid a hiding. I couldn't hear all of it but it sounded like the usual. Nag let him down just when he needed her to come through for him. When he suddenly shouted my name I jumped clear off the floor.

I never knew what to say when he shouted my name. I wanted to say nothing. If you says nothing he might think you're out. But saying nothing's asking for trouble if he comes and finds you. On the other hand you don't want to sound all keen and obedient because you'd be a cunt if you did. So this time, like all the other times, I shouted: 'What.'

He started up the stair, saying 'Right. You little bastard' under his breath. The tone of his voice set my skin itching and the hairs standing up all over my body. I wanted to cry. He tripped on the stair and fell on his face. That'd make him more mad. I stepped from foot to foot. My blood were pumping faster, getting ready for the hiding it knew were coming.

But I weren't gonna cry. I never cried no more, not since I'd worked out that crying never got us nowhere.

He'd righted himself and were stomping up the stair again. I opened the door and stepped out onto the landing. I could see him crawling on hands and knees now, afraid that he'd fall again if he walked on his hind legs like a proper man.

Then summat left me.

It were an odd feeling. Relief more than anything else. It were like I'd stepped outside of meself and left my body to do what it had to do. I could see him for what he were now. An animal, walking on all fours. I went to the top of the stair just as he were reaching it himself. I put my foot on his shoulder to stop him. He looked up and caught my eye. There were summat strange there. Just for a second I saw a flash of . . .

Not fear.

Maybe understanding.

And then the usual meanness were back.

I pushed hard on his shoulder and sent him to hell.

'Me old man's dead.'

'Alright, son. Just tell us what happened.'

'Me old man's dead.'

'Where is he now?'

'Dead.'

I put the blower down and sat on the stair. Someone came and put a blanket round us and says, 'Don't worry, feller. Someone'll come and look after you.' Folks came and went, most of em in uniform. They measured him up and looked him up and down and took a photo of him. Then they carried him away. And I felt meself coming back, stepping back inside meself.

No one asked us what had happened. They just took for granted he'd fell down the stair, drunk as he were. That's what I reckoned they thought anyhow. But later, when I were meant to be living in care but were really dossing here and there and doing as I pleased, I got to thinking on that one. I got to thinking how perhaps they hadn't assumed he'd fell at all. Maybe they knew the truth and were alright about it, being as he were a pissed-up old cunt who never done no good for no one, least of all his own son. Maybe that were the way things worked in the world. Or at least in Mangel.

I thought about it, and soon enough it weren't an

idea no more. It were a fact, like a foot being twelve inches long or water being wet. And I went on with it and made meself what I were... What I had been. And that's the way it carried on.

Until Beth died.

Everything turned around and came back at us then. See, I never killed her. I loved her, I did. We had our troubles like any couple does, but nothing so bad that I'd do that to her. The coppers asked us and asked us and shouted at us and slapped us. I never done it, and I told em so again and again.

They never believed us. But they let us go anyhow, being as they couldn't get shite to stick. No one believed us outside neither. Folks shunned us and whispered about us on the bus and sent us nasty letters. And that's when I got to thinking again. About how I'd been wrong about Mangel and the way it works.

I ain't sure what I'm getting at here. Maybe I'm just trying to tell you how I came to be how I were, how I am. But I reckon it ain't my place to do that. Fish can't say much about water cos water's all he knows. Ah, fuck it.

Where were I?

Oh aye. I were in Fenton's office, shooting Lee Munton.

But the gun weren't loaded, were it.

I pulled the trigger again.

And still the bugger weren't loaded.

The look on Lee's face went from shite your pants to well well well, what does we have here then? 'Jess?' he says, not taking his eyes off us. Jess stopped messing with the safe and gandered over his shoulder.

He clocked the scenario and grabbed his gun. I ran for the door. Lee made a swing at us but I poked the barrel at his head and caught his cheekbone, by the feels of it. I carried on pegging it. When I got to the front door Jess shouted and fired. But I were already through and closing it behind us. Buckshot peppered it from inside, but it were a solid door and soaked it all up. I kept on running. Uptown. They'd not expect us to run uptown, I hoped.

Weren't long before I had to pull up in a doorway, lungs screaming and legs like jelly. I'd always been one of them fellers built for strength and not stamina. Ain't much call for stamina in a doorman, unless you're talking about how long he can stand up for. Soon as I got my puff back I put me thinking cap on.

Alright, so the Muntons is in Hoppers, with Fenton. If I called the coppers I'd get em caught red-handed and sent down for a bit. But a bit weren't long enough. And they'd grass on us and all. No, that were a shite idea. But I had to do summat. I couldn't very well roam the streets for the rest of me borned days, hoping they'd not ever find us. They'd come after us for surely. And they'd come soon. But long as they was in there trying to pop the safe, they wasn't coming after us.

I peeked both ways out the doorway and set off again.

It were still dark when I got home. I got a bin liner and started filling it with gear. I thought about putting my doorman togs in but didn't in the end. It'd get all creased and look shite when time came to put it on. So I left it on the hanger and took it downstairs with the bag. In the kitchen I necked a couple of glasses of water and wolfed an old pork pie I found in the fridge.

No matter what shite is taking place in your life, it's important to keep your strength up. More so, in fact, when trouble is on the cards. I upturned the whisky bottle into my gob and emptied it. I stopped by the front door.

What the fuck were I playing at?

Where could I go? And how long were I planning on staying there? All my life? I knew I couldn't leave Mangel. And Mangel weren't an easy place to hide in. And who said I had to hide anyhow? Who said the Muntons'd be after us?

I opened the door and got into the Capri. Muntons after us or not, it'd do us no harm to get away for a bit. I needed some time to get my head in shape. And there were one place I knew I were always welcome, despite how she sometimes sounded.

But instead of turning into the estate where Sal lived I took a right and headed out into the country. Soon the tree-lined roads swallowed us up and coaxed us further and further away from Mangel. But I knew it were just for now. Leaving Mangel were only ever a temporary thing. Nothing seemed real outside of town. It were like Mangel were the only town that really existed, and all the rest were just illusion, blurred around the edges and hard to focus on. But real as Mangel were, it were never a place for thinking and getting your head straight. That's what the rest of the world were for. I started up the long hill on the East Bloater Road and put me foot on it.

Summat always made us floor it when I started up that hill. I wanted to keep on going and smash through the barrier and come out the other side battered and bloody but somewhere else. But it were only ever a brief urge, gone by the time I were halfway up. And there were no barrier up there to smash through anyhow. Not one you could see, leastways. I slowed up and stopped as I hit the brow of the hill, planting the left tyres on the grass verge.

I stood and admired the view, such as it were. Green and brown fields and a lot of trees. Bang in the middle of em were East Bloater – a bunch of rooftops huddled together around a spire and not much else besides. But the road went on and on past that. Up to the horizon and beyond it, like as not. And the horizon were what I always went out there to see.

When I got back to where I originally intended on going I were a couple of decisions to the good. Not that it made us feel much happier about life. I knew I were still fucked from every angle no matter what. But I were a tad less confused. And I had a wild card that might just sort us out.

The money, see. Money were all them Muntons gave a shite about. So if I let em keep my share of the sherbert they might leave us alone.

It needed working on, but that were the strength of it. Alright, it were a shite idea and I were a twat for thinking it might do the trick. Feller can hope, can't he? Feller must hope, in fact. And if he don't then he ain't a feller in my book. He's dead.

But hoping never got no one nowhere. And I weren't likely to reverse that particular trend.

'Hello?'

'S'me ennit. Let us in.'

She said nothing for a short while. Then: 'Come on up.'

I stood there stroking me tash. That hadn't

sounded like Sal at all. She'd never spoken a polite word to us since I'd known her.

Summat were up.

I walked round the corner and looked up and down the road. I kept my eye on the old fence round the back of the flats, waiting for some bastard to vault over. Plenty of cars was parked, mostly battered old shite ones. I glanced up and down em while I were waiting, fists clenched in me pockets. I were looking for summat out of the normal, summat that belonged to whoever Sal had been dogging up there. I could feel a vein sticking out on me temple, pumping hot blood into my brain. *I ain't no slapper*, she'd said. *Them days is gone*. I knew I wouldn't touch her. Hitting women ain't right. I already told you that. But you needs to hit someone. Feller can't deny his urges. 'Come on, mate,' I says, desperate for him. I needed him. My head were fit to burst, less I dropped it on some fucker soon.

And then my eyes fell on a vehicle that I hadn't noticed straight off, it being a white van, and white vans being commonplace in Mangel. It were filthier than I'd ever seen it, so much so that you could barely read the MUNTON MOTORS on the side panel.

I stepped into the road and looked up at Sal's window. A face looked back at us for a moment, then the curtain fell away. Weren't Sal's face. It were Lee's.

Bastard.

I ran to my car and fired her up. Tried to fire her up, that is. I tried three...four times and the fucker wouldn't go. I looked over at the door of Sal's building. No one coming out yet. But I knew it wouldn't stay that way. Jess were loading up his shotgun like as not. 'Come on, dozy bitch,' I says to the steering wheel. He'd be down within half a minute. Maybe I ought to get out and leg it. 'Come on . . .' The engine were flooding and soon I'd have no chance of getting her started. That were the trouble with classic cars. And birds. Push em too hard and they crosses their legs on you. I saw a movement in the corner of my eye, someone walking across the street. I didn't want to look. I wanted the motor to start so's I could piss off. But it didn't. And then there were a tap at the window. A gentle tap.

The tap of a feller who ain't in no hurry.

I looked up. Lee were standing there empty handed. 'Fret not, I ain't armed,' he shouted so's I could hear through the glass. 'But I don't like shoutin'.'

I wound down the window.

'Alright, Blake,' he says.

'Alright, Lee.'

'Just came down here to get you. Havin' a party we is. Me, Jess, and Sally. Celebratin', see. A good job well done an' that. Well, mostly well done. But we'll go over that with you and give you a few pointers, for the future like.' He grinned and stepped back. 'Come on Blake. Comin' up or what? Got yer wages up there for you we have. And you ain't seen what we found in that safe. Don't you wanna see what we found in that safe?'

'Just tell Sal to come down,' I says quietly.

'No, mate. She's enjoyin' herself. An' she wants you to join in. Look, she sent these down for you.' He got a pair of Sal's knickers out his pocket and put em to his nose. 'Mmm. She's a one, ain't she?'

He weren't getting to us. He could say what he liked, but he wouldn't get to us. He wanted us to charge up the stair like a mad fucker and burst in on

Jess, who'd be waiting there with a shotgun or summat. Couldn't see why they wanted to kill us in Sal's flat, mind. Like I says already, their style were more Hurk Wood at dead of night. Maybe they didn't want to kill us. Maybe they just wanted to shite us up a bit. They'd got away with the robbery after all. Alright, I'd pulled the trigger. But it weren't like the gun were loaded.

'Lee,' I says. 'You can keep my share. Call it forfeit, since I . . . you know, fucked up a bit. Soz about that. Dunno what happened. Reckon I were scared. See, I can't do this robbin' lark no more. I'm too old an' I . . .'

'Lost yer bottle.'

'Aye.'

'Seems you had bottle enough to shoot us though.'

'Well . . . That weren't bottle. That were . . . barminess. Aye, fuckin' insanity. I'm a bit fucked up in the head see, Lee. Doctors said so emselves. You knows about that, don't you?' I looked at him, mouth hanging open and one eye half-closed.

He weighed us up for a moment or two, then opened the door and says: 'Come on.'

I couldn't see that I had much choice, so I got out and started climbing the stair. Lee were walking just behind us. He were talking about my Capri, telling us in a polite way that it were a bit past it and I might want to think about upgrading some time soon. They could do us a good deal at Munton Motors, he reckoned, and they'd even give us a couple of ton part exchange for the Capri. He said he'd be conducting trade affairs for the time being until Baz came back from his jolly. While he were talking I pictured meself turning round and twatting him so he fell back down the stair and broke all his bones. But I kept quiet and walked on up. It were better to just let him talk, even if he did know fuck all about classic motors.

Sal's front door were a little ways open. I pushed it and walked on in.

First thing I saw were Sal. She were standing in the corner in her dressing gown, clutching it tight to her chest, looking pissed off more than frightened. She gave us eyes like she were trying to tell us summat, if only I could see what.

Second thing I noticed – briefly – were the cricket bat swinging at me face.

I didn't notice much after that.

'Don't move.'

I moved my head a bit.

'Blake, don't move. I've called the ambulance.'

'Fuck sake . . .'

'Don't speak neither.'

I opened my eyes. Everything were blurred and swimming around us like murky water, which I didn't like. But I recognised Sal's voice so I kept calm. Her face appeared in front of us, upside down. 'You called ambulance?' I says.

'Aye. Thought you was dead. Lie still.'

'Why'd you call ambulance if you reckoned us dead?' I tried to sit up. 'What good's ambulance to a dead man?'

Sal tried to push us back down but I didn't let her. She folded her arms and glared at us, lips set like a clenched arse hole. 'You never does nuthin' I says. I says don't move so you moves. Says lie still so you sits up.'

'I'm sorry, sweetheart.'

She held firm for a few seconds, then wavered. Sweet talk always worked wonders with Sal. She flung her arms round us and says: 'Oh, Blakey. Woss goin' on? You used to be so brave.'

I'd been hugging her back but my arms went limp. 'Eh?'

'You bottled it again, Blake. They told us. What this is for ennit.' She pointed at my head, grimacing. 'And this.' My arm this time, where blood were seeping through the shirt sleeve. Not so much that I might pass out, but it stung like Billy-o nonetheless.

'An' you believed em?' My head were numb, besides a throb right in the middle of it. I touched it, then looked at me fingers. Blood. I felt it again, wondering how they'd managed to get a cricket ball under the scalp like that. 'What the fuck did they do to me swede?'

'What were I meant to believe, eh? Why would they do this if it ain't true? What're you doin' knockin' around with them anyhow? I thought you hated em?'

'Never says I hated em.'

'Did.'

'Never. Says keep away from em is all.'

'Same diff'rence.'

'Ain't.'

'Is.'

'It fuckin' ain't. And what the fuck did they do to my head?' I got up. My legs was wobbly, like I'd been in the gym squatting twice my own body weight all afternoon. But they had strength enough in em to get us to the mirror. 'What the fuck has they done?'

'Keep it down. There's a babby next door.'

'A babby? Fuck the babby, what about me head?'

'Called ambulance didn't I.'

'I don't need no ambulance.'

'Does.'

'Bollocks. I'm alright. Cancel the fuckin' ambulance.'

'Why? Look at yer head. What if you've got brain damage or sum...?' She stopped and bit her lip and looked sideways. 'Sorry.'

I wondered what she were on about at first. Then I remembered: I were barmy. In the eyes of most Mangel folk I were anyhow. Even Sal.

A barmy bottler.

'Cancel the fucker.'

'Stop fuckin' swearin' at us.' She went to the window, breathing hard. When she spoke again she were a lot quieter. 'I can't anyhow. Look, they'm outside.'

'Tell em it were a false alarm.'

'Blake, yer head.'

'Fuckin' tell em.'

I stared in the mirror after she'd gone out the door. To be honest with you I didn't recognise meself. You wouldn't recognise yourself neither if you had what I had. The bump were rising up right off the top, looking like the biggest and hairiest bollock you ever seen. If I didn't have such a short barnet I'd not look so bad. But there were nothing I could do about that besides wearing a hat. Maybe I'd get a nice hat. I peeled the shirt sleeve off me skin and rolled it up. Looked like a cat had been having a go at us. The skin of me forearm were all scratched up and bleeding. But then I noticed darker stuff mixed in with the blood, like ink. And the scratches suddenly took on a pattern.

Me guts tightened up.

I went to the kitchen and ran water over it until most of the blood were off. Then I saw it clearly.

CUNT, it read. I recognised the handwriting and all. It were the same as the SUSAN on Jess's arm. I tried to wash out the ink but it were no use. They'd branded us a cunt for life.

I heard Sal shouting down in the street. Giving her a hard time about wasting council resources like as not. Giving Sal a hard time about anything were a mistake. You didn't know what a hard time were til you gave one of em to Sal.

I went back and looked again in the mirror. I couldn't see no bumps nor tats now. Just eyes. I could feel em burning into us, demanding to know what the fuck I reckoned I were up to. And how dare I let meself get knocked about in such a way?

But, do you know, I had an answer. I were able to return the stare and say just how I could let such diabolical things come to pass. Far as I seen it, I were straight with the Muntons again now. I'd walked up them stairs knowing full well summat bad'd be lurking at the top. And it were. They'd done us over good and proper. But at least I were still breathing.

Sometimes a feller's got to take it on the chin.

I'd be alright to walk around town without listening out for snapping twigs now. Long as they didn't find out about Baz. And I couldn't see that happening now. Not with his carcass vanished and all.

Come to think on it, I were wondering if that whole Baz episode hadn't all been a dream or summat. No corpse and no comeback. Maybe I hadn't topped the fucker after all. Maybe that'd all been an illusion.

What if the doctors had been right after all? All along I'd thought meself clever for tricking em. But maybe they'd seen through that. Maybe they'd thought us a mong anyhow. And to be honest, that'd be alright with me. Being a mong is a whole lot better than being a prisoner. Or a dead man.

I breathed deep, looked in the mirror again, and made meself a promise.

'Well I hopes you're happy now,' says Sal coming back through the door. 'Look at you. Head looks like an upturned light-bulb with hairs growing from it. An' woss they writ on yer arm?'

I pulled my sleeve down sharpish. 'Don't want no coppers stickin' their snouts in.'

'Didn't call coppers. I called—'

'Same diff'rence.'

'Bollocks is it. Coppers can't fix yer head.'

I looked at her in the mirror. 'I don't want no more trouble, Sal. I've had it with trouble. From now on I'm keepin' me head down and steerin' clear o' trouble. Stick to the well-trod path, and don't ever let nobody lead you astray of it.'

She looked back at us, then stomped off into the kitchen and made a lot of clattering. A while later she were back. 'What about me, eh? What about me havin' the flippin' Muntons in here makin' emselves at home? What about that?' She tugged her towelling dressing gown away from her shoulder, flashing us a bit of cleft. 'What about me wearin' nuthin' but this and hopin' they'll be nice and leave us alone? Eh?' She stepped between meself and my sorry reflection. Her breath stank of fags and vodka – one of my favourite smells as it happens. 'What about me?'

'Well,' I says, rubbing my bump. 'I reckoned you'd have telled us by now if they'd had their way with you.'

'Blake . . .' Her eyes welled up.

I felt a bit sorry for her, if I'm honest. Weren't her fault she got all het up over a mild bit of aggro. I didn't blame her that she were putting her pride before the bump on my head and the cunt on my arm. I went to put my arms around her.

She stepped away. 'Where's the old Blake?'

I looked in the mirror and rolled me eyes and smiled. Just let her get it out.

'Where's the feller used to pick fellers up and lob em out on the street? Where's the feller used to knock a man cross-eyed for comin' across cheeky? Where's the feller weren't afraid of no one, least of all coppers and Muntons?'

'That man ain't been around for some time, Sal.'

'I know.' She clackety-clacked to the kitchen door and back again. 'I know. Seems he went missin' about the time you and me hooked up.'

'That ain't the reason—'

'Know summat Blake? I don't care if it is the reason. I don't care about much no more. Don't care about yer tattoo. Don't care about the bump on yer head. Don't care about yer problems. And I don't fuckin' care about you.'

I looked in the mirror again and tried to lose meself in them eyes. If I could just do that ... If I could just get lost inside me own swede and never find my way out ...

'Blake.' She were yelling now, spit flecking up into me face. I don't like folks flobbing at us. I put my right hand out and pushed her away. She went down and landed on her back, giving us a brief view up her dressing gown that she'd rather have kept hid just then, like as not. She set her gown straight and got up, avoiding eye contact.

'Soz about that, love,' I says. 'Just that you was flobbin'...'

But she were back in the kitchen. After a bit I followed her, but she came bustling back out as I were going in. She opened the front door and says: 'Out.'

'Aw, come on—'

'Go on. Out.' She weren't shouting nor crying nor nothing. She were beyond all that. And when it gets to that, there ain't much a feller can do.

She held out a fiver as I were going past her. 'Here,' she says, blue eyes flashing. 'Save you askin' us for it.'

I took the note and stepped out. Just as she were closing the door behind us I stuck my boot back in. 'Sal,' I says, pushing the door open despite her struggling against it. 'Last night . . .'

'What about last night? What the fuck does I know about last night?'

'You were with me, right? I were with you.'

'You what?'

'I stayed here overnight. Didn't I. All night.'

Her face were white and hard like marble. Suddenly I could see what she'd look like thirty year on. 'Aye, alright.'

I leaned in to give her a peck, half expecting a belt round the chops. But none of that came. I kissed her cheek. That felt like marble and all. Cold and past caring. I moved away, then looked over me shoulder one last time. 'And Sal,' I says.

'What.'

'Couldn't make that a twenty, could you?'

12

....

You might think I'd have enough to worry about
already, but as I were driving homeward all I could
think of were scran. I'd not had but a pork pie all
morning and I had a right to consider me belly for a
change. Full English, I reckoned.

Reckoned I'd earned it and all.

So I called in at the corner shop to fetch the
essentials. It'd have helped if Sal had crashed us the
full twenty like I'd asked her, but I reckoned I could
set meself up alright with such funds as I had, which
was a fiver.

'Alright, Blake,' says Doug, the feller who stands
behind the counter.

'Alright, Doug.'

'Been chargin' brick walls, eh?'

'Wossat?'

'Yer head.'

'Oh, no. Fell down the stair.'

'Oh aye.'

'Aye.'

'Sorry state of affairs, ennit.'

'Wossat then?'

'Mangel. This blinkin' town of ours.'

I were ferreting around in me wallet as he spoke so I reckoned I hid my reaction well. It were obvious he meant the robbery of last night. He'd heard about it and he were having his old man's rant. 'Woss happened now then eh?' I says, all innocent.

'Woss happened? You, askin' woss happened?'

There were summat funny in his voice that I didn't much take to. I felt me hackles stirring before I could think. But I damped em down, took a deep breath, and says: 'You've lost us, Doug.'

'That'll be seven pound and tuppence.'

'Oh, aye. Here you go. I'll give you the two next time, eh.'

'No you will not. You pays full, like everyone else. See that sign? No credit.'

'Aw fuckin' hell, Doug. Credit? Two fuckin' pound?'

'And tuppence.'

For a moment I stood there and gave him my lairiest glare. But I knew it were useless. I'd been owing him a few squid here and there far back as memory went. He knew I were good to pay him, and he knew his till had seen a fair bit of my trade over the years. Course, he didn't know me and the lads had cleared it out once as younguns. But I reckoned I'd more than paid him back in patronage over the years.

And now he'd turned on us, the bastard.

Fuck knew what he'd heard and how many others had heard it too. But he'd heard summat. And it weren't good.

'Alright,' I says. 'Leave out the fags.'

He tilled my fiver and gave us the change without a word. I could tell he wanted us out of his shop, but I couldn't go just yet. For form's sake. 'You ain't telled us woss happened, Doug.'

'What?'

'Moanin' about Mangel an' that, you was.'

'Oh, aye. Moanin', were I?' There it were again, that hard edge to his voice that got to us like a shoe in the teeth.

'Well you tell us what you was doin' then, Doug.'

'So if a man sees things wrong all around him, and he speaks his mind about it, thass called moanin' is it?'

'Dunno. S'what it sounded like from here.'

'Well that don't surprise us. Not one bit.'

'What the fuck is you on about? Robberies is nut'n special these days. Shop owner like yerself oughta allow for one every now and then. Ain't no point whinin'. Best get yerself a good padlock and shut up.'

'Who mentioned robberies?'

'Y— Thass what you was on about wernit?'

'I were on about this town, Blake. I were on about one thing after another, crime pilin' atop crime so one day thass what Mangel becomes – one big crime that oughta be hanged by the neck until she hangs still.'

'Know what you needs, Doug? Holiday.'

'Oh aye? And who round here goes on holiday? Noticed summat missing down the High Street, Blake? Holiday shops. Mangel folk don't travel well, do us. You're born in Mangel, you stays here, whether you likes her or not. An' thass fine, ennit. Or it would be without buggers like you fowlin' her up fer decent folk.'

'Wha . . . ?' I stared at him. This were the feller sold us milk, fags and a paper every fucking day, and had done long as time went back. He'd barely spoke more than a word or two about the weather to us before today.

'I knows what you are, Royston Blake. You can't hide in a place like Mangel. No one can. A man crawls from cradle to grave and folks round here sees it all. They sees what he becomes. An' iss a wise feller who once spoke of leopards and spots.'

I were struck dumb, you might say. I could think of no words to summon, and none was coming up off their own steam.

'Go on,' he yells, breaking us out of me stupor. 'Take yer vittles and piss off.'

Climbing in the Capri and starting her up had the effect of calming me nerves no end. As I pulled into our road I were starting to think of me belly again, picturing a fork with a bit of banger, a mushroom, and some fried bread on the end of it, the whole lot dripping with runny yolk. It were quite a thought, and had me guts rumbling their appreciation loud enough to hear it above the knackered exhaust. I were still thinking on it when I pulled up outside the house and got out. But when I saw the copper's car parked across the way I forgot all about that forkful.

It were too late to back out. Two coppers was out of the car and approaching us from different angles before I knew it. One of em had a fat head and hands. Other one had bow legs. They was both lanky, but not so's they had an edge on anyone. I gave em the winningest smile I could muster. Then I recognised em and relaxed quite a bit. 'Alright, lads.'

'Alright, Blake.'

'Alright, Blake.'

'Bloody hell. If it ain't Plim and Jonah.' That's the thing about Mangel, and places like it. There ain't many folks you ain't brushed up against one time or other. 'Ain't seen you two fuckers for yonks.'

'Best not speak that way these days, Blake,' says Plim. 'Not to officers of the law, leastways.'

'Why not? Spoke to you like it at school.'

'School's a long way behind, Blake. Folks change.'

'Fuckers is fuckers.' I knew I were being a cocky cunt but I reckoned I were on safe ground. I'd come away with nothing from robbing Hoppers, and I had an alibi.

Plim shook his fat head. Jonah just stared at us.

'Hey, lads.' I says. 'You knows me. Don't mean nut'n by it, does I.'

'That looks nasty,' says Plim, looking at my head. 'Been beatin' panels with it, eh?' They both had a laugh at that.

'Fell down the stair as it happens. An' I don't reckon coppers oughta be mockin' an accident victim. Does you?'

They must have agreed with that cos they shut up and took to frowning instead. 'Woss in the bag, Blake,' says Jonah.

'Wha? Oh, scran. Don't believe us? Go on then, have a gander. Fuck sake, can't even do me shoppin' these days without—'

'We don't want no trouble, Blake,' says Plim, putting his chubby hands up. He'd always been like that at school. Soon as someone starts acting aggro he comes along and damps things down. 'Less just go on inside, eh? Can we go inside?'

Jonah grimaced like he had a mouthful of vinegar and earwigs. 'What you doin' askin' him? We don't need his permission.' Jonah hadn't changed neither. Still all mouth and no trolleys. I thought about decking the two of em right there in the street. But thinking were far as that one got. They was coppers, after all.

'Come on, Jonah.' They was whispering now, but I could still hear em. 'You knows how we're meant to conduct our investigations these days. Softly softly, an' that.'

'But we got a fuckin' search warrant, ain't us.'

'Aye, but we don't have to use it. You're settin' off on the wrong foot if you pulls—'

I stopped listening and started thinking. 'Lads,' I says. 'Less not stand out here, eh? Neighbours'll think I'm a crook.'

I led em indoors and put the kettle on. When I turned round only Plim were there, blushing. 'Jonah gone for a slash?' I says.

'Er . . . Well, he's just havin' a quick gander. That'll be alright, won' it?'

I shrugged. 'Sit.'

'Oh, ta.' He parked his arse on a wooden chair. It were the one I never sat on being as it seemed fit to break any day. It'd been that way for years, come to think on it. If it didn't give up under Plim's heft, I decided, I'd start using it again. 'So, Blake. How's it goin'?'

'Sociable visit, this?'

'Well we ain't here to arrest you, if thass what you're drivin' at.'

'I ain't drivin' nowhere.'

Plim started fiddling with the huge wart on the side of his face. It were about twice the size of how it had been at school. 'Juss got a question or two for you,' he says.

'Ask way. Milk and sugar?'

'Milk. Ta. Jonah . . . . PC Jones that is . . . has milk an' four.'

'Sweet tooth.'

'Aye. Look, seen Baz Munton of late, have you?'

I busied meself with Jonah's milk and eight sugars, thinking it over. This weren't what I'd expected at all. The body must have turned up somewhere. I might have knowed it. Folks don't just swipe corpses for a laugh. They do it to get someone into bother over it. 'Depends what you means by "of late", don' it.'

'When were the last time you seen him?'

'Couple of days. Seen him outside Hoppers.'

'Two day ago, you says?'

'Reckon so. No. Three. Aye, three.'

'And what'd you talk about with him?'

Jonah came back in the kitchen and sat down. I put his mug in front of him.

'Ta,' he says.

'Pleasure.'

'Eh, Blake?' It were Plim again. 'What'd you talk about?'

'Who says we talked?'

'Did you?'

'Well, aye. Chatted about this an' that. Can't recall zackly what.'

Jonah took a sip. 'I heared you an' Baz had a row,' he says, grimacing.

'Who telled you that?'

'Half a dozen witnesses is who.'

'Oh aye?'

'Aye.'

I drank some tea. It were too hot still and burned me tongue and lips. I drank some more. 'So?'

'Blake,' says Plim, showing us his palms. 'We're just establishin' facts is all.'

'He's givin' us aggro,' I says, pointing at Jonah.

'Come on, Blake. Jonah don't mean it that way.'

I took a deep breath. 'Alright. Me an' Baz had a . . . dispute.'

'About what?'

'Footy.' I drank some tea and looked shocked at their reaction. 'Woss funny?'

'If you an' Baz was rowin' over footy, then I'm a . . .' Jonah looked confused for a second, like the feckless streak of piss he'd been at school and still were. Then he got angry with himself. 'Never mind what I is. You weren't fightin' over no footy match.'

'Says who?'

'Says I, is who.'

'I never says it were a footy match.'

'Fuckin' did an' all. Just now you did.'

'Says footy, didn't I. Don't mean a match.'

'Oh aye? What do it mean then?'

'Anythin'. Footy rules. Footy players. Tactics an' that.'

'Bollocks.'

We batted it back and forth like that for a while, him getting more aggro and me more relaxed. I were starting to enjoy it. Then Plim stepped in with: 'Where was you lunchtime two day ago, Blake?'

'Havin' lunch.'

'Where?'

'Paul Pry.'

Well, it came out just like that. Like if it were true. And I knew they believed us cos I'd said it so innocent and matter-of-fact. But in that moment I felt the kitchen walls closing in on us, and saw bars growing up out of the window sills, and heard the teeth of Lee and Jess Munton snapping at my arse like two hungry bull terriers. I'd lied. And it wouldn't take em but a couple of hours to smell it.

Unless I could hide the hum, course.

'And what'd you eat?' says Jonah.

'Pie and chips, I reckons. Far as I knows thass all you can eat down the Paul Pry.'

'Heh heh, ain't that right,' says Plim shaking his swede. But Jonah weren't laughing. His bonfire had been well and truly pissed on.

I laughed. I laughed and laughed, looking at Jonah the whole time. By the time I noticed that Plim had shut up and were looking at us like I were a mong, I couldn't remember what were so funny.

'Right, then,' says Plim, slapping hands on knees and hauling upright. 'Thass that then, I reckons.'

Jonah gave us his look for a while longer, then got up himself.

'Ta for droppin' by, lads. Nice to see you again. We'll get together some time eh? Sink a few an' talk about old times, like.'

Neither of em replied, which were just as well. Soon as I heard their motor running I got on the blower.

'Hello. Paul Pry. Fine selection of ales and—'

'Nathan?'

'Aye. Who zat?'

'Blake. You on yer tod?'

'Aye. Why?'

'Well, you knows you done us that favour t'other day, regardin' Baz an' that? I needs summat else from you along same lines.'

'Oh aye.'

'Aye. Needs you to back us up on summat this time, that I had me lunch down the Paul Pry that day.'

'But you never. You popped in before—'

'I knows I never. That ain't the point. I needs you to make out like I did.'

'But you never.'

'Nathan, I'll make it worth yer while. Same as last time.'

'You can't get us that way, Blake.'

'You what?'

'Fifty pound I charged you. Fer a pint o' lager. Keep chargin' them prices an folks'll stop suppin' here.'

'Alright, Nathan. What'll it take?'

'I happens to know you can afford a fair bit more'n fifty pound, today.' I could picture him there with a smirk playing under his sparse tash. 'I happens to know you got a little bonus from yer boss early this mornin'. Without his say so.'

I were clutching the phone so hard I could feel me fingernails loosening. Why had I given Nathan as my alibi? Why the fuck hadn't I said Sal? 'You're wrong, Nathan. I never got no bonus.'

'Then my memory can't be jogged, then. Can it.'

If the coppers was fast they'd be getting to him in ten minutes. But they might radio someone over quicker, just to piss us off. 'Nathan, I'll give you whatever you wants.'

'Oh aye?'

'Aye. Name yer price.'

'I wants what you pulled from Fenton's safe last night, is my price.'

'Eh? The money? I ain't got it. Ain't got none o'—'

'Not that safe. T'other un.'

I frowned, wondering how the fuck Nathan had come to know about that one. But there were no time for asking him about that. And this were Nathan after all, who knew everything.

But still, I didn't have what he were after. I didn't even know what it were. And I told him as much.

'No good, boy. There's only one item I'll take in return fer this particlier favour. Thass the contents o' that there safe. Former contents, I should say.'

'Telled you already, ain't got it an' can't lay me hands on it. How about my Ford Capri?'

'The contents of the safe, boy. An' I'll give you a while to get it. A day, let us say.'

'Iss a classic, Nathan. 2.8i. The genuine article. Only one own—'

'I'll cover fer you, Blake. You heared the terms. Agree to em, does you? Or shall I tell these here coppers comin' up the path the truth?'

'Alright. I'll get you yer . . . thing.'

'Consider yerself covered, Blake. For now.' And he hung up.

Trouble with whisky is once you sits down to it you can't pull yourself up again. I can't anyhow. Well, perhaps I can at a push. But it's fucking hard. And it leaves us feeling unsatisfied and up in the air like. In fact the only place I can haul meself after getting on a whisky one, if I can be arsed, is me pit. And that's the only place I wanted to be after sitting there at the kitchen table for two solid hours and then finding the bottle to be empty.

But there's summat inside of every man, I reckons, that spurs him on at such times. My arse were heading for jail. And it'd be lucky to reach that far without the Muntons chomping off a cheek apiece. I could sit on it and until such a fate came to pass. Or I could get off it and do summat about it.

And I knew just what to do.

I went into the living room, sorted things out with the telly and video, and plonked meself down on the couch. Soon Rocky Balboa were on the screen, dancing around as Clubber Lang showered his rage down on him. Rocky were a bit ragged, which were a fair description of how I felt right then. But he got out of it. He stood back and bided his time. And when it came, he nailed it hard. He beat the odds and came out of it the bestest fighter in history.

He showed how it were to be done, for any folks who'd care to pay attention.

And that were all I needed.

Not that *Rocky III* gave us any bright ideas nor nothing. I'd be the first to confess I wouldn't know a bright idea if it did a shite in me pocket. But I had a plan, of sorts. And I were tweaking it over in my mind as I bombed across town.

I parked a couple of streets away and walked the final few yards. There were no one about, but you never knew in this part of town. I told you a bit about Norbert Green already, so you pretty much knows your way around the place by now. But what you wouldn't know is how many eyes is peeking out at you through them net curtains as you strolls past. Most every house has a couple of folks inside it who stays in all day and keeps watch. That's how it works in Norbert Green. But I were alright.

See, I were wearing a wig.

It were a smart one alright. Curly brown locks coming right down over me ears and eyebrows. And it covered up the bump on my head, which were a bonus. I'd had the wig for years. Found it in some house I were doing over and took a fancy to it. It'd been a bit baggy at the time, but I knew I'd flesh it out one day. Funny how your swede keeps on growing for a bit after your height stops. Well, the idea back then were to disguise meself in case anyone seen us popping in or out of a house. And it done the trick. My burglary arrests dropped off like a leper's toes. Course, I hadn't used it in years. Burglary were summat I'd grown out of, like sniffing glue and swinging cats. Only I seemed to be getting back into it a bit, of late.

I rang the bell and stood there, adjusting my dark glasses and looking down at me togs. I were wearing a red track suit with white piping, and a pair of black footy trainers with white stripes down the sides. All in all I didn't look a bit like meself.

Through the wobbly glass in the door I could see someone coming. A bird by the looks of her. Bollocks, I thought. I'd been banking on this being the one house with no one in it right then. I thought about running away, but that'd be asking for trouble. No, I had to bluff me way out of it. Least it weren't one of the Munton lads. The door opened.

I stood and gawped for a bit. She were Mandy Munton, younger sister to Lee, Jess, and Baz. And she'd grown up a bit since I'd last seen her.

'Alright, love,' I says, changing my voice a bit. 'I were wondering if you'd give us some directions like.'

She glared at us for a while. I glared back, wondering behind me dark glasses if she knew what I'd done to her brother. But I knew she couldn't know. Didn't even know I were meself, did she? Not with the disguise. 'Hiya Blake,' she says.

I started to say summat else, pretend it weren't us, but thought fuck it. If she'd recognised us there were nothing I could do about it. 'Alright, Mand.'

'When'd you start wearin' the hairpiece?'

'This thing? Oh, aye. Look, Mand. I were just—'
But she'd walked back into the house leaving the door
open. I followed her in and shut the door.

Like I says, I hadn't seen her in a few years. Most
folks in Mangel didn't even know the Muntons had a
sister. Stayed inside all the time she did. Afraid of the
outdoors. That's what Lee told us anyhow. Turned that
way not long after the last time I'd seen her. Must have
been twelve back then, tops. Looked a lot older, mind.
Looked sixteen if you caught her in a certain light, with
that silky dark hair and black eyes and perky chest of
hers. And she looked same now. Only more so.

'Tea?' she says, filling the kettle. She were wearing
one of them tight vest things that birds was partial to
wearing at that time and fellers was partial to looking
at. Her tight jeans barely came up over her hips,
leaving a strip of white skin and a belly button
exposed to the elements, such as they was. I thought
it a mite odd for her to be dressed up so, her being a
hermit and all. Why bother tarting up with no fellers
to appreciate it? But it were none of my business.

I looked at summat else. 'Aye. Tea'd be nice. Look,
Mand—'

'You want us to keep quiet.'

'Eh?'

'About you comin' here. S'what you was about to
ask, right? Only you never was one for comin' out
with it, was you.'

'Well, I reckon not,' I says, wondering what she
were getting at but wary of getting into any deep
conversations, her kinfolk being liable to turn up any
moment and all. I grinned.

She opened the fridge door to get the milk out. I
noticed the piles of raw meat inside, meat being all the

Muntons ever ate besides beans. Then she plonked a mug on the side near where I were stood. 'Milk and two ennit?' she says. 'Less you've changed yer ways.' She leaned on the counter and looked us up and down. 'You can take off yer hairpiece now.'

'Look Mand,' I says, leaving the hairpiece on. 'I'm in a hurry, like.' I weren't sure what I were getting at, but I had to get at summat. This were my one chance. I were in the Muntons' house, fuck sake. I could hardly climb into the dragon's mouth without making a grab for one of his gold teeth. 'There's summat—'

'What happened, Blake?'

'Wha? When?'

'With us.' Her face were down, but them dark eyes peered up at us through long black lashes. 'What happened with us?'

'What...' I stopped. I were a mite confused, naturally. There'd never been an us, far as I knew. She were twelve years old back then, for fuck sake. What do you take us for? 'Well,' I says. 'I don't rightly know.'

Her eyes stayed hard for a moment, locking onto mine like ticks on the back of an old badger. Then her face screwed up and she sobbed so hard it near knocked her over.

'Come on,' I says, putting my hand on her dainty shoulder and making an effort not to play with the thin strip of cotton that didn't cover it up.

She put her arms around us and squeezed us so tight I could taste me lungs. She were a strong lass, despite her lack of bulk. 'Oh Blake, I'm so confused,' she mumbled into my shirt. 'I been thinkin' about you all the time lately. Ever since... Since...' My hands was moving around her back, fingers slipping under her top. 'Ever since Baz went off.'

'Oh aye? An' where'd he go off to?'

'Blake, I don't know. Dunno if I care no more neither. I been doin' a lot o' thinkin', Blake.'

'Aye?' Her hard little belly were grinding up against my groin area, doing all sort of things to me concentration. But I had to keep atop it. She leaned in, pulling my head toward hers. I kept my eyes open while we snogged, watching out for her tricks, her being a Munton and all. Her eyes was closed and I recall thinking how nice her lashes was, all dark and sweeping sideways like that. Her lips was lush and all, just like I remembered em. And her tongue were tearing around me gob like a Jack Russell round a rabbit warren. She were a bit of alright, you might say.

I don't know exactly when she took it off, but suddenly little Mandy's kit were on the floor. I reached down her back to her arse cheeks, which I kneaded like two big lumps of dough. I brung me hands back up again and round her shoulders and started on her tits. It weren't long before her nipples sprung up like acorns, upon which I moved south and did some work on the lawn. When the grass were good and wet I picked her up and plonked her on the counter, and soon I were giving her what she wanted.

We slumped down panting on the floor afterwards. I closed me eyes, trolleys round ankles, shirt unbuttoned, but sleeves still down and wig in place. She snagged her jeans with her big toe and fished out a pack of fags. We sat there, smoking and sweating.

'Woss that?' she says.

'What?'

'There. Looks like a tat.' She poked us on the forearm. It fucking hurt but I held it in.

'Ah, nuthin' much.' I pulled me sleeve down a bit more. She'd have seen the NT but nothing else, I hoped.

'Looks new. Go on, show us.' She tugged at me sleeve.

I went to yank her away but turned it into summat else, pulling her close and kissing her hard. After a minute or so I reckoned she'd forgot all about the tat, so I came up for air.

She lay across my lap, looking up at us and blowing smoke rings. 'Blake,' she says. 'Why didn't you do this years ago? I knowed you wanted us. A woman can tell such a thing. But it ain't our job to do summat about it. Feller's job, ennit.'

'Well, Mand. If I ain't mistaken you was twelve year old back when I last seen you. That ain't a woman in my book.'

'Thirteen,' she shouted. I put me finger to her wet lips. When she spoke again she were quiet. 'I were thirteen. And thirteen's old enough.'

'Old enough for what?'

'You know. What we just done.'

'Says who?'

'Says . . . Everyone. Don't they?' She looked at us. She must have been nineteen by now if my sums were right. But in her eyes she were still a youngun. 'Besides, you didn't mind kissin' us.'

I lifted her off me legs and plonked her bare arse on the lino. 'I told you not to mention that,' I says, standing up now and hauling up me trolleys. 'I told you never to mention it. Mistake on my part wernit.'

'Oh aye?' She were getting her own kit back on now. 'I suppose just now were a mistake an' all?' She nodded at the counter. 'I'm to keep that quiet too am I?'

'I'd be grateful if you did, as it happens.'

She pulled her top over her head and gave us a look like she were set to flob at us.

'I mean, yer brothers might take it the wrong way like. You can see that, can't you?'

She softened a mite, but you could still cut diamond with the look on her face.

'Come on, you was fuckin' twelve.'

'Thirteen.'

'A decent feller don't meddle with birds so young as that. A decent f—'

'You kissed us.'

'Keep yer voice down. Look, yer kinfolk would've frowned upon it when you was thirteen, an' I can't see em cheerin' us on now.'

'Why? You an' me brothers is mates ennit?'

'Well . . . It don't look good, Mand.' I went over and gave her a cuddle. Her arms slipped around me back, so I knew she were alright. Which meant I'd be alright. I looked at me watch. If they was to come in and see us like this . . .

'Blake.'

'Aye,' I says, zipping up me track suit top.

'Oh . . . forget it.'

She looked like she were still bothered about summat. But I had to be hard on this one. I had to push. 'Mind if I pops up the stair for a slash, Mand?'

She turned to the sink and ran the tap. 'Go on,' she says, swilling out the mugs.

I went on up. I knew she'd be a moment or two faffing about in the kitchen so I opened a few doors and had a goose around. It had to be here somewhere. Either here or at Munton Motors. They hadn't had time to take it nowhere else I reckoned. First room I tried were Lee's by the looks of the clothes lying around the floor and the reek of stale aftershave. There weren't much to see besides togs and some furniture. Not even a couple of pictures on the wall. I opened a drawer and found nothing but socks and trolleys. Two more yielded sundry firearms and ammo. The one on the bottom contained a large collection of wank mags. I had a flick through em for a moment or two, but stopped that when I had to peel apart two pages too many. Then I looked under the bed. And I knew I were getting close.

Wads of cash. Same as Jess had pulled from the stock room safe.

'Wrong turnin', eh?'

I stood up and waved my hands about. 'Mand ... I were just—'

'Bog's t'other way. Lee won't like it if you piss down there under his bed.'

'No, I were ... Ah, fuck it. Mand, I've fallen in a pile o' shite as high as a house. If I don't find what I'm after I'm a dead man. You gotta help us, Mand. You gotta forget you seen us here.'

She were leaning up against the door frame, arms folded. It were strange to know that a few minutes ago I'd been banging her. 'Already says I would didn't I? What you lookin' for?'

'Oh, Mand. If I could tell you I would. Thing is, I dunno.'

'You dunno what you're lookin' for?'

'Aye. I mean no. See ...' I knew I were holding me knackers out for the chop here. But I were trying to forget about that. Didn't do no good to fret on such things. Not in the spot I were in. 'Lee an' Jess an' meself done a place over last night ... this mornin'. Came away with a bit o' gear. But there's—'

'You didn't though, did you. You done a runner, what I heared.'

'How'd you hear that?'

She looked down at the floor, cheeks turning a mite rosy. I were beginning to hanker for her all over again. 'I hears what they says. Walls is thin.' Suddenly she pulled herself straight. 'But I ain't blamin' you, Blake. I admires what you done. Takes a brave man to realise what he's doin' ain't right and walk away from it.'

Ran away from it more like. With a round of buck-shot coming after us. 'Well, ta for that. But it ain't workin' the way you'd hope. Got coppers after us, see. Fuck knows how but they've copped on that I were involved last night. Not your brothers, just me. An' less I can set meself up with an alibi sharpish I'm fucked good an' proper. But . . . But . . .'

I could tell I had her interested. Them black eyes was burning into us, head nodding a bit now and then.

'See, I got the alibi all set up,' I went on. 'Airtight as a nun's knickers. Only there's a snag, like. He's wantin' payin' for it. Summat in particular. Thass why I'm here lookin' for it under this here bed.'

She crossed her arms again. 'I might of knowed it. You didn't come to see us at all, did you.'

'Mand . . .' I stepped towards her. 'Mand, I can't tell a lie. I came here lookin' for the wossname. I'm tryin' to keep meself out o' jail, see. I didn't know you'd be here. But you was. An' then things happened, didn't they? Things is all different now. Here, in me heart. Do you see? You never knowed I were comin' neither, did you? You never. But them same things has happened in your heart an' all. Ain't they?'

She put her arms round me neck and pushed us onto the bed. Like I says, Mand were a strong lass.

And somehow she'd managed to pull off her top again. I thought about letting her carry on. It'd be a laugh to do it right there in Lee's pit with his own sister. But I were so close to pulling summat out of the flames.

I pushed her off us. Gently. 'Mand, don't you see? If I don't sort it out soon I'll be kissin' it all goodbye. And then we'd be apart.'

She stared at my shoulder, tongue poking out the side of her mouth. 'Woss this thing you're after?'

'Dunno. I . . . Well, iss summat they robbed last night. Summat they found in the second safe. We got the money out the first un, right? But I never seen what were in the second. I'd cleared off by then. An' whatever it were, Na— my alibi knows about it. An' thass what he wants. Won't take nuthin' else.'

She sat chewing her lip and thinking for a while. Then she says: 'Hang on . . .'

'What?'

'I knows what it is.'

I grabbed her hand and started rubbing it. 'Mand, what is it? Where is it?'

'I dunno *what* it is. But I heared em talkin' about it, sayin' things like "Where shall we hide it?" and "I can't believe we got our hands on it". And there was long bits of silence when I reckon they was just starin' at it.'

'Mandy,' I says, rubbing both her hands now, 'where is it?'

She chewed her lip a bit more, then stopped and gave us a hard look. 'Take us away.'

'Where to?'

'Away. Juss get us out of Mangel. You and me. I don't wanna be here no more. I can see that now. Iss what I been thinkin' about lately. There's gotta be more out there than this. I ain't stayin' here no more. Take us away.'

I rubbed me face. I hadn't shaved for a couple of days and it were getting rough as a cat's tongue. 'But Mand, no one leaves Mangel.'

She looked at us funny, like I'd spoke out of turn at a posh tea party or summat. Then she says: 'Eh?'

Like most birds Mandy could be thick at times. For that reason you couldn't blame her too much for not seeing everything like it truly were. I'd come across it time and again in Mangel, folks reckoning they could just hop in a motor and piss off to some other town. Aye, they said it, but none of em had done it. Ignorance were rife in this town, and concentrated mainly in the female population, I truly reckoned.

Course, Mandy hadn't barely been out of her house in donkeys, so you couldn't expect her to know what were what. 'Ah, never mind,' I says. 'So, you'd come away with us would you?'

'Oh Blake. You knows I would. If you'd only asked us all them years ago I'd of said it then an' all.' She went to pull her jeans down again.

I held em up. I had to keep her talking. Long as I kept her talking – even if it were bollocks about leaving Mangel and me running off with a Munton bird – I still had chance of saving meself. 'But Mand, it won't work out unless I pays off me alibi. Where's this doofer?'

'I can get it. Kiss us.'

'When? Can you get it now?'

'Kiss us.'

I kissed her.

'I can get it. Leave it to me.'

'Where is it?'

'Leave it to me. Meet us later on. In the graveyard. Nine o'clock.'

'The fuckin' graveyard? What for?'

'Cos no one ever goes there. An there's trees an' that to hide us.'

'But folks walks through it.'

'Aye. An thass what you'll do. Walk through at nine. I'll be waiting somewhere near the path. I'll see you.'

'Mand, I ain't sure about that. Can't we juss get the thing now?'

'Nine o'clock, Blake. And remember, you're takin' us away. Tonight. So pack a bag and have yer car ready. And Blake...'

'What?'

'You let us down an I'll tell me brothers on you.'

I kissed her again. Her kit came off easy.

I kept me wig on.

13

....

I closed my eyes.

I were in a strange place somewhere between bursting out me skin and knackered to all fuck and back. Head were pulling one way and arse the other, and I were stuck between the two. I were stuck there until I could find whatever this thing were and plonk it in Nathan's greasy paw. And then I'd only be halfway sorted. Seemed as like the only way to rid meself of one worry were to swap it for another un.

I drove around for a bit, trying to think above all the din in my head. I tried to hark back to the last time I'd felt alright, free of cares and happy to be breathing the Mangel air. Well, I don't reckon such a time had ever been. Not that I could recall anyhow. There'd been moments, when your tail's up and you can't smell the shite for roses. But moments was all they'd been. And it didn't look like there'd be many of them no more.

I found meself on the road out of town again. The Capri were giving it the big un, pushing past the ton mark on a nice clear stretch. It were always quiet out on them country roads. No bastard ever came to Mangel, and it were sure as a cat shags in the alley that no fucker ever left her. Not ones like me anyhow.

I pulled into a lay-by and checked my watch. It were getting on for late afternoon. I tried to think of all the things needed doing. But right then I couldn't put me finger on one of em. Never had been one for writing shite down, but right then I wished I were. Putting it all on paper seemed a better way forward than not knowing my arse from a burst tyre anyhow. I had a rummage in the glove box and came out with a parking ticket and a little betting pen. I scrawled around on the back of the ticket for a while, trying to get the bastard pen to work. When it started scribbling blue all over the shop I turned the ticket over and placed the nib on the paper ready to write.

But writing never got no one out of bother. Only thing that counts is action. I tossed the paper out the window and drove home. After cleaning meself up and putting on some new kit I fried up the stuff I'd bought earlier and sat down to enjoy it with a nice glass of whisky. I were down to me last bottle, and made a mental note to borrow a few more next time I were at Hoppers. And that led us to the next thing to do.

'Oh, I fell over.'

She shook her head. 'Feel alright now?'

'Aye. Thirsty, mind.'

'Pint?'

'Ta, Rache.' I lit a fag and started whistling 'Tie a Yellow Ribbon'. Stepping inside Hoppers often put that tune inside my head. Always had done and always would, far as I reckoned.

I glanced at Rachel while she were pulling the pint. There were nothing to be read on her face. Nothing

along the lines of Hoppers being robbed last night and
her boss hospitalised anyhow. So I set my eyes at chest
level and tried to switch me brain off. She dumped the
pint in front of us and started away. 'Rache.'

'Blake?' She smiled. Same sort of smile I'd got out
of her last time I got her talking. Kind of smile a feller
aims at getting from a bird.

'I were just . . . Well . . . Quiet in here tonight ennit?'

'Time of the week. You knows it's quiet this time of
week. Specially early on.'

'Aye, reckons you're right there.' I drank a bit of me
pint and licked the foam off my tash. Rache went off
down the bar. No one else needed serving but she had
some sorting to do. 'Fenton in tonight?'

'Aye.' She didn't even look up.

Fucking hell. I drank some more. 'In his office?' I
says, belching in the middle of it so it sounded all
casual like.

'Far as I knows.'

I finished me pint, stretching it out over a minute
or two.

Rache pulled us a fresh one. 'Ain't like you to spend
your free time in here.'

'Ain't it?' I weren't sure what she were getting at. If she
didn't know about last night, and Fenton were back
there in his office, then no one knew about it. Coppers
included. 'Well, I were in town anyhow, and . . .' I looked
down, smiling shyly. 'You knows how it is.'

'What? You came to see me?'

'Well . . . Aye, I did.'

'Ah . . . Royston. Gonna buy us a drink?'

She poured herself a vodka and orange and set
herself in front of us. We chatted and larked about for
a while, me thinking about Fenton back there in his

office the whole time. What were he up to? Why hadn't he hoyed the coppers? What the fuck had Lee and Jess done to him last night?

'So thass on, then? You'll meet us after work?'

'Wha? Oh, was we...?'

'Blake, you wasn't windin' us up, was you?' Her grip on my hand slackened a bit.

'Course not.' I gave her a kiss on the cheek by way of chasing doubt from her mind. She moved her face sideways so her mouth were on mine, and we sat there snogging across the bartop for a while. To be honest I were a bit shocked that Rache were behaving like that in front of all and sundry. I hadn't seen her so much as wink at a feller before, and here she were putting it all out for us in public. Perhaps she'd been saving herself for us. I liked the sound of that. Took my mind off Fenton for a second or two. But no more than that. Not even when she stuck her tongue in me ear.

I broke it off and pointed out the punter waiting for serving down the other end. While she were gone I sloped off out back. I had to know. If Fenton had clocked on to me being in on the job, it'd do us no good thinking he hadn't.

I knocked.

No answer. I wanted to walk away, fuck off somewhere else and get pissed off me swede. But I were feeling too nosy for that. I knocked again. Nothing. I tried the door.

Locked. 'Mr Fenton,' I says loud. Rachel had said he were in. 'Mr Fenton?' Then I heard summat behind the door. Furniture creaking, shite like that. 'Mr Fenton, you there, like?'

'Blake? Is that Blake?' I could barely hear it. And it didn't sound much like Fenton. Barely a whisper, just the other side of the door.

'Aye. Let us in.'

'Ah, Blake. I'm so glad you're here. I didn't think you'd be in tonight.'

'Aye, well. I popped in to... say hello to Rache. Gonna open the door or what?'

'Hang on. This isn't easy. You're sure no one else is with you?'

'Aye. Go on.'

There were a lot of scratching and grunting, and a couple of minutes later he had the door unlocked. I let meself in. Fenton padded slowly back to his chair. He looked all wrong from the back, but I couldn't see exactly how, other than that he were moving like an old man. His shirt were hanging out and his floppy hair were all messed up and wrong-looking. 'Sorry about the wait, Blake. Had to unlock the door with my teeth.' He turned about and showed us his busted face and bandaged hands. A few drops of blood dotted his shirtfront and blue tie.

I had to play it straight. 'What the fuck happened to you?'

He gave us a strange look at first, which had us wondering if I hadn't walked into a trap. But then his face gave way to other things, like pain and grief and that. He started blubbering a bit. 'I'm a weak man, Blake. I couldn't help it.'

'Help what, for fuck?'

'I gave it away. I let them get away with it.' He started crying proper now.

I shook my head and looked out the window. Fucking twat. Fancy crying. After a bit it got a bit embarrassing, so I coughed and says: 'Mr Fenton, tell us—'

'Blake . . .' He sat down a bit too hard and yelped. 'I've got so much to tell you. But I can't. I can't tell the half of it.'

'Giz the bare bones then. Like who done this to you?'

'It was those thugs who I bought this place from. Munton, their name was. The three brothers, you know? The ones I asked you to ban some time ago. But don't tell anyone okay? It's no one else's problem and I don't want the police involved. The Muntons did it, just like I always knew someone would one day. I just didn't think it would be someone . . . local. The Muntons came in here and took my...' He waved a bandaged paw at the safe in the corner. The door hung open, showing the big fat jack shite inside. 'They took it, Blake.'

'What were in it?' I says. 'Money?'

He laughed. It were a sick laugh, like a dying feller who don't give a toss no more. 'Money? Blake, it wasn't money. I wouldn't let my fingers get broken one by one for money. But . . .' He looked at us for a few seconds then shook his head. 'I can't tell you what it was. Sorry.'

'Have you been down the ozzy, Mr Fenton?' I says, knowing full well he hadn't. No doctor would bandage up his hands like that. He'd done it himself. With his teeth like as not. And hankies for bandages.

'I can't. Forget it, Blake. I don't need that kind of help. It won't mean a thing unless . . .' He looked at us. It were a look I hadn't seen on him before. He were sizing us up I reckoned, deciding whether I could do what he had in mind or no. Or if I'd be prepared to do it anyhow. 'Blake. You know how I gave you a chance, back when I first came here and bought this place? Well, I did that because I saw something in you. I saw a bit of myself there. Now, you might think that's amusing, us being

hardly similar in any way. But that's just it, Blake. I saw
in you the bit of me that I felt inside but could never let
out. I'm not big and strong like you. And I don't act on
instinct. I'm a thinker. I think everything through. But
you're different. You have your own rules and you don't
even know it. You act on them without thinking and you
don't mess about. You live by your heart, Blake. And I
live by my head. But part of me wants to live by my
heart. Part of me wants to live out there with the people
and fight and fuck with them.'

To be honest I weren't sure what he were on about.
I were looking around the room, rolling my tongue
around me teeth, noting that I hadn't been cleaning
em proper of late. You shouldn't do that. If you don't
clean your teeth regular the muck builds up on em
and then you can't shift it. I'd heard that on the telly.

'Well, anyway,' he says. 'Forget that. I guess I'm
blathering a bit. But Blake, I do need you to return
the favour now. If you're prepared to, that is.'

I were looking at the empty safe now, still wondering what could have been in there.

'Do you want to, Blake?'

'Aye. What?'

'Recover this item for me.'

'What item?'

'From the safe . . .'

'Juss tell us what it is. No fucker's tellin' us what
it . . .'

'Who's not telling you? Eh? I've not told a soul
about this.'

'Nah,' I says, kicking meself inside. 'Nah, I just
means I'm fed up of folks not tellin' us shite in
general. Nuthin' in particular. I were juss mouthin' off
like. Ignore us.'

He seemed happy with that cos he went on asking us to get it back for him. It were a relief that he hadn't rumbled us about being in on the robbery, but I can't say I liked what he had in mind. And I told him as much. 'I mean, the fuckin' Muntons?'

'But Blake, if you won't help me no one will. You know that.'

'Call the coppers.'

He shook his head. 'No police. And don't let on about this.'

I raised an eyebrow. 'This thing, knock-off is it?'

'Knock-off? Er...' He went to rub his face, but yelled out when his bandaged fingers gave way. 'Yes. It's a bit knock-off I guess. But... My fucking *fingers*. Uh, yeah, knock-off. But nothing too bad. Nothing that would interest the police too much. Unless you put it under their noses. You know what I'm getting at.'

'So tell us what it is.'

'I can't. Just trust me, Blake. I can't tell you.'

'Oh, I gets it. You don't trust us.'

'That's not true. I just can't tell you.'

'So why should I help you?'

'Because...' He went quiet, lips moving silently as his thoughts got moving. He tried to do some sums on his fingers, but gave that up. 'Ah, sod it. If you help me I'll give you a partnership in Hoppers. Joint ownership. Fifty-fifty.'

I went quiet meself for a bit. I were out there in the main hall, sitting up at the bar in a smart suit, big gold sovereign on me little finger. Folks would still say hello when they came in. Fellers'd shake my hand, birds give us that special look. But it'd all be different. I were the boss.

The boss, fuck sake.

'Blake? What do you think? Could you do it? For half of Hoppers?'

'Well, I don't like it. But seeing as it's you I reckon I'll help you out.'

He closed eyes and put hands over face, gently this time so's not to give him grief. 'Thank fuck for that.'

'But I wants it on paper.'

'Oh, contracts. Yes.' He's looking up again now. 'I'll ring my solicitor. I'll have them ready to sign the moment you deliver the, er . . .'

'And I'll get a pay rise will I? Me being joint owner an' all?'

'Of course. Assuming the business can stand it. We'll talk about all that. You'd need to replace that car—'

'There's summat else an' all.'

'What?'

'Hoppers. We keeps the name Hoppers. Alright?'

'You don't like Café Americano?'

'No. Hoppers.'

'What about Wine Bar & Bistro? We're keeping that aren't we?'

I scratched me chin. 'Aye, alright.'

'Great.'

'Oh, and one other thing.'

'What?'

I could tell he were getting narked now so I thought I'd push it a bit. 'Can you sub us a fifty?'

I were feeling good when I walked back out on the street. It were nice out. I reckon it'd been a nice day all along, but I hadn't been up to appreciating it before. I had the taste of Rachel on my tongue, paper in me wallet, and the prospect of a new life as a respected pillar of the Mangel bar-owning community lying before us. Life were looking smart. The happy wagon were coming round our way for once, and stopping right outside my door.

And all I had to do were sort out one or two trivial matters.

I walked round town for a bit, smoking fags and nodding at folks as I passed em. Most smiled back, and I found that I could read their thoughts if I looked close at their faces. *There's that Blake. He owns Hoppers. I wish I were just like him.* That were the fellers. The birds was thinking more like: *I wish he'd shag us. I heared he's smart at shagging.*

Or maybe I were wrong there. Perhaps it were more like: *Fuckin' hell. Royston Blake, the cunt who topped his own wife.*

I peered into all their eyes, searching for clues as to what were really behind em. They was all merging into the same swede, see. If one of em were thinking a thought, they all was.

Hear about him did you? It were him kicked his old man down the stair.

Aye, but he's lost his bottle now.

Fucked Mandy Munton he did. In her brother's pit.

I heared he done her when she were a youngun.

I broke into a jog, shaking my head to get all them words out. But they wouldn't budge. I ran faster, shaking my head harder and harder and smacking it with me fists.

Hear about his new tattoo?

Treats his Sally like dirt. Hit her, he did.

Coppers is onto him, mind.

★

'Look at his head.'

'Nasty, that is.'

'Looks like a big hairy knacker.'

'Don't laugh. Hurt hisself, ain't he.'

'Fuck knows how he done that, mind.'

'Fell over didn't he.'

'I knows that. But he never landed on his head.'

'Didn't he?'

'Nah, sorta floated to the ground. Like he were actin'.'

'Reckon he's puttin' it on? Fer attention an' that?'

'Wouldn't put it past him.'

'Royston Blake ennit?'

'Looks to be.'

'Hear about him did you?'

'Aye.'

'What a cunt, eh?'

'Aye. Cunt.'

'They oughta of kept him locked up, you asks me.'

'Aye. Straight jackets and barred windows, s'what he needs. Why'd they let him out, then?'

'Don't rightly know.'

'Nah, nor me neither. Funny that.'

'Straight jackets and barred windows if you asks me.'

'Juss says that, didn't I?'

'Woss that on his arm?'

'Less have a gander. Says C—'

My head were throbbing and me arms was flapping about. I were fighting for me life, see, fighting off all kinds of nasty folk coming at us out of the dark. Only now my eyes was open I could see things was a bit different. It were light, for one. But I still had two bad uns bearing down on us from above.

'Alright, Blake.'

'Alright, Blake.'

I squinted up and saw they wasn't nasty folk at all. I knew em. There weren't a soul in Mangel I didn't know. 'Alright, Don. Alright, Burt.'

'Took a fall there.'

'How'd yer head come to be like that?'

'Ah, fell down the stair. Got a fag?'

'Don?'

'Aye. Here.'

They helped us up and Don lit us a fag. Then I thanked em and went on me way. Had all sorts on my mind I did. Like how I'd come to be on the deck back there in the High Street. And what'd happened to me fags? The kip had done us good anyhow, and now my mind were good and sprightly. I thought about what I had to do. I had it all worked out. It'd go alright. I just knew it would.

Being early on only three punters was in the Paul Pry when I strolled in. But Legs and Finney'd be along just now. Never late, them two. Folks in Mangel never is, nor ever was nor would be. It's just the way round here. Everyone knows what he has to do next and sticks to it. It's a simple way of life, and one that allows a man to get the most out of his simple pleasures, without cluttering up his swede with plans stretching too far hence. 'Alright, Nathan,' I says.

'Alright, Blake. Usual, is it?'

'Aye.'

'Gat summat fer us, have you?' He didn't even look up.

'I can pay you for the drink, aye.'

'Thass good, Blake. Always likes my customers to pay up. Summat else fer us?'

'Bit o' chongy here if you wants it.'

'Not just now, eh? I'm hankerin' after summat, mind. An' I'll tell you what, if I don't gets it afore first thing the morrer I don't know what I might do. Ever get that feelin' yerself, Blake, that hankerin'?'

'All the time, Nathan. All the fuckin' time.'

'Well then you'll understand.'

He were staring at us, trying to catch my eye and hold it. But I weren't playing that game. I knew what were what and what'd be where come the next day. I looked at the peanut rack instead. When that got boring I looked at the pint he'd plonked before us. Then I drank some of it. He were still talking, far as I knew. But I'd managed to tune his words out so's they meant no more than the sounds coming from the fruit machine. It stayed like that for I don't know how long. And I quite liked it.

It were a shove in the back what brung us to. That and a sudden stink. 'Alright, Blake.'

'Alright, Fin.'

'Pint please, Nathan.'

'Had a bath lately, Fin?'

'Eh? No. Why?'

I sniffed. 'Hums like a ferret crawled up yer trouser and died in yer trolleys, you does.' He looked a mite uneasy at that, so I left it. Sometimes a feller can't help stinking. And the last thing he needs is a cocky cunt like meself pulling his plonker on it. 'Legs not with you?' I says.

'No, he's . . . Ta, Nathan. Aye, Legs. He's, well . . .'

'I were only askin' where he were, fuck sake.'

'Aye, well. As you can see he ain't with us just now. How about you? How you been keepin'?'

I looked him up and down. Dirty denim jacket. Faded England footy top. Jeans. Manky trainers.

Same old Finney as ever. 'Not too bad, Fin. I been keepin'... not too bad.'

'Smart.' He drank some of his pint and looked around the bar.

'Summat up is there, Fin?'

'Nah. I'm alright. I'm always alright, Blakey. You knows me. Keeps me head down an' looks out for me mates. Listen, Blakey. Has you... you know, has you had any trouble like?'

I were getting worried now. Then a little squirt of pain shot through my head. 'Oh, you means this,' I says, pointing at me bump.

'Aye. That.' But I could tell he were lying. Otherwise he'd be asking us how'd I got it. Instead he says: 'Sit down over here, shall us?'

I followed him to a corner table. You had to sit on benches in the Paul Pry and they was a fair bit short of comfortable. Bit like church pews I reckoned. Not that my arse had had much experience on such holy surfaces. But my guess were that God wanted to punish his flock before he were nice to em, by way of making em sit on shite furniture. And it were that way with Nathan and all. 'Fin, why the fuck is we sat down here? We always sits at the bar, fuck sake.'

'Blake...' he says, like he were struggling with the name. He craned his neck out to us and whispers: 'Blake, I gotta come clean about summat. I been meaning to for a while, but you been hard to get hold of. An' I didn't wanna tell you over the phone like, cos...'

'Spit it out, Fin. Spit the fucker out an' have done with him.'

He swigged his pint and pulled on his fag. 'Baz Munton,' he says. 'I got him, like.'

14

Finney'd always been a cunt. Far back as recollection went he'd been sticking his nose into good business and turning it to shite. He were one of that sort, see. I reckon there's one of em in every town. Like as not more than one, but one at a time is all you ever gets lumbered with. Which is a blessing, I reckon. But it didn't make Finney any less of a cunt.

Thing about them types of folks is they always means well. He wants to help you, cos he's your pal. But it never turns out that way do it. Folks like Finney'll always fuck it up in the end. Their hearts is full of goodness, but their heads is full of shite. And there's nothing you can do about it. Don't matter what your business is. Don't matter how hard you tries to keep him out of it. He'll always shoot your pigeon out of the sky and land him in the muck heap.

Mind you, life's made of such challenges. Things'd get too dull without em. That's one way of looking at it anyhow.

But Finney were still a cunt.

'You fellers alright over there?'

'Aye, Nathan.' Fin waved with his pint arm, slopping beer across the table. 'Discussin' the footy an' that.'

'Right you are Master Finney. Juss mind you keeps the cursin' to a minimum, ladies bein' present.' He looked over at us a bit longer then turned back to his tankard polishing.

'Outside,' I says to Finney. I were calmer now. I went on out without waiting for him. I stood out there in the car park. I dropped my fag and crushed it underboot.

Finney had gone for a piss or summat. I knew he were nearby cos I could smell him. It were stronger than ever out there in the car park, which I reckon were down to him opening his trolleys and the bog window being open not five foot from where I were stood. I waited and waited, smelling that smell that were somehow shitey and meaty and sweet at the same time. I lit another fag and stubbed it out. I coughed up a chewy one and sent it skyward. It came down on the windscreen of an Austin Maxi and slid slowly down, leaving a trail not unlike that of a slug. I liked that. But it didn't make us smile. Finney came out.

He started to say summat as he came forward but I swung my right at him. It landed square on his nose and knocked him on his arse. He sat there with shock on his face and blood dripping nose to mouth. That got my back up even more. I kicked him in the guts, winding him and perhaps breaking a rib or two. He went over. I stepped back so's I could get a good run-up at his back to finish him off or puncture a lung at the least, but I couldn't be arsed. I'd done what I wanted to do. Instead I knelt down beside his head and says: 'Where is he?'

He were crying like a babby. That were good and bad. I'd wanted to fuck him up and leave him ragged, and him crying were a good sign that I'd achieved that aim. But if there's one thing I can't stand it's folks blubbering. I'm a soft touch, see. Turn on the waterworks and I'm putty. 'Come on, Fin,' I says. 'Stop that, eh?'

'I were only helpin'. I were only lookin' out for you, Blake. Mates is all I got, see. I knowed you was in the shite with Baz, an'... an' when I calls round yours t'other day and finds yer door unlocked I thinks aye aye, woss up here then? Blakey leavin' his drawbridge down? An' him a master burgular and all?'

'I ain't no master burglar. Where'd you put him?'

'Like I says, I goes in and has a goose about, findin' the cellar door to be open.' Spit and blood was flying out his mouth as he spoke. You'd never have knowed he'd been weeping like a new-born a few seconds back. He looked to be enjoying himself now. 'Now, I thinks, why is this here door open? Maybe Blakey's fallen down the stair and broke his neck like? You see, Blake? Always thinkin' of me mates. An' you an' Legs is all the mates I g—'

My fists was clenching up all over again.

'Alright alright. So I goes down the stair an'... Well, fuck me if it ain't Baz Munton sat there in that corner, dead. Fair play on Blakey I says to meself. That'll learn the fucker not to mess with our Blakey. Heh heh. But then me brain gets crankin' an' I says hold up a minute there Finney. If I can walk right in here an' find Baz, woss stoppin' some other cunt doin' same? Woss stoppin' the coppers? Can't have that, can us? So I hauls his lardy arse up the stair and into the back o' me

Allegro. An I'll tell you what, lucky iss an estate ennit? That Baz were a big—'

'If you don't tell us where you put him, I'll—'

'Right you are. So we – me an Baz that is – we drives about town for a bit, wonderin' where best to plonk him. An' iss hard, see. Sun's shinin' down on us an' folks is walkin' about with smiles on their faces, an' here we is sweatin' an' frettin' over nuthin'. See, the danger were over. Baz weren't in yer house no more. I had him. An' no bastard ever pays no mind to my old Allegro. Shite brown, see. That were never a popular colour on yer Allegro. So...'

I left him to his talking, which were beginning to make the bump on my head throb. His car were in the corner of the car park, spread askew across two spaces like it always were. Everyone parks that way in Mangel. A civic duty, you might say. I went to get the boot open but the handle were gone, leaving nothing in its wake but a pair of rusty holes. Through the window you could see summat large heaped up in there under a stretch of black sheeting. You couldn't tell it were Baz just by looking at it, I supposed. Could be a heap of earth or a pile of old clothes or summat. The smell were making my eyes water.

'Ah, see?' Finney were up on his feet again and limping Blakeward. 'Thass the beauty of it. Fuckin' handle's bust off so no bastard can get in there.'

I ignored him. I reached in my leather for the monkey wrench.

'Blakey, don't open it here. Folks is about. Some cunt'll see you.'

'So what? Every bastard in Mangel's got a whiff of him by now.'

'Aye, well. He do hum a bit. Reckon it'll be time to bury him somewhere soon.'

I raised the spanner and swung it at Finney's head. He yelped and ducked. That got him away from us for a bit. I rammed one end of the wrench under the boot and started levering it. Plumes of green smoke fizzed out the cracks. But that might have been my imagination. Sometimes it's hard to tell what is and what ain't. The stink were getting worse anyhow. So bad I thought I might pass out if I . . .

The boot popped open.

'Woss that almighty hum, fellers?' Nathan were standing over by the doorway. He started slowly toward us. 'Gat folks complainin' back there.'

'Shut the boot, Blake,' whispers Finney. But it weren't much of a whisper. More like a feller with a bad cold hollering.

'I'm tryin'.' And I were. But the bastard wouldn't stick. The wrench had knacked it good.

'Alright, fellers.' Nathan were standing a little ways off now.

I pushed the boot down best I could and propped my arse up against it. 'Alright, Nathan.'

'Alright, Nathan.'

He didn't say nothing for a bit. Just stood there licking his tash and scratching his hairy belly. It struck us as strange how a man with such a hairy belly should have problems growing a proper tash. Hairy is hairy, I'd always reckoned. You're either hairy or you ain't. Well Nathan were a bit of both. 'Woss you gat in there then, eh? Smells like a butcher shop a week gone doomsday.'

I slied the wrench inside my leather and opened me gob to say summat, though I weren't sure what. But

Fin got there first. 'Ah, nuthin'. Juss some...er... Blakey, what were it you had in there?'

You could tell from the way his eyes was set in his head that Nathan knew exactly what were what. Like I says to you just now, he knew every bastard thing that ever came to pass in the Mangel area. Don't ask how. Folks had been joylessly asking about that un for yonks. Just like in every town there's a cunt like Finney, there's an oracle along the lines of Nathan the barman and all. 'What can I tell you, Nathan,' says I. 'Secret, ennit.'

He laughed. A real belly laugh like only a portly barman can do. Then he stopped. Just like that, as if he'd never been laughing nor ever had been nor would do. 'Don't you recall, Blake?' says he. 'I already promised to help you out. Gatta trust us now. Keepin' secrets from us don't make us feel right trusted.'

No one spoke for a bit. Seemed like no one in the whole of town were speaking. There were no noise at all, come to think on it. Not even cars and that. Then it all started up again.

'Only one way to make old Nathan feel trusted now. What you say, Blake? What were that thing you was plannin' on deliverin' to us?' He turned to Fin. 'Reckon he owes us a favour, Finney?'

Fin said summat. Ain't sure what. I were concentrating on meself, slipping my hand back in my jacket and wrapping me fingers around the greasy monkey wrench. My eyes was on Nathan's head, picking out the best spot to plant the heavy end. I were weighing up a knobbly bit round the back just above his hairline when Finney says: 'Ain't that right, Blakey?'

'Eh?'

'Thass a big wrench.' It were Nathan this time. I

looked at my arm. On the end of it, at about head height, were the wrench. 'Woss that fer, then?'

'The boot,' says Fin. 'Gettin' it open. Boot's knackered ennit.'

Nathan looked at Finney, then back at meself and the wrench. 'That right, Blake?'

They stood there like so for a minute or two, watching the wrench. I reckon even I had me eyes on it, wondering if any second it might jerk out of my grasp and stave Nathan's head in. 'Aye,' I says at last. 'Boot's knackered.'

'Well you'd best fix it,' he says, wandering off pubward. 'Otherwise folks'll be catchin' on you've got a dead man in there.'

'Shite.'

Finney's motor were a 1976 Austin Allegro 1300 Estate. Weren't a bad model as Allegros went, but I'd always reckoned if you went for the estate you're better off going with the 1500. I'd told Finney this time enough, but he were happy with what he had and content to shunt along at whatever pace he could get out of her. Like Finney says just now, she were mostly shite brown on the outside, with the bonnet and parts of the roof in grey primer and plenty of rust and filler elsewhere. The interior were the standard black vinyl and worn through here and there. In the middle of the sports steering wheel were a shiny Leyland centre cap. For a little car your Allegro Estate were quite roomy and if you put the rear seats down you had ample room for a dead body.

'Shite.'

We was headed north out of town. Before we'd left I put the Capri in the car park behind Strake Hill. It weren't the best of places to leave her. Cars was filched from there most every week. But there weren't many safe places to park in Mangel at the best of times. Anyhow, I jumped in with Finney and we headed north, like I says.

'S'fuckin' matter?' he says. His nose had stopped bleeding now. Lips and chin and backs of his hands was all plastered in dried blood. But blood never bothered Finney much. Which were just as well, him working in a slaughtering yard and all.

'Legs,' I says. 'We was meetin' Legs back at the Pry.'

'Nah.'

'You what? "Nah"?'

'He ain't there.'

'Says who? You knows how he's late sometimes.'

'Ain't late. Ain't comin'.'

'Why not?'

'Cos...'

I weren't really bothered about why he were or weren't there. Maybe he'd crashed his milk-float. Or dropped a barbell on himself and bust his neck. And I dunno why such nasty thoughts brung a smile to my careworn face, but bring one they did. It'd always been that way between meself and Legs. We was mates, but we still thought of each other in cuntish terms. He weren't a cunt in the Finney mould, course. His head weren't full of shite. But he were always trying to get one over on us. In a friendly manner, like. 'Why not?'

'Oh...' says Fin. 'He, er...rang us before I left. Says he were tied up with his motor, like.'

'Oh aye? Woss up with it?'

'Erm...head gasket.'

I knew this were shite and bollocks. Legs drove an

Escort Mexico. Everyone knows you can bet your pecker on them Mexican head gaskets. But a passing black Mariah reminded us of matters more pressing. I looked at me watch. 'We can't just drive around all day like bastards.'

'Aye,' he says. But I knew he'd be happy as a pig in shite to do just that.

'Turn left up yonder,' I says.

'What for?'

'Cos we can't just drive around.'

We stopped at the end of the road. Nothing but thirty yard of scrub lay between us and the River Clunge, which were tree-lined along this stretch and frequented by angling types. No one were about, far as I could see. No cars was parked anyhow. And unless they'd come on foot and was down on the bank, no anglers. 'Tell you what, Blake.'

'What?'

'Thass a fuckin' smart plan. Lob Baz in the river. Wish I'd of thought o' that.'

'Ta.'

We fell quiet. I lit a fag and froped it for a bit, thinking about being boss of Hoppers. After a while I says: 'Well, go on then.'

'What?'

I nodded at the river. 'Lug him yonder.'

'Me? Why me?'

'In your car, ain't he?'

'He were in your cellar.'

'Aye, but you took him without askin'.'

'But I were helpin' you.'

'Wants to help does you? Lug him yonder and chuck him in then. Push him out a bit an' all, catch the current. Don't want him washin' ashore ten yard downriver.'

He stared at us while I carried on smoking. Then he shook his head and got out. 'Come on, Blakey,' he says, hanging back into the car. 'Help us. He must be twenty stone if he's an ounce.' He waited for a bit, then shut the door and started making noises out back. Soon he had Baz on the ground and were lugging him slowly down to the water. I could hear him grunting and panting like a randy boar. He were right about Baz being a lump. Finney were struggling, and that were saying a lot considering he shifted dead cattle around for a living. But I were staying put. This were the way it had to be. I had responsibilities now, me being boss of Hoppers and all. If anyone clocked us putting a corpse in the river I'd be headed for more shite, just when I were clambering out of the first lot. No, it had to be this way. And besides, Finney'd said he wanted to help.

Fuck it. I got out and went to give him hand. I knew I oughtn't to. But what can you do? Mates is mates, even if they're cunts as well. I always helps a mate in need. Call it a fault in me character.

We took a leg each and dragged Baz onto the path running alongside the bank, then stopped for a little rest. Finney got his fags out and passed us one. We smoked and stood quietly, listening out for folk. Finney started kicking an old pop can around. 'No one about, is there?' I says. But Fin didn't hear us. He'd booted the can up the path and were off after it, imagining himself making a run at goal from the halfway line. All of a sudden I felt uneasy, like I were standing on a wall with a slurry pit on the one side and a sheer drop on the other. A deep sound started up somewhere in my head like the lowest note on a church organ. Unless I got shifting I'd fall off for surely. Fin were miles away now. He'd turned off into the scrub and were chasing the can back toward the car, dribbling past invisible fullbacks and shouting his own commentary. The noise in my head were getting louder, making us tremble and loosening me bowels. I flicked the fag, half-smoked. It pinged off Baz's dead face and landed in the dirt, where I stepped on it. I grabbed Baz's feet and hauled him down a little track that led to the water. I'd feel better once he were in the river.

'Alright, mate.'

I stopped dead and looked over my leather-clad shoulder. There were a feller sitting a few foot down from us on the water's edge, holding a rod. He winked at us, then saw Baz and frowned.

'Alright, mate,' I says, pleasantly enough.

It were Danny, short podgy cunt with glasses from three year above us at school. Four, perhaps. I'd never called him by name before and I weren't about to now. Anyhow, didn't much matter who he were. He were the bastard who seen me lugging Baz. He had to go.

We looked at each other a minute or two. The end of his rod started twitching this way and that but he weren't aware of it. We was staring at each other, wondering who were planning what. Then I stood up straight and pulled out the monkey wrench. It were a nice weight in my hand. Felt like it were meant for more than just servicing a wide range of nut gauges. Hitting folks' heads seemed a more proper usage right then. Specially when I swung it and caught him just above the left ear. His body lurched to the left and I thought he'd go down for surely. But his legs started wheeling under him, making up for the pull of gravity.

He scuttled off sideways. I followed and brung the wrench down on the same spot near enough. This time the sound were like batting a marrow with a crowbar.

He went down for good this time. He lay there kicking and dribbling, eyes flitting about like moths around a light-bulb. I watched him, thinking how it were a shame and all, but there hadn't been much else I could do. Then he stopped twitching and went all still.

I booted him in the guts hard as I could. Just to be sure.

I waited, and lit another un. My legs was starting to ache. I wanted to get out and stretch em a bit. But that'd be spoiling it. I'd done me bit and now I had to keep my head down. Across the river the sun were dipping behind the Deblin Hills. I looked at me watch. Eight o'clock. I had to be in the graveyard by nine to meet Mandy and get my passport to happy days. And I were fucking starving. Me guts was making noises like a pining greyhound. And where the fuck were Finney? Last time I seen him he were chasing that flipping pop can and screaming about some of the crowd being on the pitch and reckoning it were all over.

I lit another one and waited. I went over all the things might have happened to him. He'd trod in a pothole and broke his leg. He'd fallen in the water and drowned. He'd sat down and fallen akip. He'd forgot what he'd come here for and walked off homeward. I looked at the steering column. The keys was still in it. Perhaps I'd best fuck off.

But then he comes out of the trees clutching a big fish in each hand, grinning like a beered-up friar.

'Fuck me, Blakey,' he says, slotting his arse into the worn out driver's seat. 'Ever seen barbel this size? Here you go.' He dropped one in my lap.

'Well bugger me,' says I. He were right. They was the largest barbel I'd ever seen in them waters or any other waters, not that I'd ever seen waters other than them running through the Mangel area.

'Found em down there by the water,' he says. 'Someone left em there. Gear an' all, loads of it. Fancy it? I'll pop back down there if you wants it.' He went to open the door.

I pulled him back and says: 'Leave it.' He looked at us funny, so I says: 'Don't want folks seein' us round here. Case they finds Baz.'

'Aye, nice thinkin'.' He started up the Allegro and pointed her townward. 'So er...you get rid of Baz an' that?'

'No. Got up and ran off didn't he.'

'Eh?' He slammed on the brakes, making the fish fall off me lap. An old codger walking his dog stopped and clocked us.

'You means he came back to life an'...Oh.' He started laughing. 'You're joshin' us, right? Got up an' ran off, heh heh.'

The old cunt still had his bifocals on us. His hound started barking. I stared back at him until he got moving again. 'Just fuckin' shift,' I says to Fin.

He stopped laughing after a bit and says: 'Right then, thass that sorted. Fancy gettin' pissed now?'

Finney were hard to get rid of. He saw it as our duty to get plastered, being as how we'd just achieved summat. I fobbed him off by telling him I were meeting Sal for a drink, and he were welcome to come along and join us and get arsed and that. Finney'd always been funny around birds. Birds of mine anyhow. Specially Beth. He hardly ever came round ours in case she answered the door, and the one time he did try his luck she made him stand on the doorstep. She told us later she didn't want folks like him hanging around the house and bringing the place down. She had a point. Fin were a scruffy cunt if ever there were one. And he didn't speak proper like meself and Legsy. But he were a mate, weren't he. A wife ain't meant to treat her feller's mates like that. And I told her as much. But she just shrugged and says oh well, what's done is done. And she'd do it again if he came round again. But he wouldn't, would he. Not now she'd put him in his place.

Anyhow, that's how I got shot of him. He dropped us off by my car and went off somewhere. I headed for Norbert Green, stopping off at Alvin's for a bag of chips and a can of pop. I ate and drank as I drove, which weren't ideal. The bag were wedged between me thighs and the heat from the chips had us sweating like a bastard. I wolfed em down fast as I could, shutting up them pining greyhounds in me guts. Then I downed the pop in one go, which had us belching so loud folks was turning their heads as I drove past. And that were with the windows rolled up.

It were bang on nine when I pulled up outside the graveyard. No one were about, besides meself and all them deadfolk underfoot. There were a church over the far corner but I don't reckon as anyone ever used that, besides for funerals. Ain't much call for churches in Mangel, and I don't reckon as ever there were. There's a reason for that, my old man used to tell us. And this were the one thing I remembered him telling us that didn't have a wallop on the end of it. According to him, right, religion is for folks who's missing summat in their lives. There's a hole inside of em, see, and they fills it with churches and vicars and that. It's the same the world over. Big flocks of folks with holes inside of em, temples and gods to fill em with.

Well, Mangel folk ain't got that hole. Mangel folk don't need anything but bread, water, and air. And lager. And fags.

I set off down the path, getting rid of a bit more pop gas as me guts got shifting. This were it then. I were finally gonna find out what this doofer were that every bastard were after. Not that it mattered. Could be a golden calf for all I gave a toss, long as it got us my name up above the door of Hoppers. I walked past the spot where Baz had drawn his last breath. You'd never have known it. I'd covered me tracks pretty good there. It were hard to believe it'd really happened, seeing it now. I were glad of that. And Baz were off to the sea by now, which is where the River Clunge finally comes out, I hears.

Course, there were no sign of Mandy Munton. Not that I'd expected there to be. By my reckoning she'd be lurking behind a tree up the other end of the yard, ready to jump out behind us when I came past. It were only when I reached the far gate that I wondered if her brothers might have rumbled her. And by then it were too fucking late.

I barely had time to swear under me breath before Jess were atop us. He were a heavy cunt. Not as heavy as Baz, but Jess were hewn of muscle rather than lard. He were your proverbial shite house, less windows and doors, being as his eyes was always blank as a brick wall and he rarely opened his gob. But it weren't his weight what bothered us. Not even when he brung it all down into me guts via his right knee. I could handle that. Well, I'd get over it in time anyhow. It were his smell what I couldn't handle. Stank like he'd filled his trolleys he did. And I didn't take kindly to it. Fighting's a physical business, and the least he could have done were wipe his arse proper. Aye, it got my goat up alright.

He were using my head as a speedball when the thing started inside of us. It were the same thing what'd done for Baz, once he'd brung it out. It were a blackness surging outwards from somewhere in me belly, making us numb all over but mad for blood. Me arms and legs felt like cooling pig iron. I threw Jess off. It weren't that hard. He were up quick, chin stuck out like a bulldozer shovel. But he could have been swinging an axe for all I cared. I'd still have had him.

I swung my right leg at him, ignoring the right he were swinging back at me face. He connected nice and sweet with my left eyebrow. And on another day that might have stunned us good and proper. But not this time. And he knew it. My boot landed square between his legs.

No man's knacker sack is built to hold up against that much welly, and I reckon it done the trick. I pulled back to take a pot at that bulldozer blade, see if I couldn't put a dent on him on his way down.

But then I went down instead.

15
....

It were the smell what hit us first. A sweet, sickly, meaty smell. One that I'd become all too familiar with of late. Aye, it were the stench of rotting carcasses what hit us first when I came to.

'T'ain't me. The car, ennit.'

I mean, summat a lot harder than a stink had hit us already, right around where my neck joins the back of me skull. That's the way it were feeling round there when I moved me swede a bit anyhow.

'Hard to shift that kind o' stench. Had half a goat on the back seat once, from work. Only there a couple days it were. But his spirit lingered, you might say. All the way to highest heaven and back it did stink. Still comes back on hot days.'

I needed air. It were stinking, like I told you. And stuffy as a turkey come Christmas. I had to get away from it, open a window, stop breathing altogether. Anything. I opened me eyes to see which of these were achievable. And that's about the time I became aware that someone were addressing us.

'Bit of air fresh'ner'd do it. Hey Blakey, lend us a couple o' squid for some air fresh'ner?'

'Fin,' says I. 'Fin, what the fuck for am I doin' in your Allegro?'

He lowered the window and looked up and down. The stuffiness and stench gave way to the Mangel air, which weren't much better to be honest. Then he wound it up again, lit a smoke, and says: 'Hidin', ain't us.'

'From who?'

'Who? Muntons, course.'

We was parked down a back street out Muckfield way. I recognised the place straight off. As lads we'd robbed a repair shop down here. You don't forget shite like that.

'Why is we hidin' from the Muntons?'

'Wh— Can't you recall? They was doin' you over in that graveyard. Jess and Mandy, for cryin' out fuck. Saved you, I did. Mandy brained you with a big bit of headstone. Headstone, heh heh. Get it? Head—'

'Mandy?'

'Aye.'

'What for? I mean, why would Mandy—'

'You was layin' into her Jess, for one. Ain't seen you scrappin' that dirty for years, Blakey. Booted the fucker square in the plums, and no mistake.'

'But Mandy—'

'Aye? What of her? Munton, ain't she?'

'Aye, but . . .'

'But what? Muntons looks after Muntons. Besides, they all shags her. The brothers, that is. Keep it in the family an' that.'

I rubbed the back of me swede again. It were like rubbing wet turf. Least the fog in my head were starting to clear a bit. 'That right?'

'Course. Blake?'

'Aye?'

'Why was you in that graveyard anyhow?'

'Why was you there more like.'

'Follerin' you, case you got into any more bother. And lucky for you I did. What was you up to?'

'I were . . .' The thoughts flooded into my head like someone pouring hot lard into each ear hole. The coppers. Nathan the barman. Fenton and his doofer. Hoppers, my name above the door. 'What'd you do to her?'

'Who?'

'Mandy.'

'Don't fret. No one seen us. Have a fag.'

'Ta. What'd you do to her, you cunt?'

'Hey, hold up. I saved your arse again. Sticks me neck out for you time and again an' what does I get back? Meanness is what. Meanness and fuckin' nastiness. T'ain't fair.' He folded his arms and stuck out his lower lip.

We sat in silence for a bit. I smoked me fag, then flicked the stub out the window. 'Fin?'

'Aye.'

'Ta for lookin' out for us an' that.'

'S'alright. What mates is for, ennit.'

'Aye. Fin?'

'Aye?'

'What'd you do to her?'

'Oh for fuck. I juss smacked her a bit. S'all.'

'Smacked her? Where? How hard?'

'I dunno does I? Twatted her on the ear or summat. Don't matter do it? Birds goes down easy. She'd of killed you.'

'She hurt then?'

'Dunno. Went down, didn't she.'

'Blood?'

'Bit.'

'Breathin'?'

'Fuck sake, Blake.'

'Breathin'?'

'Aye. Dunno. I didn't fuckin' kill her, leastways.'

'She have summat on her? Summat in a bag or summat?'

'Sorta summat?'

'You knows. A . . . a thing. She have summat on her?'

'Well . . .' His eyes was off in the distance, concealing the hard work that were going on behind em. For most folks it ain't hard to cast the mind back an hour or so. But this were Finney. 'Fuck me,' he says.

'What?' He had us all excited. Of all folks, Finney were the one set to spill the beans on what this doofer were. 'What is it?'

'Down there.' He nods down the road. 'Thass the place we done over that time, yonks ago. Ennit?'

I sighed. 'Aye, reckon so.'

'Well, fuck me. Hey, know the old geezer we done over that time? Seen him t'other day. Sittin' on a bench in Flockford Park he were, with two or three other mongs an' a nurse. Fancy that, eh?'

'Well bugger. Mong now, is he? That were you, droppin' the battery on his head there.'

'I knows. Smart, eh? I were right proud when I seen him like that, starin' at fuck all, slobber danglin' from his lip. Right proud.' He shook his head and lit another one.

'Well?'

'Wha?'

'Mandy have summat on her?'

'Oh aye. Had a box. Dropped it on the grass when she went for you with the headstone.'

We shut up for a bit. I sat on my side looking out at that old repair shop with boarded-up windows and graffiti all over. I thought about the feller, and how one minute he were in his own premises, a mechanic on top of his game, enjoying a spot of recreation with a local slag. Next minute we waltzes in and turns it all around for him. We switched off the lights in his head, just so's we could spend a few quid down the arcade and buy a bit of lager. We switched em off for good. And it were alright. Seemed alright to fuck with folks, long as we had a laugh and got summat out of it. Folks didn't matter cos they was asking for it. Should have seen us coming shouldn't they. We was only younguns.

'Say that again,' I says, lighting up me last fag. 'Go on. Humour us. Say again what you done with the box.'

'Aw, don't be like that. Blakey. I telled you how it were. There were nut'n else I could do.'

'Say the fucker again.'

'Alright. I kicked it away. Heard some bastard comin' didn't I. Smelt fag smoke anyhow. So I hauled you up under the armpits an' starts draggin' you to the car. I sees this box on the grass near where the bitch must of been hidin' and I kicks it away. Couldn't pick it up, see. Had me hands full like.'

'And where'd it go, once you'd kicked it?'

'Well...'

'Go on. I needs a laugh.' I really did.

'Well, there were this dog, see. Mangy old bastard with one ear. Anyhow he scooped the box up in his chops... Should of seen it Blakey. You'd never believe a dog could pick up a box like that with his teeth. Heavy an' all, it were. The box that is. Me big toe still hurts like a bastard.'

'And the dog...'

'Aye. Ran off.'

'With the box.'

'Aye.'

'Blake. This ain't clever.'

I shone the torch up the alley. A cat. A bastard fucking cat. 'Go on.'

Finney pulled away again. His lights was off and he were sticking under twenty, pulling over whenever we saw a car coming. 'I tells you this ain't clever.'

I shook my head and bit me lip and counted to ten. Sitting in Finney's Allegro in the middle of Norbert Green weren't the place to have a row. But a row were coming, like it or no. 'Clever?' I bellowed. 'Clever? What the fuck does you know about clever? You wouldn't know clever if it sucked you off and gave you a tenner.'

'Calm down eh Blake? Say what you likes about me. I knows what ain't clever. And this is it.'

I sat there in the dark, trembling with rage. 'So you knows what ain't clever, eh? Reckon you do, does you? What about robbin' Baz's corpse from out my cellar? Did you spot how not clever that were? And drivin' the fucker about town for days? How's that for not clever?'

'I'll tell you what weren't clever. Keepin' him in yer cellar in the first place. And toppin' him. Not clever at all.'

'You...' It were a peculiar feeling. I were so overcome with anger that my whole body were good as paralysed. It weren't just the shite he'd got us into with Baz that were getting to us. All kinds of memories was flooding back into me swede, times when Finney had fucked up and I'd kept mum about it. 'You...You fuckin' burnt my wife. How's that for not clever? Eh? How's that for...'

Suddenly everything were silent. Then one or two noises crept into my ear holes. Breathing. Heart beating. The drip and groan of the Allegro's dormant engine. A strange urge came to us. I wanted to say sorry. But fuck that. I weren't saying sorry to Finney. He'd killed Beth and ruined my fucking life.

Alright alright. So maybe I had made that second phone call back then on the night of the Hoppers blaze. It's all a mite hazy and I had things on me mind and maybe I can't be sure either way, honest I can't. But I didn't truly reckon summat'd come of it if she did come over. How could I? Aye, messing her about and pissing her off weren't beneath us. But topping her? Come on, she were a bird weren't she. You ain't meant to top birds.

'Aye, well...' he says. 'Soz about that.'

I looked at him. He looked at his hands. Like I says before, I couldn't stand seeing folks miserable. 'Forget it,' I says. 'You weren't to know she were in there, was you.'

'Aye.'

I lit a fag. 'Aye? Aye what?'

'Aye. I did know she were in there.'

'Come again?'

'What I says. I knew she were in Hoppers. When I lit it, like.'

'Eh? How? Why...'

'Put her in there meself, didn't I. What you wanted wernit?'

I looked at Fin. He were still looking down at his hands, waiting for us to say summat. And maybe I ought to have said summat. Summat special, like such an important moment demands. But in the end I just says, 'Shut up.'

'I fuckin' done it for you, Blake. You weren't happy with her. She were bad news. An' I wanted me old mates back. Me you an' Legs. Like we is now. She were fuckin' bad news, Blakey. Trust us.'

I laughed a bit. But it weren't a proper laugh. 'Alright Fin, thass enough.'

'But I gotta tell you, Blake. Can't keep it in forever can I? I brained her with a whisky bottle and tied her up, see . . . good an' tight. Done alright there Blake, didn't I? Tied her legs together and then her arms. Then I rolled her over and tied her arms to her legs . . . '

'Fin, shut the fuck up.'

' . . . she wakes up a bit an starts blabberin' so I boots her in the swede an' gags her with me socks. Soaks her in paraffin an' leaves her behind the bar an' goes outside . . . I done all this for you, Blakey . . . Then I sets the place alight. Blake. Blake? Listen to us Blake. I had to do it that way. I—'

'Shut up.'

'Don't shout at us Blake. Done you a fuckin' favour didn't I. You'd of done it yerself sooner or later. I would and all if my wife were putting it about anyhow. Not that I ever had a—'

'You what?'

'Blake.'

'Sayin' my wife were a slapper?'

'Blake, get off us. I can't breathe like that.'

Finney's face were going slowly purple. There weren't much light but I knew it were going purple cos that's the colour a face goes when you close your hands around a throat. His hands flapped at my arms but I hardly noticed. Then summat moved out the window. Across the road there. 'See that?' I says, pointing.

Finney coughed and spluttered a bit.

'Fuckin' dog wernit. See it? Over by the park.'

I shone the torch over that way, but Finney weren't paying much heed. So I opened the door and slipped out.

I crossed the road. On the other side I stopped to spark up a fag, my lighter making a noise like a truck hitting a bridge. This weren't right. But it weren't as if I had a choice. He had to be around here somewhere. I stepped over the hedge, snagging me tracky bottoms on a thorn. 'Bastard fuck and bollocks...' I says followed by other such words. I got meself free at last, but there were a little L-shaped tear right under me knackers. I hated messing up me togs. A man's togs says a lot about him. Just look at Finney. His gear had 'cunt' wrote all over it. I flashed the torch around.

And there he were, sniffing at summat on the grass. I were sure of it. There couldn't have been two such dogs in Norbert Green.

I took a step forward. He looked up and clocked us, his one ear standing to attention. I'd been hoping it were the box he were sniffing at, but it were just a pile of old dogshite. Still, can't expect a dog to trot around all night holding a box in his chops. No, he'd hid it somewhere. He trotted off across the park.

I followed. He were walking quite slow, like Lassie when he's leading some feller with a rope and pulley to where a youngun has fallen down an old mineshaft. Maybe this here mongrel knew what I were after and were taking us to where he'd stowed it. Dogs is clever like that sometimes. I once had ten bob at eights on a hound named Ted Fletch at Blender Stadium. Half a lap to go he were second place and fading. With all the strength in my heart I willed the leader – a black and white called Pig Dodger – to fall arse over. Well, he did. Came out the last bend too hard and slid out, knackering one of his hind pins. That were the end of Pig Dodger, but it just goes to show how dogs is telepathetic sometimes. And I won eighty quid.

Anyhow, I followed this feller right up to the corner of the park. He gave us another Lassie look then slipped on through a hole in the fence.

I got down on me knees and took a gander through the hole. Looked like your typical garden on the other side. I could hear him padding off up the path and then stopping – at the spot where he'd stowed the box, I hoped. The fence were about six and half feet tall. I jumped up and got my arms over the top. I had me leather on so I weren't worried about tearing anything. But fucking up my togs were the least of it, as it turned out. I just couldn't get the rest of my arse over the fence. I kept throwing me leg over but my boot just slid helplessly down the wood. I were puffing and sweating, but there weren't no turning back now. Specially since Lassie were down there on the other side looking up at us, one ear cocked.

He were willing us over. I fucking knew he were. He were willing us over cos he were on my side. I winked at him, took a lungful, and chucked me leg up one more time.

My foot went over this time. I hauled meself upright. It were bastard uncomfortable, seventeen stone of gravity forcing a strip of wood up between my arse cheeks. But I needed a rest so I stayed like that for a bit. I had a gander down below to take me mind off the pain, seeing where were safest to land. Then the fence collapsed from under us.

Just like a cat will always land on his all fours, I always lands on my arse. Gives you a jolt but all round your arse is better than your swede for landing on. Specially when your swede's already in bad shape like mine were. Anyhow, I dusted meself off and hauled upright, noting with a shake of the head that the fence had come down all round the garden. Lights was coming on inside the house and Lassie were barking at us. 'Here boy,' I says, holding out my hand as folks does with dogs. He walked up and calmly bit us on the thumb.

Just as I were grabbing for his ear the back door opened and a feller came out in tartan dressing gown and slippers. He looked familiar. The dog ran up and started jumping up and down in front of him.

'Wh—? Wha—? Who the blinkin' flip are you?' he says. And by his voice I knew for surely he were the feller from the graveyard the other day.

'Oh,' I says, trying to recall what I'd said to him back then. But I couldn't. All I knew were that I'd had to get rid of him fast, before he stumbled on Baz. Fuck knew how I'd done it. 'Yer posts is up wrong,' I says. Had to say summat didn't I? 'Thass why the whole lot came down and not just the one panel. Ain't got em set deep enough.'

He were stepping back and forth like he weren't sure whether to come out and give us what for or go in and lock the door. It's that kind of hesitation that a feller can grab hold of and wring dry. 'This dog here,' I says, pointing at the mongrel who were now shoving his snout up the feller's dressing gown. 'Yours is it?'

'Basil? Aye, he's m . . . What of it? What you want with Basil the dog?'

'If you're his owner then you're in all kinds o' shite. See, a dog ain't responsible for his actions, is he. Far as he's concerned the world's his oyster and there ain't no such a thing as property.'

'Hang on a sec. Er...' He stuck his head back inside and says: 'Stay there, Ma.' Then he came back out and says: 'Woss he done now?'

'Woss he done? Don't tell us you don't know. Thass—'

'How ought I to know? Can't know all he gets up to, can I? He ain't, er... Ain't been bitin' arses again has he? Partial to folks' arses, he is.'

'Well, matter of fact, aye. He bit us. And other stuff besides.'

'Oh bother,' he says, looking behind him to make sure his mam couldn't hear. 'What can I say, mister? I'm sorry an' that. He's the worst flippin' zample of a dog as feller ever strapped collar on. Fourteen year old he is. I'd of had him under them roses over there long ago, but fer Ma. Her dog, see. Can't do no wrong in her eyes can Basil the dog. Even bit my own arse once an' she reckoned I'd asked fer it.'

He came a bit closer and whispers: 'When Pa left this here Earth she went out and found this puppy who were borned the same day. Same day Pa died, like. Well, cut a long un short, Basil here is Pa. Same name an' everythin'. Ma's one o' them what believes in reincoronation an' that, see. Reckons folks reaps what they sows.'

'Well I'll be buggered,' I says, glancing at Basil with a new respect. 'What do you reckon to all that?'

'Reincoronation? Bollocks ennit. But sometimes I looks at him and gets a shiver right up me spine. He behaves like Pa, see. Looks like him an' all. Right down to the...'

'Oh aye? The ear, was you gonna say?'

He peered over his shoulder and moved closer. 'He were only a puppy still. One day I come home and finds him like this, bandage wrapped round his conk. What do you reckon? Hardly fell off, did it? Same side as Pa's an' all.'

'How'd Pa lose his?'

'Same way as this un.' We both looked at the house, where you could see the old bird squinting at us out the kitchen window. Both shivered and all. I did anyhow.

'Listen pal,' I says. 'I won't give you no trouble if you helps us out with the other thing he done.'

'What other thing?'

'He robbed us. *Mugged* us. From behind. Came from nowhere he did as I were walkin' along. Run up and bit us on the arse. I lets out a cry, in agony like. An' I drops the package I were carryin'. A box it were. Well, Basil here gets it an' hares off with it before I knows what's what. Been lookin' for him ever since. Thass what led us here.'

'Box, you says?'

'Aye.'

'Sorta box?'

'Well, it were ... Squarish, like. And little enough so's a dog's jaws can haul it. But not too little. Oh, and a bit heavy. Heavy enough so's you'd hurt yer foot if you kicks it. Why, know where it is does you?'

He crossed his arms and had a quick gander over his shoulder. When he turned back he were chewing his lip and looking at the grass. 'Well ... Valuable, is it?'

'Woss it to you?'

'Er ... Thing is, er ... We had it, like.'

'Aye? And where is it?'

'Well, we...' He took a step backward. 'Look, mister, you'd of done same. How was we to know? He were—'

'Who? What?'

'Easy, mister,' he says, putting his hands up. 'Feller came by fer it earlier, didn't he. About half-nine, ten. Says a dog run off with his box an' he'd follered it here. Seemed a decent sorta feller like. So I gives it to him. What else could I do, eh? You'd of done same.'

But I weren't listening to him now. I couldn't even see him. All I could see were meself up at the bar in Hoppers, smart suited and cigar smoking, nodding at the fellers and fondling every lass that came within armshot. Only it were fading. The scene were fading.

'What were in it, eh? Little bottle o' whisky or summat? Eh? Maybe a Bible? Summat valuable? Can't think what else. Gonna tell us or what?'

'Woss this feller look like, then?'

'Well,' he smiled, thinking he were off the hook. And he were, truth be told. Doing him over wouldn't get the doofer back, would it? I ain't thick you know. 'He were about so high, with hair on his head. And long trousers on.'

'Long...? What colour hair?'

'Ain't sure. It were dark.'

'How tall?'

He put his hand up again, about a foot different from the last time.

We stood like that for a bit, me thinking up questions and him shivering in his dressing gown. But that weren't getting us nowhere. 'Soz about yer fence,' I says.

'Ah, the fence,' he says. 'Ah, sod it. Nut'n much you can do fer that. You're right though. Posts wasn't deep enough.' But I were already on my way.

I stopped just before a fallen panel, hearing summat else from him. 'You what?'

'Regals,' he shouts again. Lights was coming on upstairs in the neighbouring houses. 'He were smoking Regals.'

'For surely?'

'Aye. Sure as my mother in there's alive and not run over by a buzz like you says she was.'

I could see from across the road that Finney's car were empty. I had a gander around the park to see if he were pissing or shitting behind a bush or summat. But he weren't. Back on the street not a thing moved. Not even a cat. Or a one-eared dog. I tried the driver's door.

To Finney, your Allegro were the most desirable motor a feller could get behind the wheel of. He reckoned the sight of an Allegro would bring out the crook in a clergyman, forcing him to try the handle as he strolled by. I can't say as I agreed with him. Ain't many folks who'd argue against your Capri 2.8i being the premier motor on the road. But locking up is a good idea anyhow, even if you drives a Hillman Imp. And Finney knew that. Which had us scratching my head when the door opened.

There were nothing to be found inside. Only Finney's fags and lighter on the dash and the keys still in the slot. I got in and locked the door. He'd be back in a bit. Seen Basil the dog and run after him like as not. Be chasing for hours if he kept the dog in his sights, would Fin.

Aye, that's what'd happened.

The smell were getting to us again. I lit one up and rolled down the window a mite. I looked at the keys and thought for a bit about going after Fin. It were dark and quiet and a pleasant night all in all. Up yonder the moon were gibbous and yellow. My head were starting to feel numb rather than battered. And it felt right good when I shut me eyes for just a moment.

16

It were me and Baz and Beth at the kitchen table. My old man were sitting somewhere behind us and all but I couldn't turn my head to see him. You could hear him, mind, that heavy breathing he always done and which I hated. We was playing cards. The feller I'd killed on the riverbank came through the back door sopping wet and dripping all over. He had a barbel in each hand, both bigger than the two Finney had robbed off him. In fact they was so big they trailed along the floor, leaving big wide stripes of red on the lino. Beth glared at him and put a *Mangel Informer* on the floor for him to stand on. Then she got a mop out and started on the fish blood. 'Mind if I joins in?' says the feller.

'Aye,' says Baz, not looking up from his hand. 'I does mind. You looks like a cunt to me. Smells like one an' all. Now fuck off.'

Beth got up and dumped the cleaning-up kit on the table, but Baz didn't seem to notice. It were hard to tell what game we was playing. Seemed like I had too many cards in my hand, about two hundred by the looks of it. And all of em were the king of hearts. Only it weren't a king, it were Nathan the barman. Beth took the two barbel off the feller and wrapped em in pastry with some taters and onions and plonked it in the oven. The door were only open a second or two but I saw a few other pies in there already. Then she went back to the wet feller and started stroking his face and licking his neck. It were no sort of behaviour for a wife to be displaying, I can tell you. But this were a dream and there were nothing I could do. Beth took her top off. She were wearing no bra. She took the feller's hands and put em on her tits. The nipples was like acorns, which were not how I recalled em to be. I swallowed and blinked, and when I looked again the two of em was bare and feeling each other up, he rubbing her tits and she yanking his tadger, which looked a bit like a young barbel. Then he picked her up and plonked her on the counter and got going on her.

I looked at Baz. I didn't want to but it were a dream and what you wants don't count for shite in dreams. He were looking back at us, waggling his eyebrows and sighing and tapping his fingers on the table. It were my go, I reckoned. 'Well,' says Baz. 'What you gonna do about it eh?' I looked at me cards. They was all jokers now. Beth and the feller was moaning and groaning and humping on the counter. My old man were somewhere behind us, breathing...

I knew it were a dream straight off. So there weren't none of your waking up and thanking fuck that life weren't really like that. Besides, there were summat worse going on that made us yearn for that kitchen table and everything that went with it. There were an awful screeching racket taking place not six inches from my right ear hole.

I clapped hands over ears while I worked out that I

were in Finney's Allegro, it were light outside, and someone were shouting at us through the window. Maybe it were still a dream I were thinking as I clambered over the gearshift into the passenger seat. A fucking nightmare by the sounds of it. But if I just got this door open I could have a go at turning it into one of them running dreams. I hit the pavement and started walking up the road, me pins being too cramped up for running.

Last thing I wanted were a rumble with a resident of Norbert Green, Munton or no. Maybe if I walked on and kept my head down I could just slip away from whoever it were. But soon I heard footsteps pitter-pattering after us. Some cunt were running up to deliver us five knuckles on a hairy pole. I couldn't take no more head damage, what with the bump from Jess and the smash from Mandy and the trip on the stair and the various attentions from Baz. Anything more than a haircut and blow-dry and I'd be turning vegetable. So I turned and stuck out my arm.

'Bla—' she says, walking into me fist.

'Oh fuck . . .' I says. 'Soz about that Mand. You alright?'

After a minute she could stand up, still covering her nose with her hand. 'Got a hanky?' she says.

I gave her an old tissue I found in me pocket. 'Hold yer head back. Be stoppin' soon enough.'

I were lying, course. I'd broken plenty of noses in my time – mostly with my head, but a large number by hand – and I knew what a snapped bridge felt like. She did her best to mop some of the blood off her face and then pressed the wet mess to her nose.

'Thought you was a feller,' I says, noticing that my legs felt alright now and I'd be able to run. I had stuff to do. It were all coming back now. Basil the dog. The gravedigger in the tartan dressing gown. The box. Embassy Regal. I patted Mandy on the arm and says: 'You'll be alright now, eh?'

She glared at us, and I could see she were crying a bit. Funny that, how some birds cries silently. Most bawls like you've cut their arms off. But the odd one just lets the tears pump out like her eyes was born to do it. I also noticed her arm were in a sling. 'Who done that?' I says, prodding it.

'Ow, get off, clumsy twat,' she says, sounding like she had a heavy cold. 'Your mate done it, in the grave-yard. Skinny feller with one eyebrow going right across his head. Wossname. Finley, ennit?'

'Oh, aye. Finney. The dirty cunt... Wait till I sees him. Hurtin' a little girl such as yerself.'

'Done it for you he did, mind. Don't wanna go punishin' yer friends does you?'

'Oh, aye. He did, didn't he. So...' As if to remind us of where my priorities ought to be, a bolt of lightning passed through the back of me swede. That's what it felt like anyhow. Suddenly I weren't feeling so bad about breaking Mandy's nose. 'What the fuck you brain us for anyhow, Mand?'

She told us we couldn't talk here, it being getting on for seven and folks liable to wake up any minute. So we walked off down the road and turned into Blickett Lane, me stretching my legs and her holding the rag to her hooter. Halfway up there were an alley that came out by some lock-ups. Most of em was abandoned. Always had been, far as I recalled. They found a feller's feet in one of em years back, ankles down, boots still on. Never did find the rest of him. Coppers never found the bastard who done it neither,

this being Norbert Green. But it didn't take folks long
to chalk it up as another Munton story.

Mandy tugged at one of the up-and-over doors. It
were rusted to fuck and wouldn't budge more than an
inch or two. I gave it a good yank and got it open enough
for us to crawl inside. The garage were empty but for a
big old engine plonked on the floor. Looked like it were
from an old Rover. We sat on the dusty floor in the
corner. With her good arm she got a pair of knickers and
some fags out of her rucksack. I hadn't noticed her
rucksack before that. It didn't look that heavy. Heavy
enough so's a bird with one good arm could lug it. She
put the knickers to her bloody nose and chucked us the
fags. I lit two and passed her one. The knickers were pink
with black dots and lacy bits round the edges. Just
looking at em set off a stirring between me legs. But it
levelled off when they started soaking up the blood.

'So,' she says, like we was sitting down for
afternoon tea and crumpets.

'So what?'

'You was askin' us why I brained you yesterday.'

'Aye.' I were still half akip, to be honest. I rubbed
my face to wake meself up a bit. 'An' while you're at
it tell us why you scared the shite out of us back there
in me car.'

'Ain't your car. You drives a Capri.'

'Thass true. Finney's, it is.' I hadn't thought about
Finney. He ain't the kind you spends much time
actually thinking on. Not even when he confesses that
he murdered your wife and mentions in passing that
she were carrying on with another feller. Alright, it
bothered us. But I couldn't ponder too much on it
right now. I had other shite to sort out. And what's
past is passed, and that. But where were he?

'An' all I were doin' were wakin' you up,' she says. 'I were sittin' across the road in the park, juss thinkin'. About us. About me brothers. About me. I were walkin' past early, see, before me brothers is up. Before anyone's up round here. I were . . .' She looked at the rucksack slumped on the concrete beside her. 'I were leavin', Blake.'

'Leavin'? Where to?' I says, noting a strange pang of summat or other in my heart. It were only a pang, mind. And pangs ain't too hard to ignore.

'Anywhere. Out of Mangel. Far away from here as me legs'll carry us. Other side of the world, if they ain't lyin' about it bein' round and not flat.' She gave us a look. No, that ain't true. She weren't trying to tell us summat with her eyes, which is what giving someone a look is. She looked at us, rather. To see what I were thinking.

I gave her a look that said sorry, I ain't thinking nothing.

She closed her eyes and went on. 'Anyhow, I sees you fast akip in the car and tries to wake you up, is all. Norbert Green ain't a place where folks kips in cars. Speshly not folks like you who's in shite with locals.'

We went silent again for a bit. A black tomcat came up to the half-open door, sniffed at us, then turned tail and strolled off, showing us his little white arse.

Mandy's nose had stopped bleeding, though it didn't look right. She tossed the knickers and started wiping it up with a hanky. 'I were gonna tell you why I brained you yesterday in the graveyard, weren't I.'

'Oh aye. T'aint right to hit a feller from behind, you knows.'

'Don't count. I'm a girl ain't I.'

'Do count. We can't hit birds so they shouldn't hit us.'

'Anyhow, I didn't wanna do it. Honest I didn't Blake. An' I tried to do it gentle. But you was beatin' our Jess. You was killin' him. If I hadn't of thought that, I w—'

'He fuckin' jumped us. What about that eh? An' what were he doin' there? Set us up like a good un you did.'

'Stop that right now, Royston Blake. You knows I wouldn't do such a thing. Not to you anyhow. It surprised me as much as you, him turnin' up like that. Telled us after that he were just passin' by an' spotted you. Dunno how else it could be. He surely didn't foller us. But there's summat you should understand about me and my brothers. We . . .'

Fucks each other. Aye, I knows that.

'We has a special relationship. We . . . We're close. Always has been.'

Aye, ever since they found a hole in you.

'Iss funny, an' I can't expect you to understand. But thass the reason for me leavin' town like I am. I've had enough of it. An' you knows what Blake? Seein' you yesterday made me mind up for us. Ain't sure why. Lookin' in your eyes juss gave us a different view on things, made us wanna get out there an' do things for meself.'

I nodded and got another couple of fags out.

'So?' she says.

I passes her a fag and says: 'So what?'

'Comin' with us or not?'

I sucked on the fag and looked at her, holding the smoke in me lungs. She had a bust nose, bust arm, messy hair and dried blood across her face. But right then I'd still have had her above any other bird I knew or ever had known. Maybe she were made like me. Maybe she were made for me, and I for her. There's one out there for everyone, they says. If you can find em. Well, I'd bet me eyebrows that this un here were mine.

Drying blood were gathered thick and dark under her nostrils and round her mouth. She didn't seem bothered. I pulled the dark hair back off her face and kissed her cheek, which were mostly clean. Then I says: 'Sweetheart, there's summat you oughta know.'

She looked at us with her big dark glistening eyes. It broke my heart to say what I were about to. But I had to. If I didn't tell her, she'd go and find out for herself and get herself into all kinds of bother into the bargain. Still, it shouldn't ought to be me doing the telling here. If her brothers'd let her out more she'd have found it out for herself. She'd have learned it from an early age like other Mangel folk.

'You can't leave Mangel,' I says gently. I took her hand and stroked it. Anything to soften the blow. 'No one can. See, we're all leaves on the same tree. And when a leaf drops off the tree it withers and dies. We can't live without the tree, and it can't get by without us, like. Understand us, does you?'

She were looking at us still. Them eyes of hers was stuck to mine like a couple of lampreys. It were a lot for her to take in, I knows. And I felt sorry for her. The truth hurts. But it's there, like it or not.

'Course, folks from outside can get in if they wants. There's Fenton, who bought Hoppers from yer brothers. An' Finney, believe it or not. They says Fin's grandpa were a mad gypo strayed through the gates lookin' for dogs and cats to eat.'

I went on like that, laying it all out for her and trying not to miss anything. And she seemed to take it well. She sat nice and quiet and listened, appreciating the effort I were putting into it, I reckoned. And then I stopped, and it were her turn. Her turn to tell us how fucking surprising it all were and she couldn't take it all in and thank you so much Blake for setting us straight, that is. But that weren't what happened.

You know what she said?

She says: 'Oh . . . right.' And she smiled a bit and all. A thin smile that never touched her eyes. But that were down to me, like as not. I'd messed up a bit hadn't I. Dumped too much on her brain in one go. 'So you're not comin' then?'

I smiled and shook me swede. She were catching on.

She looked at the engine in front of us for a bit. The sun were creeping into the garage, touching up the dark greasy metal with a few drops of white gold. It made you squint to look at it. Then she had another one-handed rummage in her rucksack. 'Here,' she says, turning to us, face set like a mask. She held out a pistol. 'If you stays in Mangel you'll need this.'

I took it and turned it over and over in me hands. Looked like a new un. Not that I'd seen many old uns. Nor new uns neither. Guns is seldom seen in Mangel, less you're a farmer or a member of the Munton clan. Just ain't much call for em. Plenty of aggro takes place, but folks is happier using fists and heads. And blades. And coshes.

No, can't say as I'd ever coveted a firearm. Never liked the idea of em. Takes all the fun out of things, don't it. But now I had one in my hands, well . . . 'Fuckin' smart,' I says. 'Loaded is it?'

'Aye. Here . . .' She showed us how to flick the

safety and get to the chamber. Then she got a little box of bullets out of her bag. Or shells as she called em. There couldn't have been much left in that rucksack of hers. 'Hold it like this, see. An' use both hands. Till you gets used to it anyhow.'

I took it and aimed at an old beer can out in the yard. I didn't fire it, mind. I weren't that barmy.

'Blake?'

'Fuckin' smart.'

'Blake, you knows why I'm givin' you this, right?'

I had a go at spinning it on me finger by the trigger guard, like they does in cowboy films on telly. It weren't as easy as you might think. A real pistol's a lot heavier than a pretend one, for starters.

'Blake?'

It occurred to us that acting like a cowboy weren't too clever. So I packed that in. For some reason Lee Munton's words of advice on how to handle a firearm were coming back to us. Never point it at someone you'd rather not shoot, he'd said. Don't rest your finger on the trigger. Keep it unloaded till you're ready to use it.

'Well, I'll be off then, Blake.'

I opened her up and took all the shells out of her, rolling em around in the palm of my hand. They didn't look like they'd pass through a man's chest and chalk him up dead. Truth were I couldn't wait to try it out. On a tree. Maybe a cat. Dog perhaps. I put the bullets in one pocket and the pistol in the other.

'Mand?' I says. 'Mand? Where you off?' She had the door up and were halfway across the yard before I caught up with her. 'Mand? Where you headed? Want a lift?'

'Best I walk. I wanna feel meself walkin' away. I'll get a bus at Furzel and go on from there.'

'Well . . . Want us to walk with you for a bit?'

'No. Bye, Blake.'

She kissed us. We had a long kiss. But when she pulled away it didn't feel like it had been so long.

I stood in the yard and watched her disappear up the alley, her little rucksack slung across her shoulder. She were only a little girl really, and she didn't have a hope. Part of us wanted to go with her. But you knows about that part by now. It weren't very big and it didn't have much say. So I went back into the garage.

Luckily she'd left her fags behind, so I smoked em while I bided me time. It were risky for us now, see. On top of me not being welcome in Norbert Green at the best of times, I now had the hardest family in Mangel after us. That's how I reckoned it anyhow. I'd lost track of what were what, to be honest and fair. I knew I'd done some things that wouldn't sit well with a few folks but I had to think hard to recall exactly what they was. And even then I'd leave a few bits out like as not, my mind being the way it were right then.

But there were one thing sitting shiny and solid behind my eyelids whenever I closed em. A thing that I couldn't forget, even if forgetting's what I wanted for it. It were the answer to everything, see. That's how it looked from my angle anyhow. What were that thing, you asks?

The box, course.

The fucking doofer.

Only I didn't know who had it now. A smoker with arms and legs and hair, by the sounds of it. Regals, he'd said. Plenty of folks smokes Regals. Can't say I goes for em meself. Too short, for starters. But there's no accounting for other folks' taste. Who the fuck smokes Regals that I knows? Only one person I could think of. And it couldn't be... Nah. Unless...

I stubbed me fifth fag and got up. My hand were on the door to pull it up when I heard the noise outside. Someone out there. Two of em. Three, perhaps.

They wasn't saying much. Mostly grunts and swearing. But they didn't sound too happy about things in general. I looked around for a stick or summat to protect meself with, but there were nothing but the big engine, and that were too heavy even for a big feller like meself. But I were fretting unduly as it turned out. Sounded like they was opening up the next garage along. And once inside they shut it.

I stayed put. Best to wait a bit before chancing it. And besides, I were feeling nosy. Summat about it weren't right. Why would they be shutting emselves up in one of them manky old lock-ups this time of morning?

I walked along the wall, looking for the spot where sound carried best. Most building work in Mangel is done by the same firm, see, and every bastard knows their habit of splitting the odd breeze block down the middle and calling it two. Another little trick they do is to mix up too much sand with the cement, so here and there the mortar crumbles away, giving you gaping holes in the wall. And that's what I found near the middle of this un. I looked through it. The gap were about three inch high and half a one across. And through it I saw the top of Lee Munton's shaven swede.

And heard his voice: 'Alright, Jess. Take it off.' For a bit all I heard were slow footsteps and heavy breathing. Then someone were gasping, like he'd been underwater too long. Then someone else spoke, someone I couldn't see.

Our Finney, none less than.

17

....

'You can't scare us,' says Fin, still gasping. But you could tell in his voice he were already cacking himself. 'Whatever you does to us ... you ... you'll get back ten times more worser. Aye, Blake'll find out an'...'

'An' what, eh?' I could see the spit flying off Lee's lips. 'What'll Blakey boy do when he finds out?'

There were nothing for a while. Nothing but breathing and background hum of far-flung folk going about their business. Then Finney says: 'He'll kill you.'

'How's that ten times worser'n what we got planned for you?'

'Alright, maybe not ten times. Worser though.'

'But you dunno what we've got planned, do you.'

'Aye but I knows Blake an' he's me mate an'... an' whatever you does he'll find out an'—'

'Show him, Jess.'

Finney's heavy breathing filled the silence for a bit, then, with a final gasp, stopped. I tried to bend my eyesight round the corner to see what Jess were up to. But bending your eyesight had never worked for us and it weren't working now.

'What you reckon now, eh?' says Lee. I could see his

meaty face grinning down at where Finney must have been reclining. 'Reckon Blake could do ten times worser'n Susan?'

Jess came into view. He were circling Lee and Fin, holding Susan out in front of him. Susan, as it turned out, were a chainsaw. A fucking big old chainsaw with nasty teeth.

Things was silent for a bit. When Lee spoke his voice came over all booming, though he were talking no louder than before. 'Got summat to say now, Fin? This'll be yer last chance.'

'I told you, Lee. I dunno nuthin' about Baz. Ain't seen him for days. Honest I ain't.'

'Ain't what I heared. Know what I heared? You killed him. You topped him and put him in yer boot. Been luggin' him round in there for days is what I heared. Luggin' me little bruvver round lookin' for a place to dump him. Thass what I heared, Fin. What should I make o' that, eh? Eh?' Lee's face were turning pink. It were the shape and size of a pumpkin and the colour of a ripening tomato. 'Where is he? Where's our bruvver? Why'd you kill him? Who helped you? Were it Blake? Come on, where is he?' He were screaming now. Screaming and punching Finney's head. When he stopped all you could hear were his breathing and Finney's whimpering. They all stood like that for about ten seconds. Then he gave the nod to Jess.

It were loud. To any bastard outside it'd sound like someone working on his motorbike I reckoned. Lee's face stayed pink and fat and glowering. But Jess's changed. He'd come to life, sort of. You could see the sparkle in his eye, the radiance of his yellow smile. I'd never seen him smile before. Never seen him waving a chainsaw about neither. It were a funny moment all in all. I could stand there and peer through a little crack in the wall and laugh at it all. I mean, slicing up Finney with a chainsaw in a lock-up in Norbert Green? Come off it.

Then Jess brung Susan down slowly. And red stuff sprayed up into Lee's smirking face.

I fell away from the wall. I sat there on my arse for a while, hearing Susan roaring and Finney screaming. Then I turned over and heaved. Nothing came out, which weren't surprising being as I hadn't been eating proper of late. Then I crawled across the floor and under the door.

I stood outside for a bit, thinking about this and mulling over that. Finney were a mate. Muntons was in there right now chopping him up. Chopping my mate up. I ought to do summat about it. Finney'd said I would, hadn't he? You'll get it back ten times worser he'd said. Well then I ought to. I ought to come down on their heads like a ton of shite, chainsaw or no. But how could I pull it off? How could I fuck with the Muntons and save Finney?

I scanned around the yard. No one about. Mandy's bullets rattled in me pocket, bringing emselves to my attention. It's easy to forget about a gun when you ain't carried one before. I got it out and loaded it, hoping I were doing it proper.

What a twat I were, faffing around wondering what to do when all the while the answer's in me pocket, courtesy of Mandy Munton. Meanwhile Finney had like as not lost an arm or a foot or summat. Still, doctors can sew bits of your body back on by all accounts, long as you got em delivered to the ozzy along with the feller they came off of.

I held the pistol out in front of us, clutching it with both paws. It felt alright. And I reckoned if Clint Eastwood could shoot straight then so could I.

I went to the lock-up where the racket were coming from and put my ear against the door. Behind the roaring chainsaw I could hear Finney's screams getting weaker and weaker. I grasped the handle and turned.

Locked.

'Fuck,' I says, and pointed the gun at the keyhole. But that were no good. You couldn't lock them doors from the inside. Locking yourself in ain't what they're designed for. No, the Muntons had jammed it from the inside or summat. Bullets wouldn't help us get through a sheet metal door. Not fast enough anyhow. I crawled back into the other garage.

Susan had stopped roaring for the time being. In her place you had Finney jabbering and wheezing, which you couldn't blame the poor cunt for really. I reckoned the Muntons was working slow. Cut him up a bit, somewhere that wouldn't kill him. Then give him a break. Then cut him some more. Ain't no point in torturing someone less you gives em chance to tell tales. I peered again through the hole.

Right enough, Lee were just opening his gob to speak: 'Fun, ain't it Fin. Me an Jess here'd be happy to entertain you like this all day. How long you reckon yer hide can take it for, eh? Maybe Jess'll try cutting a mite deeper next time. Course, you don't like it, all you has to do is say. Say what happened to Baz.'

'I told you.' Finney didn't sound too bad considering. But that were our Fin for you – he'd be enjoying himself like as not. 'You been talkin' to liars. I ain't had Baz in me boot. Honest I ain't.'

'Callin' my mate a liar now?'

It went on like that. I stepped back from the wall and rubbed hard on my stubbly chin. Summat needed doing. If I did fuck all Finney might grass on us. I went back to the crack and tried to aim the pistol through it. Nah. I'd never fired a gun in me life. And even if I brung Lee down I couldn't be sure Jess'd still be in firing range.

Susan started up again.

I turned and saw the engine on the floor. Like I says, it were an old Rover un. V8 or summat. Them things is heavy as fuck, even if there's three of you and a winch. But fuck it. There were nothing else for it.

I skipped around for a bit, punching the air and slapping me face. 'Eye of the tiger,' I says to meself. 'Eye of the tiger. Eye of the fuckin' tiger.' I glared at the engine on the floor in front of us, and from somewhere came the opening bars of Survivor's theme song, slamming into that engine like Rocky's fist into a punchbag.

Bam.

Bam bam bam.

Bam bam bam.

Bam bam baa...I took a deep one and bent down to get a grip on the fucker. I squatted there, thinking of all the times I'd been down the gym in the old days and squatted more'n any other cunt in Mangel ever had done. I remembered my old man smacking us in the teeth and the way I always wanted to give him one right back but never did. I thought about them kids calling us bottler round at Sal's house. I pictured Rocky decking Clubber Lang in the last round. Then I stood up, nice and slow, bringing the engine with us.

I turned. I weren't thinking of the strain on me

biceps and shoulders and legs. Fuck the sharp bit that were digging into me guts. There were only one place that engine were headed. I heaved high as I could and lobbed it wallward.

It were hard to see anything for a while, the air being full of dust. I felt for my pistol and flicked off the safety, backing away towards the door where it were easier to breathe. Susan's roaring had stopped. But you couldn't hear much from Finney neither. A bit of coughing and spluttering, but that could have been anyone. I had a bad feeling about that. If Finney were still alive I reckoned he'd be screaming. I crouched down and rested me finger on the trigger, itching to pull it but waiting for the moment.

I stayed crouched. For too fucking long. Crouching's alright if you can shift around a bit on your haunches. But I couldn't move. I didn't dare. It were as much as I could do to blink and breathe, besides pointing the gun and watching as the dust cleared up.

After a minute or two you could see the hole. It were a big un, like a doorway with an arched top. Unless I were imagining it that is. Sometimes you stares at a spot for too long and starts seeing things as they ain't. Weren't much noise from the other side. Once or twice I reckoned I'd heard a whisper or two, but nothing else. I were starting to wonder if I hadn't flattened em all with the engine and falling breeze blocks and that. Then Susan started up again.

She came through the wall, Jess right behind her. Susan were roaring. Jess were roaring. I were roaring and all, like as not.

I pulled the trigger.

But it didn't do much besides give my arm a jolt.

Jess were still coming at us, chainsaw aloft and yelling like Billy-o. I could smell the petrol. Bits of this and that was flying off the saw, splatting on me face. I collapsed sideways.

It were one of my wiser moves, all things considered. Jess kept on going, shagging the wall with his weapon and making an awful racket as metal chewed breeze block. Then he sort of slumped, buckling under the weight. I were hoping Susan'd land atop him and cut him right through, but she fell to his side and went quiet. I could see what he were yelling for now. His hands was jammed between his legs, slick with blood.

I thought about the kick I'd dealt him in the graveyard, and how he weren't having much luck in the knacker area of late. It were for the best, mind. Someone like Jess Munton is best keeping his oats to himself.

'Blakey.' It were Finney. Only it didn't sound much like the Finney I knew and put up with. More like an old cunt in the later stages of a heart attack. I got up and walked to the hole, pointing the gun and bearing in mind that Lee might well aim summat at us any moment. I got to the hole and looked through it nice and careful. I spent about a minute edging slowly closer. All the while Fin were going 'Blakey, Blakey...' I took another gander back at Jess. He were lying stiller now and looking like he'd carked it, which spurred us on a bit.

Bollocks to it.

I climbed on through.

There were a fair bit of light in there, a bulb shining overhead and the door being now half open. Lee must have got away, short of a weapon and feeling a mite naked. I could feel the floor wet and sticky underfoot. The air smelt of two-stroke and summat else, summat that reminded us of the time Finney showed us the slaughtering yard. I swallowed hard and turned.

He were tied to a metal chair in the middle of the floor, body slumped, head drooping, eyes shut. But you could see he were still alive. His chest were going up and down. I counted his hands and feet and accounted for all of em. But both ears was gone and his head and shoulders was cut to hell and back. Every visible inch of his body were slick with blood. A pool of the stuff were spreading out under the chair. I stuck the gun down me pants and took the straps off him slowly, worried he might fall apart. In the event he just fell against us and let out a grunt. I were feeling strong. I were feeling like I could do anything and beat any odds. I still had the eye of the tiger, I reckoned. I breathed deep through my nose and hauled Fin across me shoulder.

He weren't as heavy as I thought he'd be. I found that I could balance him with the one arm and hold the pistol with the other. That were good, seeing as I'd just shot the one Munton and the other were still at large. I headbutted the door fully open and went outside.

I looked around the yard, eyes popping out my head. No fucker were there. I pulled up the door of the next garage, expecting to see a dead Jess lying there next to his chainsaw. But Susan weren't there.

Nor Jess neither.

Finney were light as a stillborn kitten. I wished he were heavier. I wished he were so heavy his weight pulled us down and made him hard to carry. But carrying him weren't a problem for us. I could have carried two of him right then. I walked up the path to the street, saying his name quietly over and over, asking him to wake up and stop fucking about. But he just carried on being light and limp and covered in blood.

A car were coming up from the right. I stepped into the road and pointed the gun at the driver, who were a lad of sixteen or so. He stopped and got out, leaving her running. I put Finney down on the back seat and drove us out of Norbert Green. I carried on talking to him the whole while, telling him what a thick cunt he were and how he were gonna get himself killed one of them days with his twattery. He didn't have much to say back. I reckoned he were kipping.

When I got to the Infirmary I pulled up behind an ambulance and got him out. I kicked the glass doors open – cracking one of em – and carried him inside. He were heavier now, which were a good sign I reckoned. The place were packed with sick and lame of Mangel, moaning and yelling. They all shut up when I waved the pistol at em. I laid Fin out on the front desk and told the nurse he'd had an industrial and could they sort him out sharpish cos he's got an important game of footy in two days' time. She said nothing but I knew me and her understood one another.

When I got out front again a feller in a green and yellow tunic were shouting at us about parking. I aimed at his head and fired. I thought I'd nailed the fucker but he ran off, so perhaps I missed. I got in the car and had away, noting with interest that it were a Morris Marina. The commonly held view of Marinas is that they goes like a combine harvester through a forest. But this one were fair nippy – an 1800 I reckoned – and not at all uncomfortable to drive. I took it around the block a couple of times before I recalled what I were meant to be doing.

I turned the radio on to see what kind of output it had. The news feller came on and said a lad in Norbert Green had had his purple Marina hijacked by a large armed feller in a black leather carrying a blood-soaked and possibly deceased third party across his shoulder. Coppers said the man were highly emotional and warned folks not to fuck with him in case he shot em. I pulled in, got out, and started walking.

It were only half a minute or so before an old feller came chuntering along on his moped. Soon as I seen it I knew it were the right transport for us at that particular time. I ran into the road and waved him down, but he went right on past us. I ran after him, thinking how it were a good job he were going uphill. Any folks could tell you how nippy I were over thirty yards. Further than that and me lungs always started screaming. I reckoned I had asthma or summat, but I couldn't ever be arsed to go along to the doctor and find out for surely. Weren't as if it bothered us anyhow. A feller can run away from you, but where's there to hide in Mangel?

Anyhow, I caught the old feller after ten yard or so and wrenched his hand off the throttle. That's all I meant to do, mind. Weren't my fault he fell off. Took a swing at us, didn't he. Cheeky old sod. As I were riding off on his bike I looked back at him. He were lying still in the road. But he'd be alright there. Someone'd find him.

I reached where I were headed a few minutes later and without further mishap. I parked her round back and went on up the fire escape. His light were on, so

I were sure he were in. Legs weren't the sort to waste nothing, not even a couple of pennies on the leccy bill. I rapped me knuckles on the door-frame and waited. No one came. I lit a smoke and knocked harder. Perhaps he were in the bath or summat. I couldn't hear no music so he'd be sure to hear us sooner or later. But no one came to the door. I knocked again for good measure but still got no avail. I walked slowly back down the stair, feeling a bit cheesed off. Alright, he were my mate and I had to trust him at the end of the day. But he were in. I fucking knew he were in. Why didn't he open the door for us? Cunt.

I stopped dead when I saw a feller running up the stair at us, hood up and head down. I didn't have much time to think, so as he came close and looked up I thumped him full bore on the forehead, knocking him cold and hurting me knuckles a bit. I had a look at him as he lay sprawled on the metal steps, head hanging over the side. He were only about thirteen by the looks of him. What the fuck were he playing at, taking a run at us like that? I looked inside the big orange bag over his shoulder. It were full of newspapers. I picked one of em out and had a look at it. It were the *Informer*. The headline were KILLER, and under it were a photo of meself. I squinted at the writing.

Mangel Police are after Royston Roger Blake in connection with the death of Daniel Herbert Draper of Mangel.

Going by the testimony of a witness who was walking his dog by the River Clunge yesterday, police believe Blake dealt Draper a series of blows over the head with a large metallic object and pushed him into the water. He then dumped an unidentified body in the water after him.

Draper's body was found further down the river near Higgis Wharf. The other one remains at large.

Blake, of South Mangel, was arrested two years ago for the murder of his wife Beth. The case was dropped due to lack of evidence, but not before Blake was diagnosed clinically insane. He was released back into the community eighteen months ago after a spell at Parpham General Asylum. 'Quite a nice chap, I thought,' said Dr Lawrence Gelding, who treated Blake at Parpham. 'I can't believe he'd so much as swat a fly, let alone murder a person. Oh well, there's no accounting for folk is there?'

Members of the public are warned not to approach Blake should they see him. Just phone the police and let them sort it out.

Only thing I didn't like about it were the photo. It were an old one, from when I were eighteen and half stone of solid beef. Don't get us wrong, it were a good picture. But that were the problem. Showed how much I'd let meself go in the past couple of years didn't it. I tucked the paper back in the kid's bag and trotted down the stair.

I didn't fancy getting on the moped again. My arse were aching still from the ride into town. Besides, coppers'd be on the lookout for it and I couldn't be doing with none of that bollocks right then. I pushed it into the corner and hid it behind a load of rubbish bags. Then I walked round front.

Before stepping into the street I hesitated. What the fuck were I playing at? My face were plastered all over the bastard paper, for fuck. Walking round town with me chin in the air wouldn't be clever. Folks'd spot us – despite me not comparing well to the photo of meself – and sooner or later I'd end up in an interview room with two hard coppers and a truncheon. I stepped into the shadows and felt inside my pockets. There were a lot of gear in em, I can tell you. Any trouble cropped up I'd be alright. Short term anyhow. But trouble were what I aimed to avoid, long as I could. I fished out the wig and pulled it on, then looked at meself in a window. It were alright, but I needed summat else if I were to pass meself off as not meself.

I walked back up Legsy's fire escape and had a look at the kid's anorak. It were nice and baggy on him, but it'd be a bit of a stretch around my generous girth. Still, it were that or nothing. And it were a disguise alright. Folks'd never expect to see Royston Blake wearing such twat-wear. I pulled it off him careful as I could. He grunted and wheezed a bit but didn't wake. I put it on. I couldn't zip it up without bursting the seams, but hanging free it looked alright, if you likes that sort of thing. And with the wig on I looked nothing like meself.

I took everything out of me jacket and put it in the anorak, then dumped the leather in the bins. I thought about putting it on the kid, as a little thank you, like. But that'd be leaving evidence. And it were a warm day anyhow so he'd be alright.

I walked off up the street, humming 'My Way'. When I saw Hoppers off up the way a thirst took hold of us that shrivelled me tongue and made my hair ache. I gave meself a once over in the window of a junk shop. I looked like a twat alright, but nothing like Blake. Not even Rachel'd recognise us. I walked in.

It were mid-afternoon and slow. A few lunchtime stragglers was laughing and getting pissed over by the back wall, but no one else were there. Besides Rachel, course. But she were always there. I stepped up to her, trying to walk different to what were my habit. I wished I'd practised that one beforehand cos all it did were make us look more of a twat. The fellers at the back laughed a bit louder and I knew they was pointing at us. Fuckers. If they knew who I were they'd not find it so funny.

'Hiya Blake,' says Rachel, not even looking up from her paper.

'Alright, R— How the fuck did you know who I were?'

She looked at us. 'Oh, I see. Incognito is it? Sorry, should of looked first. Pint is it?'

'But how'd you know?'

'Dunno Blake. Reckon there's summat about you that walks before you, like. Know what I means?'

'No, Rache, I don't.' I looked at meself in the mirror behind the bar. It were a fucking marvellous disguise in my opinion. 'Hey, got a pair of sunglasses behind there?'

'Aye. Here.'

'No, fellers' sunglasses.'

'What would I be doin' with fellers' sunglasses?'

Eventually I got her to have a look in that drawer down the bottom where all kinds of shite is stowed. She rummaged through it for a while, cooing at this and turning her nose up at that. At last she came up with two pair of fellers' shades. One had only one arm. The other were alright. I put em on and had another gander in the mirror. It were perfect. The shades and hairpiece did such a job that I had to move my head side to side to make sure it were meself I were looking at. Did look a mite strange, mind, which were like as not why Rachel were giggling. I reached over and gave her a slap on the arse.

'Hey you, get off,' she says.

'Weren't what you says yes'dy.'

'Yesterday were a different day, before all this came out.' She nodded at the paper spread out on the bartop. It were the same one I'd already seen just now. 'Got summat to say about it, eh?'

She were looking at us funny, not like you'd expect her to. But it weren't bad. It weren't a bad look at all in fact. No, her eyes told us that she thought I were summat special. She were looking at us, to be honest, as if I'd got out a foot-long tadger and waved it at her. 'Know what I oughta do?' she says, not blinking nor taking em off us. 'Pick up this phone and call the coppers.'

'What would you do that for, Rache?'

'Why not? You don't care for us.'

'Rache, that ain't true.' I took her hand in mine. I could hear the fellers laughing behind us. 'Why'd you reckon such a thing?'

'Feller who cared for us'd turn up when he said he would. Like last night.'

'Last night? Oh . . . I were—'

'Aye, I've read about what you was up to.'

'Rache, t'aint like you thinks. Coppers just wants to talk to us is all. I ain't done nuthin'. Ever knew us to lay a finger on a feller other than to keep the peace?'

'Well . . .'

'No, course you ain't. S'why I'm a doorman ennit. Cool head.'

'What about the, uh . . .' She frowned at the wig.

'Juss don't want coppers botherin' us right now is all. Got other business to —.'

'Other business? Blake, you weren't involved in the . . .' She nodded at Fenton's office. 'The robbery?'

'Come on, Rache.' I squeezed her hand harder, wondering what Fenton might have told her about it. She winced a bit, so I let go and started rubbing up and down her arm. 'You knows that weren't me. Wouldn't Fenton know if I'd ripped him off? Course he fuckin' would.'

'What other business then, Blake?' I could tell she wanted to believe us. Rachel were a good un, and there weren't many of that kind in Mangel. She were the sort who'd walk through walls for you once you'd got her in your corner.

And I wanted her in my corner. I weren't sure why. With all the shite rising up around my ankles right then you'd reckon I'd be more concerned about other matters. But, looking right back at her as I were then, nothing were more important than making things straight with her. 'Rache,' I says. 'Rache, sometimes there's a time when a feller's gotta put his life aside and do a few things so's he can . . . Well, iss like that story about the fox and the . . . er . . . What were that story about? You know . . . '

She put her fingers up to my lips. 'Shut up,' she says. Then she leaned over the counter and kissed us.

I looked over her shoulder and got a fright when I saw the mop-haired gimp in shades and anorak in the mirror. Didn't look right for such a one to be kissing a bird like Rachel. But I weren't complaining.

Things was alright for a bit after that. I drank me pint and we chatted about this and that, without getting heavy nor her letting slip that I were Blake. Course, us having a snog might have drawn a few eyes. But it didn't give us away. After a while a skinny cunt with thick glasses, sticky-out ears and pigeon toes came in and told her he'd come for the interview. It were Mick Runter, a useless cunt who'd never had a job in his life, far as I knew. You wanted Mick Runter, you'd find him down the bookies or Blender Stadium, or kipping under a bus shelter when his mam wouldn't have him. Though why you'd want Mick Runter I don't know. She sent him out back to Fenton's office, then went bright red and turned to her glass polishing. 'Interview?' I says. 'For what?'

'Your job.' She were still blushing but there were a defiant tone to her voice that I didn't much care for.

'My job? How fuckin' come? S'goin' on, Rache?'

'Well you can't hardly do it, can you? Shouldn't even be here now, coppers after you and all.'

'But I'm Royston Blake, Head Doorman of—'

'Who's gonna man the door tonight then? Clint Eastwood?'

I didn't answer. She shook her head a bit and went off to serve someone. I felt bad. I felt like everyone were ganging up on us and setting us up for summat. And I didn't like feeling that way. I were Blake, Head Door...

Ah, you knows who I were. And so did every cunt in Mangel.

I pissed off. I walked down Friar Street for a bit, thinking how right it all weren't. I snapped out of it when a feller coming up on the pavement decided to step to the right just when I stepped to the left, and vicey-versa. Before long we was nose-to-nose, a pair of totems deathing each other out. I could feel the sinews in me neck tense, getting ready for the head I were about to drop on him. But I stopped it right on the point of letting go. His eyes was a bit funny, like he were pissed. Only I knew he weren't cos I couldn't smell it on him. And a pissed-up feller'd surely have said summat by now.

It weren't much of a surprise when I finally recognised him. Weren't many folks I didn't know in the Mangel area. This were the feller from the repair shop, the one whose head Finney had dropped a battery on. Funny how that happens. You think of someone for the first time in donkeys, then next day you sees em. Shite like that always happens to me. Used to reckon I were special that way. But now I knows better. Way of the world ennit. You can't get away from folks. Not properly. Not even when they're dead. 'Alright, mate,' I says.

He says nothing.

I waved my hand in front of his face. His eyes moved a bit. He were a mong alright. Finney'd not been wrong there. I stepped aside.

The feller shunted slowly on like a bus pulling away.

I tagged alongside, peering at his face. His mouth hung agape. A trickle of flob dangled from his lower lip. 'You alright, mate? Know where you're goin'?'

Still he says nothing.

'Who let you out?' I says, and a few other such enquiries after his welfare. There's one type of feller I always looks out for, and that's the one whose mind ain't straight. Poor fuckers has got enough on their plates without worrying about folks wanting to fight em. But it were clear my solicitations was all for nothing. The cock were crowing but the farmer weren't home. We walked a bit more. He crossed the road and went up a side street. Seemed like he knew where he were going. 'Hey mate,' I says. 'You used to run that car shop on down by the Muckfield Road, right?'

His eyes didn't move. But I could have sworn his ears did a bit.

'Packed it in in the end, didn't you? Younguns broke in and gave you a proper hidin'. That right? One of the little cunts dropped battery on yer swede, eh?'

I reckoned a touch of pink came to his cheek. Might have been wrong, mind.

'Well, you won't believe this, but . . .' Now I might be wrong again here, but if his eyes didn't flick over to us and back then I weren't born in Mangel. 'Them young fellers – the ones what done yer head in – s'me, ennit. I fuckin' done it. With Legs an' Fin.' I laughed. I laughed all the way to buggery and back. It were funny. It were funny as fuck painted blue and stuck atop a maypole.

The feller stopped. He looked at us in that same sad way. The flob hanging off his lip dropped off and landed on his shirt. I wondered what he were thinking, if anything. You hears things about mongs. Superhuman strength, so they says. I stopped laughing.

Things stayed like so a moment or two, then he went on his way. I watched him walk twenty yard up the road and turn into a courtyard. There was a couple of nurses walking around the yard with other mongs, ones who couldn't walk proper. One of the nurses took his arm and made him sit down on a bench. I stood staring at him over the wall. A feller like him ain't a real man, they says. Can't make his own judgements, can't choose his own path. He's stuck where his arse is until someone decides otherwise. That's what I'd heard anyhow. But I reckoned he had it about right. His arse might be stuck in Mangel. But he weren't. He were off in the clouds, doing fuck knew what and bugger the consequence.

My arse were stuck in Mangel and all. My arse and

the rest of us. 'I done you a favour, mate,' I whispers. 'I done you the biggest favour a feller can do. An' you didn't even say ta.'

I took off when the nurses started pointing at us and whispering to each other. Wig felt askew so I looked in a shop window and set it straight. I were fucking starving so I headed down to Alvin's. I thought about Hoppers and this new feller on the door. They was trying to get rid of us, clear as day. I risks me life to fetch his doofer back and Fenton gives us the boot.

'Kebab in yer chilli sauce, sir?'

'Aye, but go easy on the rabbit food eh?'

'Right you is, Blakey.'

'Fuck sake, why do every cunt think I'm Blake? I don't look nuthin' like him. Look at me fuckin' hair, for starters.'

'Right you is, Blakey. Nice hair.'

I took me scran and walked off down the road. Down by the meat market there were an old bench covered in pigeon shite. I dusted it off best I could and parked my arse. It were a funny spot for a bench, facing as it did the high wall round back of the market. I recalled sitting there once or twice as a nipper, like as not bunking off school and at a loose end. Always seemed to be trading or slaughtering going on back in them days. I'd sit there and listen to the drone of the auctioneer on market days. He'd talk so fast it were hard to keep up with him most times. Plus half his words was drowned out by the bellow of cattle in the killing shop next door. After a while I'd stop hearing him and just listen to them cows. It were a hell of a sound, let me tell you. A bit hard on the ear holes at first, but once you got yourself accustomed it came across almost like music. They knew they was up for the chop, them cattle did, and this were all the noise they had left to make. I'd sit there on me tod and listen to it, letting it sink right into me bones. They wasn't crying, see. They was singing. Singing cos not five yard away were a feller with a poleaxe waiting to dispatch em from Mangel and this here Earth.

I thought about the folk I'd killed. I'd poleaxed em all, for one reason or another. And I'd paid for em. I'd been paying for em all me life it seemed, what with guilt and feeling out of sorts and running round Mangel like a horsefly around a nag's arse, trying to cover me tracks and sort it all out.

And for why? Why were I shelling out for doing em a favour? The feller with the poleaxe in the slaughtering yard never paid. They fucking paid him. He sent the bastards to a better place and got his reward for it.

So why ought I to pay?

Well, I can't answer that. But I can tell you summat else.

I weren't paying no more.

I looked at the market again. There were no singing cows in there now. Market these days were five or six fellers in flat caps standing round an old bull. Slaughtering yard were hardly worth the space. Finney were one of the handful they had left working there, and he only went in now and then. Farms had been shutting down steady for years, and the folks who worked on em had up and moved here. There's Mangel for you.

Town full of sprout pickers and shite shovellers.

Sun were getting low and I could hear voices coming up the alley from the river. Lads, out for a night on the pop. I screwed up me kebab wrapper, lobbed it over me shoulder, and got walking again. I weren't afraid of no one. I reckon you knows that by now. But I knew how I looked, sitting there all alone in me wig and sunglasses. I looked like a cunt, and a bunch of lads up for a laugh can't very well walk past a cunt without making summat of it. No, I weren't in the market for aggro just yet.

Weren't long before I would be, mind.

18

....

I hadn't long to wait. I'd only been there a few minutes when he pulled up in a muck brown Viva that were white underneath if I recalled it right. No pride, that Mick Runter. How he got my job were beyond us. Fenton must have been taking the piss.

He got out and slammed the door behind him, then stood there shaking the cramp out his skinny legs and yawning. As he strutted past the stinking doorway where I were hid I stepped out.

'Oh, alright Blake.'

'Alright, Mick.' I twocked him with the wrench.

Piece of piss.

He went down nice and clean. Just like they always does if you hits em hard enough. I dragged him into the shadows and set about swapping kit with him. His togs was fucking tight. I couldn't do the trousers up proper but they had to do. I didn't have no mirror nor nothing but I looked at the brick wall and saw meself in that. I looked dapper, I reckoned, despite the tight kit. And when you looks good you feels good. I winked at meself and laughed. It were good to be head doorman again. It were good to be Blake again. I went round the front.

Rachel turned the colour of washed tripe when she clocked us. 'Know what you needs,' I says, pulling up a stool and nodding at my choice of lager. 'Bit of blusher round yer cheekbones. Our Beth always got the blusher out when she were feelin' peaky.'

'Blake...' she says. I nodded at the lager again. She got a glass and started pulling. 'Blake, ain't you...'

'Head Doorman? Aye. Too fuckin' right I is.'

'But the coppers...'

I put the glass to me lips and didn't let up until it were empty. I couldn't recall ever having a nicer beverage in all me borned days.

'Blake, the coppers is after you. You can't come in here.'

'Some bastard's gotta man the door ain't he?' I says, struggling to get the words out between belches.

'You knows we got someone in for that.'

'Don't look like he's turnin' up, do it. And Mick Runter? Why the fuck him, fuck sake?'

'No one else applied.'

'Scared of steppin' in me boots.'

'Er... summat like that. What's you smilin' like that for?'

'Smilin' am I? Just happy, I reckon. Life's a laugh, and Mangel's the place to live it in.'

She glared at us, pulling us another pint. 'Have to make this me last un for now,' I says. 'On duty.' I necked the lager and went out back to see Fenton. Doors required manning up front and all, but I had a feeling Fenton needed a bit of buttering up, what with me not getting the doofer for him yet.

Dunno what I'd been expecting, but it weren't what I found. Fenton were sat at his desk, phone in one hand, scribbling on a bit of paper with the other. A businessman at work, you might say. Both hands still had a bit of strapping on em but nothing suggesting the kind of fucking up the Muntons had done him. The cigar lay smouldering in the big ashtray on his desk. It were a big fuck off one like you don't often see round these parts. He put the phone down and picked the cigar up, taking a nice long pull on it.

'Alright,' I says.

'Evening Blake.' From just them two words I could tell he'd be hard work. In one of his moods weren't he. Me poor heart sank. I didn't have the energy to pull him out of it. 'Take a seat,' he says.

This weren't right. Weren't just his moodiness neither. Him being moody weren't unheard of. It were the other stuff. Last time I'd seen him he'd been a wreck. Fucking desperate one and all. But now he looked alright. He opened a wooden box and offered us a stogie. I took one and sparked it up with the lighter he offered us. He hadn't looked us in the eye yet.

'Blake. There's some things we need to sort out.'

'Oh aye?'

'Yes. First of all, what are you doing here?'

I asked him what he meant by that. I were Blake, Head Doorman of—

'That's not true, Blake. We've got a new doorman. Mick, his name is. You'd like him. He's starting tonight, though I'm not sure where he's got to . . .'

'You ain't got no new doorman. I'm the doorman.'

He clocked us proper for the first time. 'What have you done to Mick?'

'Who says I done summat?'

'You're wanted by the police, Blake. Your picture is plastered all over the paper. You're a . . .' His cigar had gone out. He lit it again. There were no point him going on as he were. He knew the score as well as I did. I were doorman. *Head* Doorman. Some things you just can't go tampering with.

'I ain't forgot our deal, Fenton.'

'Deal?' He looked at us like I'd just flobbed on his carpet. His lower lip were quivering and his nostrils was going in and out like a pair of bellows. 'Well I have forgotten it,' he says. You could tell he were trying to sound hard. It didn't work. 'I have forgotten about our... "deal".'

'Woss matter, Fenton? Gaggin' for us to get yer doofer back you was, last time I—'

'Yeah, I was.' He got up and went and stood in the corner near the window. 'But when I asked you I didn't realise you were the cunt who—'

'Hey now, mind yer tongue.'

'—who stole it in the first place. You and your cohorts.' He were yelling at us now. His yelling voice were all shrill and warbly and I wished he'd do my ears the honour of shutting his cake hole.

'Well I dunno where you heared that, Fenton. I ain't...' I trailed off. Not cos I'd forgot what I were saying, mind. I were looking at the marble ashtray on his desk. It were the one Lee had used on his fingers. But that weren't the clever bit. Clever bit were the two fag butts in it. Regals, they was. Fenton only smoked cigars. I wondered if Mick Runter smoked Regals. I doubted it. Couldn't think of no one smoked Regals in Mangel. Except...

'You what?' I says. Just cos a feller ain't listening don't mean he ain't aware he's missed summat. 'What d'you say?'

'I said,' he says, all slow like I were thick. 'I said I

know you did it because someone told me. And I believe him. Want to know why I believe him? Because he gave me back what you stole. The doofer, as you call it.'

'Who?' I says, trying to get the Regals out of my head. 'Who the fuck?'

But it were his turn to not listen now. I heard the door open behind us and Fenton stood up, saying: 'Who the fuck . . . ?'

The thing about getting coshed from behind is you don't know about it. Not even when you comes to, pushing yourself off the floor and spitting the taste of rusty nails out your gob. Too much lager is your first thought. Too much lager tasting like rusty nails. Only later does you put two and two together and come up with a cosh.

I got hold of the chair I'd been sitting on and hauled meself up, putting two and two together and coming up with the rusty lager still. My skull were vibrating, which were a bit of a clue. But when me eyes came together and I could see what were happening across the desk I forgot about skulls and sums and lager and the lot of it.

'No,' Fenton were saying, sat down behind his desk with his face bleeding and his eyes weeping. A feller were behind him, dressed in black. It were that feller from the big city. You know, cunt asking Rache about Hoppers t'other day and suggesting I were a shite doorman. He were steadying Fenton's head with one arm and holding a blade to his throat with the other. Over in the corner the safe door were hanging open.

I clocked all this in the space of a couple of seconds, still hanging off the back of the chair with my head vibrating. Then the feller jerked the blade and opened Fenton's neck, spilling blood across the desk and causing Fenton's hair to fall clean off his head. A little jet of the stuff squirted sideways, arced a bit through the air and sprayed one of his poncey pictures on the wall. It pumped out like that for a while, a red rainbow across one side of the room. Fenton's eyes was rolling, mouth opening and closing. Then his blood pressure eased off and the jet slowed to a trickle. His shaved head still had a bit of tape atop it for holding the wig in place. It were odd to see him without his poncey hair. But once you got over the shock it were alright. Better than the wig anyhow. Why some fellers wears hairpiece I never will understand.

Didn't have much time to think about it before the feller had me face in the carpet. He pinned us down with his hefty frame and poked the blade into the side of me neck. 'Give me one good reason why I shouldn't do the same to you,' he growled into me left lug-hole. 'Go on, I'm waitin'. Ain't waitin' all night neither. No? Ain't got a reason? Right . . .'

'Eh,' I says, mouth full of rug. 'Hold up a sec, mate.' I tried to twist my head round to see him, but he pressed the metal into me neck all the harder, which hurt a lot I can tell you. 'Alright. Fuckin' calm it, right? No need to lose yer rag.'

'One reason. Ten. Nine.'

'Me birthday ennit.'

'Eight. Seven.'

'I got kids. Eight of the fuckers.'

'Six. Five.'

'Coppers is on their way, you know.'

'Four. Three.'

'Er . . .'

'Two.'

'I'm Royston Blake, Head Doorman of Hoppers Wine Bar & Bistro, and you can't kill us.' I shut me eyes tight and hoped for the best.

He didn't get off us, but the blade didn't go in no further neither, which pleased us no end. Then his hulking body started bouncing up and down a bit, shoving the wind out of us in little bursts. I frowned and wondered what manner of hanky panky he were up to, when finally he made a barking sound and it dawned on us that he were laughing, in his own way.

'Doorman,' he says, barking and bouncing. After a bit he got off us, using the back of my head as a push-off. 'Go on and get up, doorman. Let's see you.'

I rolled over. Me ribs hurt pretty bad. I tried to take a deep un but they kept screaming once I got so much in. 'Who the fuck's you?' I says soon as I could manage it.

He were sat on one of the plastic chairs on the side of the room that weren't covered in Fenton's blood. He started cleaning his nails with the blade – a lock knife with a thin shaft and black handle. Jutting out the side pocket of his jacket were the chewed corner of a little brown box. He laughed again a bit, shoulders going up and down like a pair of humping cows. 'I was a doorman for a bit when I was younger,' he says after he'd calmed down. 'Not for long, mind. No one stays doorman for long where I come from. You either move on to better things or you end up an old security guard with his Thermos and his fuckin' Woodbines. Nah, pal. That ain't for me.'

It were a bit odd, watching him talking and picking his nails and Fenton sat behind him, throat slashed, trap open, eyes on the ceiling. But the feller seemed happy.

And it made me a bit happy to see him so at ease.

'Don't a doorman got career opportunities round here? Good doorman down our way gets noticed. He's useful, innit. Soon he's in demand for a bit of action, spot of enforcement or problem solving or summink more his level than standin' at a door lettin' pissed-up slag-rakers and leather-faced mingers inside. Ain't that the way round here?'

'Well,' I says, getting up carefully. I glanced at Fenton to make sure he weren't listening, conversation taking a turn for the sensitive and all. But I knew he weren't. No man could lose that much sap and keep ticking. 'Matter of fact,' I went on, 'I have done a bit of . . . Action, d'you call it? Aye, I done a bit o' that but I never took to it.'

'So a doorman you'll stay.'

'S'alright with me. A doorman I were borned and a doorman I will stay. I likes the sound o' that.'

'Sounds alright dunnit. But who says you'll stay a doorman?'

'Eh?'

'Me, ennit. I'm the one says yay or nay, alright? And right now my head says nay. Know why?'

I slid my hand inside me jacket, all casual like. 'Reckon I don't.'

'See, that's the trouble with all you sprout pickers – no brains. 'Stead of brains you got turnips. You walked in on us dincha. I ain't gonna let a bloke see me do a job and go on breathin'.'

I had me finger and thumb around the top end of the gun barrel. If I moved my arm in any more he'd notice for surely. My eyes was flitting between him and the box in his pocket. I let him rabbit on, waiting my moment.

'That's the difference between you and me innit. I'm a professional. You're a turnip. I cover my tracks and get a job done clean. You go round messin' with folks you don't know and gettin' yourself in the shit big time. And for what? Cos you don't like a bloke's face? Cos he makes you feel small? Fuckin'—'

He'd stopped and gave us his full and undivided. He nigh on had to, me having a gun on him and all. That fucking shut him up, didn't it. Until he started smiling.

I were pointing a bloody monkey wrench at him, weren't I.

'Don't shoot,' he says, putting his hands up and barking like an uppity spaniel. Then he jumped up and stood legs apart, tossing the knife hand to hand without taking his eyes off us. I reached me left arm behind us and tried the door. He'd locked it, the fucker. He lunged at us.

I jumped sideways, clattering a filing cabinet and giving meself a dead leg. I limped on around the desk to the window. He stayed by the door, watching and laughing. I laughed and all as I pulled out Mandy's pistol. Good old Mandy.

'Who's the perfeshnal now, eh?' I says. 'Who's got the turnip on his head now? Eh? Eh?'

He aimed the knife to lob at us. Looked like he knew how to do it and all. 'Put the fuckin' weapon down or I bury this in your throat,' he says, not moving his lips.

Well, I had no choice, did I. I were a professional, see. I didn't give a runny shite about him killing Fenton. But I wouldn't stand for no flash cunt from the big city coming down here and likening my head to a turnip.

I pulled the trigger.

The gun were bust or summat. Must have been. It went pop and that, but sort of whipped out of my hand and flew under the desk. Fucking firearms. I hadn't never seen a monkey wrench do that.

He lobbed the knife at us.

It were more a lurch than a side-step, but I moved to the left anyhow just as the blade were due to stick us between the eyes. Glass shattered behind us.

'Lucky bastard,' he says, rooting around for summat in his jacket.

But I didn't fancy hanging about to give him another aim at bull. I punched aside the rest of the glass and jumped out the window.

It were only a ground floor window but I landed sort of wrong, right shoulder touching tarmac first followed by my poor head. But I managed to turn it into a roly-poly and hit my feet running, which were good news being as the feller were just then making an appearance at the window shouting 'Hoy'. I ran and I kept on running, up the side and round back into the little car park. I ran round looking for my car for a bit, which shouldn't have been so hard considering there was only five cars there and a gold Capri with black vinyl roof stands out amongst a thousand. I couldn't recall if I'd parked her there or not, but the upshot were that I didn't find her.

Alright, I thought, trying the nearest door handle.

Just my fucking luck, I were thinking as I pulled the fascia off and started fucking around with the wires. Mick Runter's Viva, weren't it. If there's one motor I can't fucking stick it's your Vauxhall Viva. Just can't rely on em, can you. I know I'd had a few glitches with my Capri, but that's different. Your Capri, as I've said many a time, offers a sensual experience not unlike going at it with a bird. Your Viva offers a fucking headache. And that's if you can get her started.

Well, luck were with us right then. I weren't sure which wire were what to be honest, but somehow she spluttered into life. I pointed her up the side lane and gave her some shoe, whispering encouraging words to her.

'Hoy,' yells the feller again, now in the road blocking me way. I slammed the throttle down and went straight for him. Well, what would you do? Asking to get run down he were, silly fucker. And him calling himself a professional?

But somehow he sort of jumped up and sideways and got out the way, which were good for him. I turned right into Friar Street and went up town, just as a couple of black Mariahs was turning in from the right.

19

Town were nigh on empty, most folks being in or outside Hoppers. I drove around it for the best part of an hour – getting better acquainted with the Viva's handling and changing my view of her a mite for the better – before settling on the notion that I had no place to go. Home were being rifled through by coppers like as not. Sal weren't in. Finney were laid up. Legs were . . . I didn't want to think about him just yet.

All I needed were somewhere to crash. Just for a bit. If I could just clap eyes on a friendly face and talk about footy for half of an hour, I'd be alright.

I went down the Paul Pry.

Nathan the barman had a face for us but it weren't friendly. It were a frown that stretched halfway round his head, which he shook solemnly when I stepped up to the bar and says, 'Alright, Nathan.' I ordered meself a pint of the usual, which drew from him nothing but a folding of the arms.

'Not in my bar you won't drink lager,' he says.

'Why not?' I saw meself in the mirror behind the bar and noted that I were still wearing Mick Runter's tight doorman ensemble with the filthy shirt hanging out the front. 'Oh,' I says, tucking meself in. 'Bit scruffy is it?'

'Scruffiness don't bother us. This is a working man's tavern and one that don't turn up its nose at an honest day's grime.' He unfolded his hairy arms and leaned em atop the bar. 'Iss the actions of a man that interests us more. Show us a man's actions and I'll show you his character. You, Royston Blake, I ain't sure as you've got a character at all.'

'I ain't got . . . ?' But I didn't say no more. I'd been prepared for him being a bit surly over us not giving him the doofer and that. I'd even half expected him to give us a public bollocking and boot us out. But this were a bit different. I weren't sure what he were getting at, you see. Normally if a feller's words passed over me swede I'd switch off and turn my attention elsewhere. But it didn't work like that this time. There were summat about Nathan that made him hard to ignore. I felt confused and more than a tad uneasy. I wanted to know what he were getting at, but couldn't ask him in case it turned out to be summat I didn't much care for. 'Eh, but Nathan,' I says, trying hard to brighten up. 'I got yer doofer for you.'

As hoped, his face changed at that. 'Doofer?' he whispers, pulling us around a bit so's to get us out of public earshot.

'You know, the doofer you asked for. Remember? You asked for Fenton's doofer in return—'

'Aye aye. Juss checkin' we was talkin' same language. So you gat it on you, eh boy?'

'Aye. Well, out back ennit. In me motor.'

'In yer motor? Bring him on in, son. Bring him on in.'

'Well . . .' I scratched me chin. It were getting to be

a proper beard and as such were causing us no end of itching. I reckoned a drink would go some ways to rectifying that problem, along with a few more after it. I looked at the pump and raised me eyebrows, hoping Nathan'd take the hint. Being a barman, he did. He plonked a tankard of the stuff before us and set to watching us again. I picked up the brew and swilled it down me neck without a drop of it touching the sides it seemed to me. Deciding that it'd be a mite cheeky to press Nathan for a refill, I went on: 'Well, ain't as simple as all that is it. In a safe it is, see. Fuckin' heavy one with a combination that I ain't acquainted with.'

He smiled. Then he frowned again. 'Ain't takin' the piss, are you? I bet you have got a safe out there in the car park. I knows all about you Blake, and I knows you're tapped enough to do just such a thing as that.'

'Ain't cos I'm tapped, Nathan. I juss dunno the combination. Had to take the whole safe, see. It were that or never get another chance.'

He nodded slowly. 'Ain't my problem though is it. All I wants is what I asked for. I don't want no big bastard safe locked up around it. Give us what I asked for and nut'n else. Give it us soon, Blake, or you'll rue this day. There's a lot of things I knows about you, and the coppers'd be interested in all of it.' He turned and picked up a tankard and started polishing it with a dirty rag. For a minute or so the tankard got shinier and the rag got dirtier.

'Woss so good about a doofer that you wants it so bad, eh?' I says.

'Keep yer counsel,' he whispers loud enough to wake a drunk on a Sunday morning. 'Keep yer blasted counsel.'

'Go on though, Nathan,' I went on a bit lower. But

not that low. I wanted him on the back trotter, so to speak. 'Tell us why you wants it. I don't even know what it is. No one'll tell us will they.'

'Never you mind why I wants it. Juss give it us or—'

'Tell us or I won't give it you. How's that, eh?'

'Don't give it us and I'll tell on you.'

'An' I'll go to jail an' you'll miss out. Woss that prove? Tell us why you wants it and I'll give it you and we'll all be happy. Come on, you knows summat, don't you. Got ears like radars an' you hears it all.'

He drew his face so close his eyebrows was tickling me forehead. 'A barman can't keep bar forever. And a man with knowledge from which he can't profit is a poor man indeed, says I. Well, Blakey, I knows a lot. You're right there. But it ain't me ears. Thass where you been gettin' it wrong. Ain't me eyes neither. Seein' and hearin' things is easy, but any man can do that. This, ennit.' He tapped his left sideburn.

I looked hard at that sideburn, trying to see what were so special about it.

But then he went on: 'I uses me swede, see. And I ain't braggin' there. Don't take a genius to work out why a feller from out o' town chooses Mangel to settle in. A feller who wears hairpiece and buys Hoppers cash up front? Why would someone like him come to Mangel, eh? Well I'll tell you why: Cos no one else ever comes here. Cos Mangel folk never leaves town and can't let on about him. Only one reason to come to Mangel, Blake. To hide. Mangel's like the underside of a boulder, all damp and crawlin' with woodlice. No one'd ever know it were there, less they took trouble to lift the boulder. But no one ever lifts the boulder, Blake. Too heavy ennit. So the lice runs round and round in the dark and damp.'

Another pint of lager had appeared in front of us at some stage during all this. I picked it up and knocked it back, trying to wash my head clean of the confusion that Nathan's words had caused. And I reckon it done the trick, being as when I plonked glass atop bar I couldn't recall half of what he'd said. Summat about woodlice, were it?

'Yer mate were in here askin' after you not long since,' says Nathan, back to his tankard polishing.

'Oh aye,' I splutters. 'Which un?'

'Which un? How many mates you gat, Blakey? How many real mates you gat?'

I clocked meself in the mirror again. I didn't enjoy it. The feller in the mirror were too big. His head were too big and his clothes was too bright and his cheeks was too pink. He looked like a cunt and I wished he weren't there. I wanted to go over and drop my head on him, then drag him out back and leave him for the rats. But I couldn't do that. So I tried hard to ignore him instead. That didn't work neither. 'How many friends you got then, Nathan?'

'Me?' He laughed. Spit flew from his face like a wet sheepdog shaking himself dry. None of it seemed to land on meself though, which were fair play. 'Me? I ain't gat no friends, Blake. What do I need friends fer? A man stands alone.'

I turned and headed for the back door, same as I always done. Nathan shouted summat after us but I hardly paid it no heed. It were only once I were pulling out into the road that his echoes come back to us. 'Legs,' he'd said. 'It were Legs after you.'

I killed the engine.

I were in Cutler Road a few yard up from Legsy's

flat. I didn't want him to hear us coming, see. I reckoned he'd be on his guard if he heard a motor pull up right outside. I got out and walked.

Ain't sure why I didn't want him on his guard. I were just following me instincts, see, same as I always done. I followed em round the side of the offy and over to the bins in the corner. My leather coat were still there, right where I'd left it. It warmed me heart to see it so, and I felt more meself the moment I put it on. I chucked Mick Runter's black jacket in the bin and closed the lid. Then I opened it again and felt about for the pistol and monkey wrench. I found the wrench alright but not the gun. I searched and searched, digging deep into the rubbish in case it'd slipped out. But all I found were old tea bags and broken glass. Bollocks, I thought. Must have left it in Fenton's office, beside his dead body. That'd look good when the coppers found it.

Ah well, fuck it.

I walked over and trudged up the stair, wondering what had happened to the youngun I'd laid out on em earlier. Like as not he'd woke up soon after, putting his misfortune down to slippery steps and an anorak thief. At the top I took a deep un and rung the bell.

Lights was on behind the frosted door. I could hear some music coming from inside. Sounded like 'Devil in Disguise'. It ended suddenly, right before the slow verse kicks into the fast chorus. I rung again. Legs opened the door. 'Alright, Blake,' he says.

'Alright, Legs.'

We stood like that for a while or two, eyeing each other up. You couldn't see much of him. His face were swathed in darkness, hiding all but the faint smile on his chops. My face couldn't have been much more visible neither, which were good. He stepped aside.

I went on in.

I sat on the sofa and looked at the telly, same as what I always done. Some folks was walking about and talking and music were playing in the background. Same as always happened on the telly. Legs came in and lobbed us a cold un from the fridge. I caught it without looking up. Everything were taking place the way it always had done. I didn't want it to. I hadn't come to sit around and have a laugh. I'd come cos I were in deep shite and the wind had carried us here. But now I were here all I knew were the old routine. Legs sat down.

We looked at the telly for a long stretch, chugging ale and farting quietly. It were Legs who spoke first. He looked over at us, then back at the telly. He says: 'Seen Finney?'

'Not since he went in,' I says. 'Yerself?'

'Nah. Heared about him on the radio, mind. What the fuck happened?'

I looked at him. It were hard to tell if he were joshing us or not, it being so dark. I knew he hadn't been there, but I had a feeling Legs knew everything that had happened. 'Got done over by the Muntons, didn't he,' I says, watching him.

He raised a couple of eyebrows. 'Fuckin' bastards,' he says.

'Aye, brung him over the ozzy meself. Covered in blood he were. And cut to fuck. They was torcherin' him, see.'

His eyes was on the telly. A bird were taking her kit off and any second her tits'd be out. We both watched for a bit until she did just that. It were a fleeting moment. Soon as it were over I turned back to Legs.

'Aye, had a mind to kill him they did. But they was doin' it slow, draggin' it out like.'

His eyes was still on the telly, but I could tell he weren't paying it no heed now.

'Looks like Finney killed Baz, see,' I went on. 'Thass how the Muntons'd reckoned it anyhow. Some bastard telled em it were Finney, so they went after him. Can't blame em though, eh? Some fucker tops my brother I'd like as not be after em with a chainsaw an' all. Know what I'm wonderin' though, eh Legsy? I'm wonderin' who telled em.'

He rubbed his chin and puffed his cheeks out, still saying nothing. He got up and went into the kitchen.

I followed him. When he opened the fridge door it lit up his face and showed how white it were, like he'd had a nasty shock. But he had had a nasty shock, hearing about Finney like that. 'Legs,' I says. 'What was you wantin' us for?'

He got a couple of tins out and lobbed us one. We cracked em open and started chugging. He leaned back against the fridge and looked at his watch. Then he says: 'I know what you done.'

'Done what?' I says. 'Woss I done?'

'Killed her.'

He were watching us now, just like I'd been watching him earlier, telling him about Fin. He were looking for summat in me face.

I didn't know what he were after, but whatever it were I knew he'd not find it. My face felt like it were made of wood. Nothing'd show on it. 'Killed who?'

'Beth.'

'Killed Beth?' I says. The words fizzed up somewhere in my head and bounced off the walls, echoing like a dog barking in a warehouse. But I didn't feel much else. Sounds echo in hollow places. 'Course I never,' I were gonna say. Cos I fucking never, did I.

But I didn't say that. Wouldn't sound right, would it. Be as good as saying: 'Aye, course I killed her.' And there were summat else and all. Finney had clocked onto it but I'd told him to piss off out of my business. I didn't want to hear it, see. Not from meself nor no one else. But maybe it were time I did hear it. A problem shared and all that bollocks. And if you can't trust your mates, who can you trust. Eh?

There were a feller once who found a pack of fags in his bedroom. Same bedroom he shared with his dear wedded wife it were. Only they wasn't his fags. He smoked Bennys and these was Regals. Weren't his wife's neither, her smoking Consulate. So he scratched his head and wondered how come a pack of strange fags had come to be there, peaking out from under the bed.

And no matter how hard he scratched, no answer came. Sore head were all he got. So he went to his wife aiming to ask her. Only when he got to her – when he stood in front of her and looked her in the eyes – his mouth dried up and his tongue went all limp. He didn't need to ask her, did he. There were the answer for him, right there in her blue eyes, behind all that smudge she'd taken to applying of late. And you know what he done?

You knows what he ought to have done, like as not. He ought to have got it all sorted there and then. Are you my wife or are you a slapper? Do you know who I am? I'm Royston Fucking Blake and no wife of mine puts out behind me back. And what about this pack of Regals, eh? Who's this gentleman you've been entertaining? Tell us now. He'll be smoking em out his arse when I'm finished with the fucker, I can tell you.

But that's not what he done. What he done is walk away like a sick old dog.

The twat.

And he tried to forget all about it. He tried to think of all the innocent little accidents might have led to a pack of Regals being there in the bedroom. There was tons of em when you came to think on it. And when you came to think on it you saw how twattish you was behaving. That's your fucking wife, mate. Not a tuppenny whore from down the arcade. Course she ain't putting out to all and sundry.

So this feller started being nice to his wife instead. He weren't sure why, but summat told him that he'd better, just in case. He brung her flowers and perfume. He done a bit of cooking once until it were plain as day that cooking weren't summat he were born to do. And he started paying her a bit more attention in the pit. Just like the old days, when they was newlyweds and at it like a couple of rabbits in spring.

Only it weren't the same now. The more he pressed himself on her, the more she turned away. And the perfume sat on the shelf and the flowers died.

Meanwhile he ate and drank and slept and crapped and pissed and went to work and stewed on it. And one evening it all got a bit too much. Folks was taking advantage. Kids was getting past him. Fights was kicking off and playing out without him noticing. And when his boss – a big feller with a scarred meaty face and shaved head – told him to piss off home cos he were no use to man nor beast standing at the door with his eyes on his boots, that's what he done. And as he rode his Capri homeward he pushed her harder and harder. Summat were driving him on, summat red hot and knotted in his guts. And as he got closer it coiled tighter and tighter.

He let himself in nice and quiet, nice and slow, though his head felt like it had a hurricane in it. He wanted to turn and run. He wanted to peg it into town and neck twenty pints of lager. Maybe he could have a crack at that new stripper they had in on Thursdays. But it were too late.

It were too late for him to keep his head down and get on with it. He'd stood in the hall long enough to smell it. There were a feller in the house. A feller smoking Regals. And then he heard it and all. Breathing. Grunting. Bumping. Fucking.

Upstairs.

Just as quiet as he'd come in, he let himself out.

Legs lit a Regal and looked at us. It were a funny look he had on his face. Not smiling, not frowning, and not much else besides. Aye, it were a look that I hadn't seen much of before. Not only on Legs, but on anyone in the Mangel area. He held out his arm and offered us a fag.

'No ta,' I says. 'I don't smoke Regals. Didn't I just tell you? You don't catch on quick do you Legsy, eh?' I laughed. I stopped.

We caught each other's eyes.

It were a funny old feeling. Sort of like a rusty old gate closing shut after banging in the wind for years. And soon as it's shut it's like it were never open.

'You always knew though, eh?' says Legs. 'An' you always knew I knew, about you killin' her.' He drew deep on his fag and let it out through his nose and never took his eyes off us.

I wondered about saying aye, course I always knew you was shagging Beth. But it didn't seem right to come out and say such a thing. Felt like it'd make it true if I said it, even though I knew it were true. I'd sat on it for years and got on with things. And here were Legsy coming along and spoiling it all. What right had he to spoil it for us? Him, the cunt who'd started it all.

But this were all confined to my head and I didn't say none of it out loud. What I said were: 'Finney tell you, did he?'

'Finney?' Legsy pushed himself off the fridge and looked at his watch. He sauntered back into the living room like this were a typical night.

I followed him.

'Finney?' He were on his couch now. Sitting up for a change and not spread out on his back like normal. One leg were stretched out across it but the other were grounded and jumping up and down. 'Finney's your mate, Blake. He wouldn't dob on you. Take yer secrets to the grave he would. Thass juss what he will do, in fact.'

My eyes was on the telly. Greyhounds was tearing round the track and a voice were shouting the odds. 'How'd you know then?'

His eyes was on me. 'Really wanna know?'

I moved my head a bit.

'I were with her, when you rung her up that night and called her out to Hoppers. I told her not to go. Let him fuckin' walk home, I says. Iss a warm night and the exercise'll do him good. But she says no. Never understood that about her meself, how she still done right by you even when you treated her bad and forced her into the arms of another feller. Looked after you she did. An' look what you done to her in return.'

The news came on next. The feller were carping on about summat or other but like always I weren't paying him no heed. Too many words and you get confused. I just looked at the pictures. It were a bit dark and grainy, and shot from overhead like the cameraman were in a big hot air balloon. But you could see what they was up to down there alright. They was taking that big bastard of a bomb out of the silo and loading him into an airplane. You'd never have thought he'd fit into her, big and nasty as he were and small and flighty like she looked. Then the feller's face filled the screen and I heard what he said this time. He were telling folks to go on about their business and not to panic like a bunch of jessies.

'Woss that s'posed to mean?' I says. '"Thass just what he will do"?'

'Eh?' he says, loud and a bit lairy.

'Finney. Said he'd take em to the grave with him, you did. My secrets an' that.'

'Aye, well. He killed her too didn't he. Your idea, but he lit the fire. I seen him. I waited up the road from yer house, see. Had a bad feelin' and I wanted to see her back in one piece. Well, she didn't come back did she. I sees you pull up in yer fuckin' rusty old nail but no Beth. So I goes down there. Still had a bad feelin', see, and it were gettin' worser as I got nearer. Then when I drives past the back of Hoppers I clocks Finney jumpin' over the back fence. And by the time I gets round front the whole place is blazin'. An' there's Beth's car parked round back.' His leg were jumping up and down like a road drill. It were all I could see, though me eyes was on the telly. I reckoned he'd be putting his boot through the floor any moment. 'So I told the Muntons all about it.'

Five planes was flying across the screen in formation, like a little flock of giant geese. 'When?'

His hand went to his nose and then back to where it had been – clutching the arm rest. 'T'other day. Then I told em about you killin' Baz an' all. Well, told em to go ask Fin about it.'

'Why?' I were gonna ask. But then I recalled my bodged headbutt and it all pieced together. 'You grassed us cos I dropped one on you, by accident?'

'Don't be fuckin' thick. I grassed you cos you was gettin' cocky. I'd not done it till then cos you was contrite before, wanderin' round like a lost soul. Looked like you was doin' a life sentence in yer head. Plus the Muntons was leanin' on you more and more anyhow, you carryin' on as doorman of their old place and all. An' long as things stayed like that I couldn't bring meself to open me gob about it. Let him stew, I thinks. He's done his crime an' he's payin' for it. But that night in the Pry – when you nutted us like that . . . Well, seemed to me you was lettin' yerself out on remand.'

I got up. I couldn't stay sat no more. I stood up and shook the cramp out me legs.

Legsy stood up and all. 'And look woss happened now. All the Muntons would of done is use you a bit. Bit of donkey work an' that.'

I stuck my hands in me pockets. The monkey wrench slipped into the right one like water down a thirsty man's gullet. I looked at Legsy while he rabbitted on. It's different now, I were thinking. I'm a proper killer, not just a foul weather one. I'm wanted by the coppers and feared by all and sundry. And what are you? A fucking milkman. A fucking milkman who fucked my wife.

He looked at his watch. 'But you wasn't up for that, was you. You was cocky. You had to kill Baz. Why'd you go and do that eh? Another of yer accidents, like droppin' yer nut on me? And then you fucked up robbin' Hoppers. Couldn't even get that right could you. And you, a feller who spent his youth climbin' through folks' windows. How'd I know all this? See these? Ears, mate. Folks talk.'

I wished I still had that pistol on us. No matter how hard I gripped it, the wrench just didn't seem enough for Legsy. His head were too big I reckoned. You'd have to bash it from all sides before he'd go cross-eyed on you. And besides, he were a mate. I couldn't very well brain a mate with a monkey wrench.

He looked at his watch again.

'Why the fuck do you keep ganderin' that watch?' I shouted.

He looked a bit rattled at that, which were summat at least. He'd been having it all his own way so far while I'd sat quiet asking a polite question here and there. But, like I always used to say about Legsy, he don't stay rattled long. He sparked up another Regal and sucked it deep, looking at the window like he were working up to an answer. But there were a wallop at the door before one came. He shrugged at us as if to say folks at the door – what can a feller do eh? Then he walked out leaving us clutching the monkey wrench and scratching my head and boiling up inside.

I had a quick think while he were in the hall getting rid of whoever it were. If I got up now and stood behind the living room door I could brain him coming back in. I started to get up, thinking about the weight of the steel pulling on my arm as I swung it through the farty air. Then I sat down again. What were I thinking of? Legs were a . . .

He were a mate, weren't he?

Alright, we was having a bit of a to-do about this and that. We had a few problems to straighten out for surely. But nothing that time and a few piss-ups couldn't see right.

Right?

So I sat tight and awaited his return. I were feeling alright about it all, considering. I were feeling lighter in meself, and confident that we'd be getting all of me problems sorted this very night, one way or another. But then Legsy came back, followed by Lee and Jess Munton.

20
....

Lee comes in first wearing the same long leather coat he always wore. It were a bit tatty now. There were a dull area down the left arm where he must have fallen hard and slid along the concrete for a while. Also he hadn't shaved of late so his goatee were now lost in the undergrowth. Like my tash.

Jess pulled up the rear, looking a bit odd. What he were wearing didn't add up, see. It were one of them dirty white smocks they makes folks wear in hospital. On his feet were tartan slippers, same ones everyone's Uncle Bob wears. A bit higher up you could see loose bandages dangling down from between his legs. They was yellowish and a bit bloody. His face were white as cows' milk and made the smock look even pissier. Piss is what he stank of, come to think on it. You could even smell it over the top of Lee's aftershave when the two stood side-by-side.

'Fungcun...' says Jess. Gave him summat strong for his pain at the ozzy, like as not. 'Fungkillyuh.'

Legs stood behind the two of em, grinning at us in a way that I didn't much care for. Not sure what to do meself, I grinned back. I grinned at all three of em. I grinned like me life were dependent on it, and right there and then I reckon it were. If only I could make em believe in that grin I might be alright. Everything'd be tidy. Folks wouldn't really be dead. Finney wouldn't be fucked up. And Jess Munton wouldn't be wobbling on his pins and staring chainsaws at us.

Lee grinned back. But not in a nice way. I'd have preferred a frown, all in all. Then he got a sawn-off out and pointed it at me knackers. 'An eye for an eye,' he says, putting his free arm around Jess to hold him up. 'A knacker for a knacker. Right Jess?' The both of em glared at us a moment or two, then lowered their eyes to trouser level. The rough-nosed barrel wavered a bit as Lee curled his finger round the trigger.

'Hold up, hold up,' says Legs, bringing a couple of tears to me eyes. I knew he'd pull through, see. I knew he wouldn't stand by and let the Muntons shoot me knackers off, followed like as not by my head. 'You can't do that,' he says.

Lee relaxed his finger but didn't take his eye off us. 'Why not? He's gettin' what he's got comin'. Nuthin' I can do is bad enough for him. Look what he done. Look what he done to my family.'

'Aye, I knows all that.' Legs came round and put himself in front of the shotgun, bless him. I'd be alright. I just knew it. Legs had the kind of voice you listened to and acted upon. Even if you was the Muntons. 'But you can't do it here. Not in my flat. The offy downstairs is still open and folks'll hear. Take him out somewhere quiet. Got yer van out there ain't you? Take him out to Hurk Wood and have some fun with him. Don't want blood all over me walls an' carpet does I.'

Lee tightened his grip on the gun. 'You reckon, Jess?'

'Aye. Fungurk Wood.'

'Heh heh.' Lee squeezed his brother's shoulder and patted his back, making him wobble on his pins a bit. 'Eh Blake? Fancy a little drive out to the country?'

There weren't much to say. So that's what I said.

'Go on then.' Lee jerked his head at the door. 'Shift.'

I tried to lift me foot but it were stuck to the floor. Yours would have been and all. And don't fucking go saying it wouldn't. It fucking would.

'Shift.'

I looked at Legs. He were standing behind Lee again now, arms folded and lips pursed. He looked down when my eyes met his. Then he looked back at us and shrugged. 'I'd shift if I were you,' he says.

I closed me eyes. When I opened em again I were halfway down the fire escape. Jess were tottering in front of us, taking one stair at a time. Lee were behind us prodding us on with the gun. As we stepped off the last stair I opened my gob and licked me lips and found I had summat to say at last.

'The doofer.'

Lee poked us hard in the back. 'Fuckin' move.'

'The doofer. You was after it, right?'

'Go on. Move.' He smacked us across the right ear with the gun, then stuck the barrel in it. 'Tell yer story walkin'.'

My ear were ringing and felt like it were filled with ice cubes and hot coals, but I turned and faced him anyhow. What did I have to lose? Besides I knew he wouldn't shoot us. Not with what I had to tell him. 'Nah, nah, just listen. The thing in the box. From the safe, like, at Hoppers. You was after it, right?'

It were hard to see what were going on behind his

fat face, but I reckon I spotted a bit of confusion in them piggy eyes. And that gave us hope. 'Oh aye?' he says, face turning hard again. 'Know summat about that, does you?'

'Aye, I fuckin' do an' all.'

'Go on then.'

'Legs.'

'What about him?'

'Legs. Legsy. Had yer doofer didn't he. Stole it off Mandy he did. An' you know what he done with it then? Gave it to Fenton.'

'Bollocks. Legs is alright. Been helpin' us out of late he has. Ain't that right our Jess?'

'Fuh.'

'S'right. He's a good lad and we'll be bringin' him into the fold at Hoppers once we gets her back.'

'Get her back?'

'Aye. Course. Fenton can't keep it, can he?'

'Why not?'

'Fuckin' dead ennit. Feller from the big city got him. Always on the cards mind. Ripped off the wrong feller I hears. But some folks you can't hide from. Not even in Mangel. What you make of that eh? Your boss, a crook.'

I puffed out me cheeks and shook my head. 'Don't seem the type, do he.'

'Just how he wanted it, that is. Hidin', see. New identity an' that.'

'Ah. But it don't make Hoppers yours now do it.'

'Don't you fuckin' worry about that. Go on. Move it, you cunt.' He stuck the gun barrel in me ribs, quite possibly breaking one of em.

'Hang on, what about Legs?'

'What about him? Shift.'

'Gave the doofer back to Fenton he did.'

'Bollocks did he. You did. You're the one who stole it off our Mandy. Telled us all about it she did. You took it off her and brained her with a big rock. Got a lot to answer for, you has. An' you'll be answerin' for it tonight. I can tell you that much for nuthin'.'

'It were Legs. Fenton told us it were. Legsy swiped it off Mandy and gave it back to him.'

I shut up for a bit to see if Lee had summat to say about that. But he didn't. That meant I had him. All I had to do now were reel him in.

'Know what else, Lee? You oughta listen careful here cos it concerns you. You wanna own Hoppers again? Wanna see the name MUNTON above the door? Well you'll have a problem, cos in return for handin' back his doofer Fenton signed over half of Hoppers to Legs. What about that eh? Legsy such a good lad now, eh?'

Lee scratched his chin and chewed his lip and looked at Jess. 'What about it Jess? Believe him does you?'

'No. Fungcunt. Killthfugger . . .' He went on like that.

When I turned back to Lee he punched us in the guts and told us to fucking move or I'd die there and then. I lurched up the side road, him kicking us up the arse and Jess barking nonsense at us. The Meat Wagon were parked out in the road, being as it were too wide to get up the side lane. Jess opened the back up while Lee shoved the shotgun up me nose. I looked inside the offy and made eye contact with the feller there. He shook his head and got on with reading his paper. A second or two later I were in the back of the Meat Wagon for the first time in my life. The doors slammed.

I squeezed me eyes shut and tried not to think about it at first. It's just a fucking van like any other,

I says to meself. I listened for two doors opening and slamming up front and the engine firing up. But none of that happened. I sat dead still for about four hours it seemed, although it might well have been half a minute. Nothing happened, and soon enough I got cramp in me right leg and had to stretch a bit.

I were still trying to josh meself that I were lying on a park bench. It weren't working so well now. Bits and bobs about the van was seeping into my head and making emselves known. The smell first off. Dried blood and diesel.

I opened me eyes and found that it weren't pitch black like I'd reckoned it would be. A dim light were threading through from up front. I looked up there and found a little oblong window smeared in muck. Not much light came through it but enough to show us that the back of the van were near empty. Besides a lot of dirt and crap lying around, the only other thing in there were a rolled up bit of tarpaulin shoved up against the front. I tottered over to the back door to see if I could get it open. It were shut tight and I couldn't find no handle. That had us panicking and I lost it a bit. I started booting the metal again and again like it were a tractor tyre. Only it weren't no tractor tyre. It were a metal door and it fucking hurt. After a bit I stopped and fell over, hurting me shoulder. I might have cried out in pain just a tad, things being as they was, and I aired a few choice words for surely. While I were lying there in agony I opened me eyes and clocked summat moving up front, behind the glass window. I got up and hobbled closer.

I went to give the glass a wipe but stopped when I noticed the grime were more like fingerprints. Greasy new ones atop dark and flaky old ones. I didn't want to touch em so I got up close and peered through. There were nothing to see, just a big blur with a bit of windscreen wiper across the one side. Summat inside us said lean over and peer to the right, so I did just that. And surely enough there were the top of someone's head, straight dark hair covering a neat little head.

'Hoy,' I yells. 'Who's there?'

The head moved back so I couldn't see it. But I had seen it, hadn't I. So I kicked the panel with me good foot and yelled again. Didn't see no reason not to. I were fucked, far as I could see. And this feller up front couldn't be one of the Muntons, being as I hadn't heard Lee and Jess get back in. And if it weren't a Munton...Well, I didn't rightly know what. But it were someone, weren't it?

'Hey, answer us, fuck sake. I'm Royston Blake, Head Doorman of—'

'I knows who you are,' comes back a bird's voice. A familiar one, like all voices are in the Mangel area. And then a face loomed up t'other side of the mucky glass. It were so close I couldn't make much of it out. But I knew who she were alright. 'An' I knows what yer job is. An'...Oh, just shut up.'

You ain't meant to yell or curse at birds. Not even when they does same to you. Not even when you're hurting and locked in the back of the Meat Wagon and she's up front all warm and smug. It's one of them things separates us from the monkeys, so they says. And I happens to agree. So when I spoke I did so in a calm and reasonable manner. 'Now Mandy,' I says. 'I dunno just what you're doin' up yonder. Seems to me you oughtn't to be there, bein' as the last time I seen you you was—'

'Just shut up Blake.' She were sitting back in the driver's seat again so I couldn't see her. But her voice came from not two feet away. 'I heared all about what you done. The less said the better, far as I sees it.'

'Woss you heared? Whatever it is, Mand, I tells you it ain't true. It weren't—'

'Woss you done? Woss you done, you says? You killed my brother. Killed little Barry an'... an' all I can say is I'm glad Lee and Jess picked me up on the road to Furzel. I'm glad cos now I gets to drive you out to Hurk Wood meself.'

'Hurk Wood? But Mand, what about all that stuff we talked about?'

'What stuff?'

'You know, in the lock-up there. Over in Norbert Green.'

'What did we talk about?'

'Oh, come on. You remembers.'

'What? You come on.'

'You know... Stuff.'

'Like what?'

'Well alright. I don't rightly recall what particular words was said. But—'

'Well there's yer answer then ennit. It ain't important enough to recall.'

'Mand, come on girl. Let us out an I'll...' To be honest I weren't sure what I'd do if she let us out. And while I were thinking of summat the back doors swung open and the van filled up with cold air.

'Company for you,' says Lee as he and Jess heaved Legs into the van. Legs were unconscious or thereabouts, and the heaving weren't coming easy on Jess's side. But Lee bore the brunt and after a bit they got the whole of Legs in and slammed the doors once again. Then they climbed up front and started her up.

Legs lay where he'd fell for a long while. I thought about getting up and having a go at kicking him to death, him being the cause of all this and all. But what were the point of that? We was both fucked. No use bickering now. So I ignored him and closed me eyes and tried to shut my brain off.

I normally finds it easy to do that, long as there's nothing to distract us. But there were a grating noise coming from somewhere and it were fucking annoying. Legs were sat still, so it couldn't be him. I looked around and saw the tarp. It were rubbing against itself as the van rocked this way and that. It were getting cold in there, and I wondered about stretching some of that tarp over us blanket-like. But nothing came of such thinking. No point having warm legs when I were about to cark it, were there?

Suddenly the van swerved hard left, sending us arse over. My back hit the front panel and I fell down on the tarp. I pushed meself up off of it, noting with interest that it weren't just a tarp after all. Summat were in it. Summat soft and hard at same time. Just like folks is soft and hard at same time.

That and the van swerving to the right just then made us fall over. I landed on my arse back where I'd been sat. A bit of the tarp had come away at one end, revealing what looked to be a shiny black shoe.

'Who the fuck is in there?' says Legsy.

The van went over a huge pothole a bit fast, sending the tarp in the air. When it came down a dead feller popped out, his big right arm lopped off and strapped upside his body. He lay there staring at us, face lit up grey by dim moonlight through the greasy little window, same dopey look on his face as when I'd tried to run him down outside Hoppers just now.

'Who the fuck is that?' says Legsy again, voice all high-pitched and womanish now.

'Outsider ennit,' I says. 'Reckons he's a doorman. Serves him fuckin' right, you asks me. Called us a turnip he did.'

I sniffed and wiped me nose. Road were getting rougher under us, which had my arse slamming up and down on the metal floor. We'd be going into the woods now, driving slow up the dirt track. I weren't scared. You'd reckon I would be, this being the end. But you know what? I couldn't give a toss.

The Meat Wagon stopped. Legs were looking at us. Some light were getting in from somewhere, showing his eyes up as all wet and glistening. 'Blake,' he says, voice cracking. 'I loves you.'

Well, I didn't very well know what to say to that. Ain't the sort of thing one feller says to another is it. But I reckon he were cacking himself a bit so I had to make allowances. I opened me gob to say, 'You're alright mate,' but the door opened just then and a lovely cool breeze rushed in and took the words away.

Jess's movements was different. Didn't seem so doped up now. He came in first, waving the fucking chainsaw about like a fucking tennis racket.

Lee came in behind him holding a shotgun.

Legs started crying.

Jess laughed.

Lee grinned and slapped his brother on the shoulder. Then he slammed the door and grinned at us all. He kicked the dead feller aside and sat atop him. 'Got a job for you,' he says, looking at me. 'If you ain't too busy.'

Jess laughed again. Then he put the chainsaw on the floor in front of us.

Lee got a sawn-off out of his coat and passed it him. He nodded at Susan and looked at me. 'Pick her up.'

She were heavier than I'd reckoned her to be. And up close she stank. It were the same whiff as the rest of the Meat Wagon, only more so. 'Why?' I says.

Lee pointed the gun at me face. 'Go on, start up Susan.'

I touched the chord. It were damp and greasy. She started first time.

'Wha—' I heard Legs say, but the rest were drowned out. He shut up when Jess smacked him across the back of the head with the sawn-off. His lips said 'Ow' and his arm went up as he started to turn.

Jess got him again, bang on his left ear hole.

Legs went down cold this time.

Susan were roaring and gnashing her teeth. Lee's knees were a couple of feet away at most. While I were thinking about that he stepped back and aimed the gun more closely at my head. Jess aimed at us and all. They'd have had my head sprayed across the panel before I could reach em with the chainsaw. And it were too heavy to lob. They'd shoot me arms off anyhow if I tried.

Jess squatted and pointed at Legsy's throat. Then he mimed like he were bringing Susan down on it, all the way to the floor. He got up, swinging an invisible head from his hand by the hair.

I shook my head. Thoughts was coming into it that I didn't much care for. Had no space for em did I. Not here, in the Meat Wagon. I were thinking about when I used to go up Legsy's flat and moan about Beth. He never started it. It were always me, cracking a tin open and shaking my head and telling him how he ought never to get wedded. Or if he did, choose a bit more careful than I did.

Lee were shouting summat. It were hard to hear. He were waving the gun around and kicking Legs and spraying flob all over us.

I hadn't always slagged her off, mind. When me and Beth was newlyweds I couldn't stop talking her up. Specially to Legs. I'd tell him what she could do, how her body felt, what noises she made, how she liked it, what her tricks was. Maybe it weren't right to say all that, looking back. Maybe, if I hadn't, things'd be alright now.

Lee raised the gun a couple of inches and fired. Buckshot raked across me scalp. Blood trickled down my forehead into me eyebrows and gathered in em like a couple of thunder clouds. A blast of cool air came through the new hole behind us. Jess lowered his gun and aimed between my legs. I reckoned this were it.

I walked toward Legs. I knelt beside him. Cold metal pushed into the back of me neck. Hot stinking breath bellowed in my ear: 'Chop his block off.' I looked at Susan. She were massive. And if I held her like so her blade blotted out Legsy's face. I brung her down close, close to . . .

'Chop his block off.'

Legsy's eyes was shut. Didn't look like they'd ever be open again. Maybe Jess'd knocked him too hard just now with the sawn-off and killed him. Maybe it wouldn't matter so much if I . . .

The blunt barrel of Jess's sawn-off prodded against my stretched trousers from underneath, right on me tightening knacker sack. The clouds burst above my

eyes, filling em with blood. Legsy were a mate.
Alright, we had a few problems. But he had shagged
me missus, hadn't he.

I mean, fucking come on.

Someone fired. I didn't know who. All I knew were
the broken glass flying and blood spraying everywhere. I didn't care. The darkness were already in us.

I were filled with it.

It were an odd noise to wake up to, a sound not often
heard in the Mangel area. Airplanes. I opened me eyes
and clocked five of em passing overhead in formation.
I'd seen em like that somewhere else of late, but
couldn't recall where. Don't matter. They wasn't
stopping in Mangel so it didn't concern us, did it. I
shifted up on me elbows.

She didn't speak. Didn't smile neither. Didn't even
look us in the eye. Not that I looked in hers. I stayed
where I were and watched her walk over to the
driver's door. She opened it and reached up inside the
cab, holding her leg out behind her for balance. When
she jumped back down she had her little rucksack.
She slung it over her shoulder and stood facing us,
eyes down.

'Mand...' I says.

She didn't speak nor smile nor look at us. Her nose
looked alright now. Maybe I hadn't broke it. I were
glad of that. Shame to mar such prettiness. Arm were
still in a sling, mind. Finney had a lot to answer for.

'Mand,' I says again. 'Ta for that.'

She said nothing.

'Helpin' us out there.' It weren't easy, but I had to
say summat. 'I mean like, shootin' yer own bro—'

'Blake.'

'Aye?'

'Don't.'

'An' Legsy... You knows I never meant to—'

'Please Blake...'

'It were your two. Fuckin' made us do it they did. You saw em with them shotguns, didn't you? Bastards.'

Summat rustled in the bushes behind us. I looked and saw a badger come out of the bushes following a scent. He stopped and sniffed the air in my direction, then turned arse and went back in the thicket. I turned back to Mandy. She were twenty yard away, off up the path that carries on past Hurk Wood and through the fields the other side. If you goes far enough along there you reaches the big city, they says. But I wouldn't know about that.

I tried to get up but me shoes and trousers was all wet and slippery and I fell on my arse. I tried again, more carefully. My leather were drenched in blood and all. I took it off and dropped it on the grass. But summat told us leaving it on the grass weren't clever, so I picked it up and looked around.

The back of the Meat Wagon were shut. I took a deep un and opened her up. It were a meat wagon alright. And it'd take a lot of cleaning up. I put Legsy's head where it belonged and draped me leather over him. Fuck the others, Muntons and that feller. They could lie where they was, eyeballs drying up.

I shut the doors, wiped my hands on the grass, and went up front.

The keys was in the slot. I started her up and let her rumble for a bit. I had a look around the cab. Weren't much to see. Dirty old spade on the floor, copy of the *Informer* with my photo on the front in the door pocket, little box on the dashboard. It were wrapped in brown paper and sticky tape. I turned it over in me hands, weighing it up and shaking it a bit. Felt like a doofer to me, though I couldn't be sure without opening it. I put it back on the dash and cut the engine. I grabbed the spade and headed out into the wood.

Sky were getting lighter behind the trees. Be dawn soon. Folks'd be getting up and going about their business, keeping their heads down and hoping nothing too bad happened to em. A bit later the pubs'd be opening for the day. And I aimed to be at the Paul Pry when they did, doofer in hand. Hard morning's graft deserves a pint, don't it?

Fucking right it do.

In memory of Gerald Ashby

Other Serpent's Tail titles of interest

David Peace's Red Riding Quartet

Nineteen Seventy Four

'Breathless, extravagant, ultra-violent . . . Vinnie Jones should buy
the film rights fast' *Independent on Sunday*

'Quite simply, this is the future of British crime fiction'
Time Out

'Peace has found his own voice – full of dazzling, intense poetry
and visceral violence' *Uncut*

'Peace's storytelling may be unrelentingly dark, at times even
nightmarish, but what impresses most about the books . . . is the
author's literary ambition. Peace uses prose like a blunt weapon.
His sentences are hypnotic, repetitive, incantatory. Pages seem
to fly by. Sharpened dialogue jostles with drifting thoughts.
Snatches of pop lyrics wrestle with the fractured ravings of the
killer. Victims swirl through the text, alive, dead, alive
again . . . Peace is at the forefront of a generation of hard-boiled
crime writers pushing the genre into new and difficult territory'
Sydney Morning Herald

'Peace's Boschian landscape of West Yorkshire's all-out dystopia
began with *Nineteen Seventy Four* and a young girl's murdered
body, found in a ditch with swan's wings sewn to its shoulder
blades. While atmospheric with '70s music and ads, that first
installment set the quartet's bleak Orwellian tone, though with
echoes of the complex modes of Dos Passos' *USA* and the
demonic grimness, violence, corruption and conspiracies of
James Ellroy' *Kirkus Reviews*

'His Red Riding quartet . . . set a new high-water mark for
British crime writing. Their pace, tension, plotting, sheer in-
your-face brutality and evocation of how corruption twists lives
served notice that an utterly distinctive and prodigiously
talented new writer had arrived.'
Writing Magazine

Nineteen Seventy Seven

'Quite simply, this is the future of British crime fiction . . . the finest work of literature I've read this year - and its ending is as extraordinary and original as what precedes it'
Time Out

'With a human landscape that is violent and unrelentingly bleak, Peace's fiction is two or three shades the other side of noir' *New Statesman*

'David Peace's stunning debut has done for the county what Raymond Chandler and James Ellroy did for Los Angeles . . . This is a brilliant first novel, written with tremendous pace and passion' *Yorkshire Post*

'One hell of a read' *Crime Time*

Nineteen Eighty

Nineteen Eighty Three

'Will undoubtedly stand as a major achievement in British dark fiction . . . the pace is relentless, the violence gut-wrenching, the style staccato-plus and the morality bleak and forlorn, but Peace's voice is powerful and unique. This is compelling stuff that will leave no one indifferent' *Guardian*

'This is fiction that comes with a sense of moral gravity, clearly opposed to diluting the horrific effects of crime for the sake of bland entertainment. There is no light relief and, for most of the characters, no hope. Peace's series offers a fierce indictment of the era' *Independent*

'British crime fiction's most exciting new voice in decades' *GQ*

'Peace is a manic James Joyce of the crime novel . . . jump cutting like a celluloid magus through space and time, reciting incantations and prayers, invoking the horror of grim lives, grim crimes, grim times' *Sleazenation*

'Beautifully crafted, almost poetic prose isn't what you would expect from a crime novel, but David Peace isn't an ordinary crime writer' *Big Issue*

'The novel's power lies in its poetic depictions of violence and in its flawless period detail, which grounds it convincingly in the Eighties. Fiction and history merge, and the personal and the political mirror each other, creating a disturbing portrait of social decay. Rarely has the crime novel managed to say something more serious and enduring than in Peace's masterful quartet' *New Statesman*

'If you like your fiction to be vicious and chaotic, the Red Riding Quartet reveals Peace to be one of the masters of the form' *Sunday Herald*

'This is the final instalment, and it is magnificent. The three years since his debut have seen Ossett-born Peace grow into one of the most distinctive and compelling crime novelists in the world . . . *Nineteen Eighty Three* is Peace's best yet' *Yorkshire Post*

'A raw and furious wade through the Valley of Death that understates its big sweet hell of pages chock-a-block with violated corpses and red rain running with blood' *Kirkus Reviews*

'*Nineteen Eighty Three* is a profound piece of British crime fiction that howls with the horror of its subject matter' *Leeds Guide*

'The final instalment of David Peace's Red Riding Quartet arrives with a sickening thud, the flutter of leathery wings and an ominous darkening of the skies ... terrible. And magnificent' *Big Issue in the North*

'A gripping read, written in short breathless sentences – at times a sort of hardcore poetry ... Not for the faint-hearted, this is as hard as a Leeds pavement on a Saturday night' *Birmingham Post*

'*Nineteen Eighty Three* is every bit as powerful as the books that have preceded it' *Flux*

'Fans will be pleased with this finale' *Metro*

'David Peace is the obvious successor to Derek Raymond's title of King of British noir ... Dark, depressing but important fiction from a very fine writer' *Time Out*

'Stunning ... Each novel powerfully evokes the period surrounding the crimes and capture of the Yorkshire Ripper' *Crime Time*

Deadwater
Sean Burke

Deadwater begins with the murder of a prostitute in Cardiff's Tiger Bay. The novel's protagonist, the alcoholic pharmacist Jack Farissey, wakes up next morning in blood-stained clothes on a plastic sheet and no memory of what happened the night before. Lucky for Jack that the police soon finger local gangster Carl Baja for the murder.

What follows is a bleak journey through the dying Cardiff docklands as Farissey looks into his own heart of darkness and that of his childhood friend, the musician Jess Simmonds. Both Jack and Jess love the same woman, who is bent on proving Baja's innocence. Baja's release from prison will be the beginning of the end for all three of them.

'A strong, disturbing novel. As crime writers we forever want to achieve what seem (but are not) contradictory things: to document in as much detail as possible this most particular world about us, this life of the streets, and at the same time to represent the whole of an urban environment. Sean Burke's Cardiff ranks with Jonathan Lethem's Brooklyn, John Harvey's Nottingham or George Pelecanos' Washington — which is to say, among the best' James Sallis

'Downbeat but beautiful' *Guardian*

'A haunting, impressive novel, hardly suitable for the fainthearted' *Western Mail*

'A notable entry in the genre of modern British noir, with characters hardened and almost dehumanised by the unforgiving city, but drawn with enough depth to suggest that redemption is still an option' *Leeds Guide*

'Disturbingly beautiful' *City Life (Manchester)*

'Now Cardiff has its chronicler. Now that powerful and political, blood-soaked and beautiful city has the ferociously talented observer it deserves and needs. Sean shares with James Lee Burke not just a surname but a lyrical despair, a committed wrestling with God, an unflinching endoscopic eye into the black chambers of our hearts and an ability to completely convince. He is a necessary alternative historian, a dark and barometric moralist. *Deadwater* will haunt me for years' Niall Griffiths